THE SECRETS ON FOREST BEND

SUSAN C. MULLER

CO-AZH-957

SOUL MATE PUBLISHING

New York

THE SECRETS ON FOREST BEND
Copyright©2011
SUSAN C. MULLER

Cover Design by Rae Monet, Inc.

Published in the United States of America by
Soul Mate Publishing
P.O. Box 24
Macedon, New York, 14502

ISBN: 978-1-61935-124-0
eBook ISBN: 978-1-61935-045-8

www.SoulMatePublishing.com

For my family;

those who are here

and those who have passed on.

Acknowledgements

Thanks to my husband for putting up with my long hours on the computer, and to my son, Ron Muller, and my daughter, Angela Rehm, for trudging through my first drafts.

Thanks to Delma Neeley and Tess Grillo, for their work as my early readers, and to Jason Rehm, Keno Henderson, and John Foxjohn for their assistance.

Thanks to my critique partners, Jenn, Allison, Jan, Jaye, Stella, and especially Shawnna Perigo for looking at every change and making such valuable suggestions.

Thanks to my good friend Christie Craig for so much more than I can say in one line.

I appreciate the work of all the contest judges who offered helpful suggestions and encouragement.

Prologue

September, 1986

The house didn't feel right. It was too quiet. Where was everyone?

Jillie padded softly down the silent hall. The door to her parents' room creaked as she pushed it open to peek in. Her older sister, Heather, sat cross-legged on the big four-poster bed.

Talking made Jillie's throat hurt, so she took a deep swallow. "You're not supposed to be in here. Mommy won't like it."

"Mommy's not here." Heather glared at her. "She went to the store to get your medicine. I'm in charge. You should be in bed. If you get sick again and I miss my pageant, I'll make you wish you hadn't gotten up."

Jillie ignored her and climbed onto the bed. If Heather could sit there, so could she.

"What're you doing?" Jillie clamped her hand over her mouth when she saw the gun in Heather's hand. "Umm. Daddy said never touch that. Grandpa brought that home special from the war. You're gonna be in sooo much trouble."

Heather rolled her eyes. "You don't know anything. Daddy said I could look at it because I'm a big girl. Thirteen is almost grown."

"I'm big," Jillie said, straightening her shoulders. "I had my birthday, and Daddy said six was big."

"Not where it counts." Heather poked her in the

stomach and said in the sing-song voice Jillie hated, "Silly Jillie, jelly belly."

Jillie bit her lip. She wouldn't cry. Heather always got a funny smile when she cried. It made her want to run and hide.

"Let me see it," she begged. "I want my turn." Jillie reached for the gun, but stopped and wrinkled her nose. "You smell funny. Did you get into Mommy's perfume?"

"I did not. This is my perfume. I won it at my last pageant." Heather wouldn't look at her when she said it.

That wasn't right. Jillie didn't pay much attention to Heather's pageants, but she never came home with anything except another stupid trophy. Now she remembered. "You didn't win last time. You came in second."

Jillie sat back. Her eyes went wide. "You stole that perfume, didn't you?" Jillie couldn't prove it, but she knew that's what happened.

Heather's face began to change colors. "You don't know what you're talking about, you fat little brat." She waved the gun in Jillie's face. "If you say one word, I'll take this gun and shoot that kitten you have hidden in the woods. The one you think nobody knows about."

Jillie's heart stopped. Not her kitten. She couldn't let Heather hurt her kitten. She reached out to grab the gun, but as soon as her fingers touched it, Heather gave her a hard shove.

Jillie tried to cry out, but her head hit the bedpost with a loud crack and the air rushed out of her chest. She slipped to the floor, landing with a thud. She was sleepy and her head hurt—bad.

A big firecracker shook the room and her eyes flew open. Heather collapsed onto the floor beside her. Heather's shirt was all dirty. She must have spilled strawberry jelly on it. Mommy wouldn't like that. The room went dark, but that was okay because then her head didn't hurt anymore.

Suddenly a cloud of perfume enveloped Jillie and a breeze stirred her hair as Heather seemed to float above her. Jillie's breath came in short gasps and her skin prickled.

Heather leaned down and whispered in her ear with that mean voice she used when Mommy wasn't close. "Look what you've done. I'll miss my pageant, and it's all your fault. I'll make you pay for this."

Chapter 1

April, Twenty-six years later

"Another day, another dead body." Detective Adam Campbell immediately regretted his words. The fatigue must be getting to him. As soon as he reached the victim, his adrenaline would kick in. He took one last swallow of stale coffee and pushed out of his city-issued Taurus.

Hours past the end of his shift and he was still on the streets. Three long days in a row with no partner to share the load. And now this case, smack in the middle of Montrose, the most difficult section of Houston to work. Skirting the edge of downtown, the area was a grab bag of museumgoers, fancy restaurants, gay bars, and vagrants.

He nodded to the uniformed officer nearest the body. "Hey, Fredericks, what're you doing here this late? Aren't you supposed to be working days?"

"It's the fucking economy. My wife got laid off. Now I have to take all the OT I can manage. What about you? Are you sure this is a case for Homicide? Looks more like one of those misdemeanor killings to me."

Heat raced up the back of Adam's neck as he struggled to keep his face impassive. He despised the saying and the lazy cops who used it. *I must be tired if I'm letting a little attitude like that get under my skin.*

Stepping closer, he draped his arm around the young officer's shoulder and pitched his voice low. "In my book, there's no such thing as a misdemeanor killing. Every victim—prostitute, drug dealer, or church deacon—deserves my best efforts. And the perp, dealer or deacon, deserves my worst."

He patted Fredericks on the back with a hearty laugh and a wink. Let Fredericks wonder if he'd been chastised or punked, as long as he showed more respect in the future.

Adam shifted and scanned the area for first impressions while the wind played havoc with his unruly hair. As he approached the crime scene tape, his eyes registered every detail. Fatigue drained away with each step.

Despite the steady breeze, the area reeked of garbage and urine. Evening traffic roared overhead while red and blue flashing lights reflected off the walls and ceiling of the overpass like the neon lights of a fancy club. Chains rattled as a police wrecker prepared to tow an ancient clunker held together by rust and unfounded hope.

To Adam, these were the sights and sounds of death.

He shoved his glasses back into place, cursing the flimsy wire rims as he shifted to get a better view. Worn, dirty clothes, arms covered with tats, and an old sleeping bag beside the body probably meant the victim lived under the bridge where he died. Adam's gut clenched when his eyes reached the head. He confronted the ugliness of death every day, but few things trumped a gunshot to the face.

Runoff from the afternoon rain formed a moat around the body. At his first step, water sloshed over his feet and wicked up his socks. Christ, what a day to wear new shoes. At least it smelled better over here. Too much better in fact.

He glanced around quickly. Were any women working the scene? They weren't supposed to wear perfume on duty. The two uniformed officers guarding the location were both male, and the CSU van was parked on the far side of the overpass. Maybe it was his imagination, but the feeling of being watched, coupled with the cloying scent of perfume, had the hairs on the back of his neck standing at attention.

Shaking his head, he shifted his attention back to the crime scene. An old Luger lying beside the body was a surprise. Maybe the wound was self-inflicted. About time he caught an easy case.

He took a step forward and his foot squished. Water traveled up his pant leg and the clammy fabric stuck to his shin. No, things weren't looking up. With the luck he'd been having lately, ten bucks said the gun would turn out to be more of a roadblock than a short cut. Old guns were impossible to trace. He'd been banging his head against a wall for months on a similar case with a World War II weapon.

"So, Detective Campbell," Fredericks stammered. "Looks like you've had a long day."

Adam didn't take his eyes off the evidence as he mentally catalogued it all. "Series of long days, actually."

"Shit, man. That sucks."

"Nature of the job." Adam shrugged. No point worrying about it. The only thing he had to go home to was a frozen dinner and a sick cat. He checked his watch. After nine o'clock. He needed to give Rover his shot in less than two hours. Time to get to work. He knelt on the wet pavement beside the body. "Okay, Fredericks, what can you tell me about this?"

"White male named Manny Dewitt, age forty-five according to his ID. The guy over by the patrol car claims to have been driving by when he spotted the body, but his driver's license puts him living in the same run down motel as the vic. Not to mention that the cash and Ecstasy crammed in his pockets was covered in blood."

Fredericks tapped the notebook against his pant leg. "You want to talk to him?"

"Well, I don't *want* to, but my boss might think poorly of me if I didn't. What's his name?"

Fredericks consulted his spiral. "Eddie Coleman."

Adam groaned as he glanced toward the patrol car

where Eddie stood in handcuffs. He remembered Eddie. During his days in uniform, he'd regularly peeled him off a barstool and sent him home.

To call Eddie an unattractive man was doing him a favor. His nose was the size and shape of an antique glass doorknob and covered with broken blood vessels. His entire physique suggested a man who'd spent a lifetime courting a bottle or a needle, probably both. He could be thirty or ninety. He hadn't changed since the day Adam first saw him.

As he neared the patrol car where Eddie was being processed by a crime scene technician, Eddie spotted him and called out, "Campbell, thank goodness it's you. You know I wouldn't hurt nobody. Sure, I told the other officers I didn't recognize the guy, but that's 'cuz he didn't have no face. I've known Manny for years. In fact, I was driving around looking for him. He disappeared from his room a couple of days ago and I was worried about him."

The technician, finished with Eddie, left, and a uniformed officer sat him in the back of the car, then moved a few feet away so Adam could begin his interview.

"You were innocently driving past and spotted your good friend's body beside the road." The absurdity of the statement made him smile.

"Yeah, I didn't see nothing. I didn't even know it was Manny till they told me. I guess that shows I was right about it being dangerous to live here. I heard a gunshot, drove around the corner, and saw him there. I was only checking for a pulse when the officers drove up and found me leaning over him. I woulda called 911 myself, but I don't have no cell phone."

If Eddie was in a talkative mood, Adam wanted all his bases covered. He grabbed a card from his pocket and read Eddie his Miranda rights before continuing. "What about the gun? Have you seen it before?"

"Manny showed up with it a few months back. I mighta

touched it, just to move it out of the way."

"Okay, but I understand you had one pocket full of Ecstasy and the other bulging with cash, and both were covered in blood."

"I musta cut myself shaving." Eddie squirmed behind the metal divider. "I did take the X, but only to keep it outta the way of kids till I could turn it in to the proper authorities."

"You haven't shaved in a week." Adam sank into the front seat of the patrol car as Eddie's aroma hit him. *Or taken a bath.* "And you could have given the X to the first officers on the scene."

Eddie shrugged. "Hey, they pointed a gun at me. I got a little nervous. Is this what I get for trying to be a good citizen?"

"Eddie, if your story holds up, and I honestly hope it does, I'll buy you a medal myself."

Adam rubbed a hand over his chin, rough with stubble. He didn't put much stock in intuition, preferring to let the facts speak for themselves. Of course Eddie had taken the X and the cash, that was a given, but he'd always liked Eddie and had never known him to carry a weapon of any kind. He'd hate to see him go down if there was any way his story could be true.

This case wasn't going to be the slam-dunk he'd hoped for.

A few hours sleep and Adam was a new man. He could even shut out most of the racket in the squad room. The constant ringing of telephones, the voices, even the beeping that signaled a paper jam in the printer, were white noise that floated at the back of his mind. Two Times Tommy, sitting six feet away, was another matter altogether. Tommy leaned back in his chair, one foot resting on an open desk drawer, and rocked back and forth while he read an autopsy report.

The chair protested with a loud squeak each time he moved.

"I'll give you fifty bucks right now if you'll stop that." Tommy was so cheap, Adam worried he might actually accept the offer.

Tommy looked directly across the aisle at Adam and rocked forward slowly, causing the chair to emit a painful squeal.

A low growl escaped from somewhere near the back of Adam's throat.

Tommy laughed and dropped the report on his desk. He twisted his chair and called across the room to Frank Nelson. "Two minutes twenty-seven seconds. You owe me ten bucks. Ten bucks."

Adam slammed a file folder on his desk. Why had he agreed to take the case? He'd been off duty and heading home. Eddie, the only witness, still claimed he hadn't seen anything, the lab work wasn't back, and a copy of the victim's records should have been on his desk hours ago. He did have hopes for some type of information on the gun, but that might be days away. Now he was stuck in the office with a bunch of jokers placing bets on how long it would take to make him growl. Did that say more about them or about him? He almost growled again, but stopped himself in time.

"Campbell. You close the DB under I-59 at Montrose last night?" His boss, Lieutenant Harvey "Hard Luck" Luchak, appeared beside Adam's desk, as if out of smoke.

"I'm waiting to hear from Records, sir. They should be here shortly."

"If you can't get information from Records in a reasonable amount of time, that's your hard luck. You brought it on yourself. Next time look a little farther from home for your entertainment."

Adam shifted uncomfortably, his chair designed for a shorter man. He immediately felt the need to rearrange the papers on his desk. Months since his breakup with Mai, the sexy Records clerk he'd been so infatuated with, and the repercussions still echoed through his world. How long would it take for the gossip to run its course? Until someone else made a bigger fool of himself, that's how long. Why did sexy and crazy always seem to come in the same package?

"Wrap this one up fast, Campbell. I don't want it hanging around. Remember, you've already got your limit of open cases." Hard Luck disappeared as silently as he came.

Adam glanced around the squad room. Ignoring the two jokers, his eyes settled on the ample frame of Tommy's partner, Tenequa. She was chewing gum and using one finger to hunt-and-peck on the computer keyboard. He tried to stroll over casually, but the snickers behind his back said he wasn't fooling anyone.

"I'll bring you coffee and a donut from the break room if you'll call Records for me and get the information I need."

Tenequa blew a bubble and studied him. "Make it a Diet Coke and two donuts, and we got a deal."

Within the hour, he had a rap sheet on the vic. Manny Dewitt had been in and out of jail for drugs and petty theft for thirty years or more. The only surprise was that he lasted as long as he did. It looked more and more as if the only way Eddie hadn't seen anything was if he closed his eyes when he pulled the trigger.

A good lawyer could argue that Eddie's prints on the weapon and the gunshot residue on his hands resulted from moving the gun and checking the body. His inability to ID the vic as someone he'd known and associated with for years could be explained by the fact that Manny no longer had a face. But face or no face, Manny's arms were intact, and they sported full-length sleeves of intricate, geometric tattoos that should have been recognizable to anyone who knew him. And even a lawyer like Racehorse Haines couldn't argue away blowback blood spatters on top of the grime that was

Eddie's shirt.

Once he traced the gun, he could put the case to bed. Barring some unforeseen factor, there wasn't much he could do to help Eddie.

Two days passed before Adam stumbled across a report detailing the long and disturbing life of the murder weapon. It was buried under a report on another case. He bit back a growl directed at Mai, still trying to get even with him by hiding his paperwork.

The report caused him an entirely new set of problems. How did the weapon from his earlier homicide end up in the middle of this murder case? He knew it was trouble when he saw it lying there. He could have sworn he heard it laughing at him. Now he needed to do all kinds of legwork tracing the murder weapon to give Eddie any chance at a defense.

His head said let it go. If Eddie had lied to him, he deserved anything he got. His gut urged him to dig a little deeper. He growled at himself as he pushed back from his desk. Probably a wasted effort, but he'd never be able to put it aside until he knew all the answers. He wasn't sure which would haunt him more; the thought of an innocent man in prison or a guilty one walking free to kill again.

Frustrated, Adam pulled out his cell and dialed his partner. Ruben Marquez would be out for several weeks, the result of a ruptured appendix. With all the budget cuts lately he'd be working alone until Ruben recovered.

"Hey, buddy. *Que p*asa? How you feeling?"

"I'm coming along. I'll be fine if my mother and I can keep from killing each other until I'm able to go back to my own apartment." Ruben's voice still lacked its usual deep rumble.

"That's what you get for not having a lady in your life. Or should I say just one lady? Speaking of ladies, how's your scar look? Will they be impressed with your bravery?"

"It's not as big as I'd hoped. I'll tell them I was in a knife fight. There's some truth to that. The doc had a knife, and I put up a fight. How's it going there? You miss me yet?"

"Only because you're better at deciphering a paper trail. I have to run all over town chasing down a gun with a history as long as my dick."

"That short, huh?" Ruben chuckled. "Quit bellyaching and get to work. I don't want to find a big stack of open cases waiting on my desk when I get back."

"I don't bellyache," Adam shot back.

"Only to me and that dopey cat. If the cat starts answering you, we need to change places and you can lie in bed for a while. Talk about needing a lady in your life."

"I tried that. Then I really had things to complain about." Adam stopped short and changed the subject before Ruben had a chance to remind him how many times he'd been warned to avoid Mai. "It looks like I'm not going to have time to stop by today. Take it easy and do what Mamacita says."

"Come for supper tomorrow night. I think she's making chicken *mole*."

"You don't have to ask me twice." Adam's mouth started watering at the thought of Mamacita's chicken *mole*. His own mother had always worked outside the home. While she usually prepared their meals, they were only something to fuel the body and stave off hunger, not the expressions of love Mamacita put on the table. He hadn't realized the difference until he met Ruben.

"I usually don't have to ask once. Anyway, having you here will keep her off my back for an hour or two. I think she likes you more than me."

"Most people do, *compadre*. Most people do."

Adam snapped his phone shut as he hurried to the car. He needed to wrap this case up quickly. At thirty-four, he was young for a homicide detective. With Ruben out of commission and his feud with Mai well-known, if he let a two-bit drunk with a drug habit scam him, he'd become a laughing stock in no time.

Once that happened, his effectiveness would be compromised and he might as well work traffic.

Chapter 2

Some detectives liked to trace a thread from the end back to the beginning. Adam preferred to start at the beginning and move forward. If there were gaps in the story, they were easier to fill in when moving in chronological order. The history of the gun used in his latest homicide had gaps he could have driven the prisoner transport bus through, backed it up, and gone through again. With his own reputation at risk, he decided to start in the middle, with the last known owner, and let him explain how he had managed to misplace the weapon.

Warm sunlight filled the spring afternoon. Adam's spirits lifted as he slipped on his sunglasses. He breathed in the fresh, clean scent leftover from a recent rainstorm, and relished the excuse to get out of downtown with its noise, traffic, and exhaust fumes.

He headed north on I-45, just past the Houston city limits. Bluebonnets and Indian paintbrushes carpeted every available space. Beside the feeder road, a sign read "No Mowing, Wildflower Area." Even the ever-present construction couldn't keep him from enjoying the ride.

Hidden between a used car dealership and a boat and RV storage area, a county road wound back off the freeway. Adam nearly missed his turn. The street sign was obscured by American flags of all sizes, flapping loudly in the breeze. He couldn't figure out what buying a used car or clogging the road with an RV had to do with patriotism, but the idea of a boat did have some allure. Maybe he could afford one, now that he was out of debt.

J. R.'s Guns and Firing Range backed up to a heavily wooded area with no other businesses in the vicinity. Several spotlights meant the area was well-lit at night. The building itself was old, but well maintained. The right side was two-stories and contained the gun shop. The other section had its own entrance, but was connected by an enclosed hall or breezeway. A freshly painted sign over the door read "Firing Range."

How could someone who took so much care with a building be negligent enough to lose a dangerous weapon? Where were the owner's priorities? His good mood began to turn sour and a growl built up in his throat.

He strolled in slowly, not wishing to announce himself until he had time to look around. The sales room was large, with well-placed glass cabinets and wall displays. A hint of gun oil and Windex lingered in the air. Not a smudge or fingerprint was visible on any cabinet. The merchandise was easy to view and arranged in logical groupings. Definitely the nicest gun store he'd ever seen.

When a display of SIG-Sauers caught his eye, he stopped to study them.

A woman's voice called from the back of the room. "I hope you're here to replace that shoulder holster. It makes your jacket bunch up on one side. Not a good idea if you ever want to go undercover."

Shit. Barely in the door and he was already made. His cop mode took over as he studied her. Early thirties, tall and slim, dark hair worn in some type of spiky arrangement, not a speck of makeup—why should she with that skin—and eyes like melted chocolate.

"Besides," she went on, those eyes measuring him, "it has to be uncomfortable after a long day. You're rather large through the chest, but I've got a Falco double magazine that would be a perfect fit for you. It's not cheap, but we offer a standard fifteen percent discount to all military and law enforcement personnel."

"No, thanks, that's not why I'm here." She was rather large through the chest herself, he noticed. A dark brown tank top revealed arms that were toned and strong. She certainly looked tough enough to belong in a gun store. He wouldn't be surprised to find she could chew nails and spit out thumbtacks.

She nodded toward the case he'd been studying. "You're not planning to switch to a SIG, are you?"

"No, I'm happy with my Glock." This conversation was not going the way he planned. *Maybe I should go outside and start over.*

"Good. I know the Coast Guard and Homeland Security are going with the SIG, and it has a certain sex appeal, but in my opinion you can't beat the dependability of the Glock for someone in your profession. Now, I could upgrade you to a newer model if you're interested." She held his gaze and her eyes drew him in.

Time to get this interview under control, although any woman who described a firearm as sexy had a definite appeal of her own. His ex-wife had never liked having a gun around, despite knowing what he did for a living when she married him. She claimed that was why she left him. He figured it had more to do with the lawyer she was seeing on the nights he worked late. Just one more in a long list of reasons to distrust attorneys.

He held up his badge. "I'm Detective Adam Campbell, Homicide. I need to speak to J. R. Whitmeyer."

"I'm J. R. Whitmeyer."

"I'm looking for James Robert Whitmeyer, owner of this establishment. He's listed in my records as a fifty-nine-year-old white male."

"That's my father. He passed away about eighteen months ago." A shadow crossed her face, but she blinked twice and it was gone. Adam knew instinctively she wouldn't appreciate condolences.

"I'm Jillian Rose Whitmeyer, the new owner." She spread her arms, indicating the shop and merchandise. "What can I do to help you?"

Plenty, but not while I'm on duty.

He took out a photo of a large, matte black pistol with a distinctive toggle bolt on top and placed it on the counter in front of her. "What can you tell me about this gun? It's a Luger P08. Our records show it once belonged to your father."

Eyes that had been open and friendly a moment before were now dark and cold. She still wore a half smile, but it didn't go past her lips. She pivoted and took two steps toward a small door. "Billy, I need you out here to take care of the store."

A young man stepped around the corner, and Adam immediately began an appraisal. His eyes appeared clear, if a little vacant, but his arms showed signs of former drug use. He might be clean now, but how long would that last? Any time an obvious drug user appeared in a case, Adam's radar kicked into overdrive.

Billy didn't look like the brightest bulb in the four-pack. In fact, he wasn't sure Billy would even make a good nightlight, but it wasn't his store, so he kept his mouth shut. Billy glared at him, and Adam gave him props for loyalty.

"Sure thing, J. R.," Billy said. He crossed his arms, as if protecting the store from the devil himself.

Interesting. Did she use initials so she wouldn't have to change the sign, or so she wouldn't confuse Billy by making him learn a new name?

She pointed to a coffee pot on the back counter. "Grab

yourself a cup and let's go upstairs where we can talk in private."

No problem. A caffeine boost was always welcome, and he never minded following a well-shaped ass up a flight of stairs.

When she opened the door, not into her office as he'd expected, but into what was obviously her apartment, he was surprised. It was small, probably one bedroom and bath, along with the living area and a small eat-in kitchen. The furnishings weren't new by many years, but they were clean and looked comfortable. In fact, the whole apartment felt warm and appealing. Not surprising, considering the effort that had gone into arranging the store downstairs.

She pointed to an old-fashioned Formica table like the one his grandparents had used. He eased himself into the nearest chair, testing the old chrome legs before he put his full weight on them.

As soon as he sat, she put her hands on the table and leaned forward. "Now, would you like to explain to me what the fuck the HPD is doing letting a gun that has caused so much misery get back on the street again?"

He raised his eyebrows, but didn't answer. Let her tell the story her own way.

"Don't give me that look. You wouldn't have come here if something hadn't happened. I know, a gun is just a piece of metal. It has no soul. But that gun is evil." Her lips compressed into a thin line and her eyes narrowed to slits.

The coffee was scalding hot—just the way he liked it—with a hint of hazelnut flavoring, resembling the tepid, burned sludge from the coffee machine at work in name only. He leaned back and took a sip. "I'll take that to mean you're familiar with the weapon in question. So what can you tell me about it?"

"It's killed three people that I'm aware of, and that's in this country."

Whoa, who else was she counting that he didn't know about? He hadn't mentioned the teenage girl who was one of his open cases. He could live with Mai hassling him by delaying reports, but if he discovered she had intentionally withheld information on a case, he'd have to pursue it, no matter how much it pained him to report someone he'd once cared about.

"Why don't you start at the beginning? I find I can follow better that way."

Her shoulders relaxed slightly, but her eyes remained hard. "It belonged to my grandfather originally. He brought it back from the war. I have no idea how he got it, or why he kept it, but it was the only thing of his my father had."

"Yeah, a lot of returning servicemen smuggled weapons home in those days." He'd seen plenty in collections and at gun shows. An unfortunate number made it onto the streets.

"One day, when I was six and my sister Heather was thirteen, she got the gun out to play with." Her face was impassive, not a flicker of emotion showed. "Someone, I'm not sure how it worked, decided her death was an accident, and must have given the gun back to my father because my mother used it several years later to blow her own head off. Since that wasn't a crime, some idiot let my father take it back again. I found it last year when I was cleaning out his things."

She repeated the story calmly, as if she'd told it many times and it meant nothing to her. She didn't fool him. He'd had years of experience reading people's hidden emotions. The undercurrent of anger floating in the background might as well have been a neon sign.

He sat his cup down, crossed his arms, and leaned back in his chair. This was a murder investigation. He couldn't afford to let feelings of sympathy distract him. "That's two. You said three."

"Whoever you're here investigating. You did say you were from Homicide, didn't you?"

She was quick. He had to give her that. "When was the last time you saw it?"

"About an hour after I found it." Her words were clipped, but her voice was steady. "I drove straight downtown. No way would I allow that gun to cause any more misery. I marched into 1200 Travis Street, handed it to the sergeant at the desk, and asked him to have it destroyed. Now you've let it out again and it's killed someone else."

Uh-oh. That was a development he hadn't counted on. If she had turned it in, there should be a record. "Do you have any paperwork on that?"

She pushed back slowly and stepped into the living area a few feet away. When she leaned over to search through a file cabinet, the edges of an intricate tat peeked from beneath the strap of her tank top. He suddenly had an overwhelming desire to know if she had any others. If she did, where were they and what would they feel like, what would they taste like? By the time she turned around, he had his cop face back on.

The form was bright pink, like the ones he remembered. He hadn't seen one in a while, and it was possible they had changed. He held it up to the light. The signature was illegible, but he could make out the date and that should be enough to start with.

"I'll take this back to the office and check it out. Will you be around tomorrow? I can return it then."

"Most of the day. I have to go to my little sister's volleyball game at three-thirty, and then we'll probably get something to eat. I should be back by six."

"So you have another sister?" Why wasn't that in his

records? These games with Mai were undermining his work. He'd have to find out if the sister also had access to the gun.

"Little Sister, as in Big Brothers and Big Sisters. I'm terribly proud of her. She has a scholarship to North Texas for next year. She'll be the first in her family to go to college, actually, the first to graduate from high school."

She didn't look like the mentoring type. His opinion of her had taken a nosedive when he met Billy. Now it began to edge back up. "I'll be here before you leave. I've been trying to figure out what to call you. Do you usually go by J. R.?"

"I was Jillie when I was little, and Rose in school. When I took over this place, which was several years before my father died, I needed to be tough to deal with some of the characters around here so I've always answered to J. R."

"Why don't I call you Jillian? It's a beautiful name. If you don't mind."

"Sure, that would be fine." This time she wore a full smile, and it hit him like a punch in the gut.

He left through the store, nodding to Billy on his way out, but his mind drifted elsewhere. If Jillian's story was true, and he didn't doubt her, then this case didn't revolve around a lost or stolen gun. It hinted at a dirty cop on the force, someone working in his own building, someone he probably knew, and that set his teeth on edge. The possibility chased away his earlier concerns for his own reputation, along with daydreams of a bass boat and fantasies about Jillian's possible hidden tattoos.

Well, maybe not thoughts of tattoos.

Chapter 3

Jillian watched through the window until Detective Campbell pulled away. He was a big man, tall and solidly built, with a five o'clock shadow that probably appeared two hours after his morning shave. Even an expensive, well-cut suit couldn't hide the width of those shoulders. The cheap knock-off he wore didn't even promise to try. Everything about his expression and demeanor said, *tough guy, don't mess with me*. It was a look he had most likely cultivated for his job.

That didn't impress Jillian. She was used to dealing with tough men. She generally tried to appear tough herself. It was his soft hazel eyes, hidden behind wire-rimmed glasses, that had caught her attention, along with the light brown hair, which seemed to escape any attempt at discipline. She'd seen him brush it down with his hand when he came in the door. How hard a man could he be if he couldn't control his own hair?

Who was she kidding—a police detective? There couldn't be a worse choice for someone holding as many secrets as she did. Better that she should keep her vow to stay away from men until she could call her life her own. Who knew? Maybe she could find a way to bump into him then.

She went back to the store and spent the next half hour straightening out the mess Billy had made in only fifteen minutes. When she couldn't think of anything else to do, she poured herself another cup of coffee, told Billy she was going to the park for some fresh air, and headed out the back door to her car.

She chewed on her lip as she drove. She hadn't actually lied to Detective Campbell. Everything she'd said was true. It was the things she'd omitted that would have caused him to question her sanity.

Twice on the short drive she almost turned back, but she gripped the wheel and kept driving. Avoidance wasn't the answer. She couldn't live this way any longer. Always in limbo, never knowing for certain. She'd sworn she would never do this again, but she had to find out what had happened.

In less than ten minutes, she sat at her usual spot in the park. She tilted her face to the sun. In a couple of months it would be too hot to enjoy, but for now, its rays felt soft and the breeze refreshing. Birds and squirrels chirped and chattered while going about their daily business. Traffic sounds were far enough away that she could ignore them.

She took a deep breath and called, her voice shaky, "I'm waiting, Heather, but not for long. If you want to talk to me, you better come out."

For one long moment, she let herself believe Heather wouldn't show, that she was finally safe.

As usual, Heather's perfume arrived before she did. "You don't have to be so prissy about it. You haven't talked to me in months, and now you think I should appear the minute you decide to show up." Heather sat beside her on the table, tossing her long blond hair and showing off a flawless profile, hidden beneath heavy makeup. Her white linen outfit hugged her hourglass figure and the stones on her sandals matched the colors in her low cut blouse.

"What're you drinking? Is that a Coke?" Heather asked.

"No, it's coffee."

"I used to like Coke. Why don't you drink it anymore? I remember the way it fizzed in my mouth. Is the coffee hot? Does it smell good?" Heather leaned over, as if inhaling the aroma.

"Yeah. It smells good." *Although, your perfume drowns it out.* "It has special flavoring, hazelnut."

"What's that?"

"It doesn't matter. That's not what we need to talk about." Jillian tossed the cup in a trashcan near the table and forced herself to remain calm. "Did you do something with Daddy's gun?"

"What could I have done to Daddy's gun? I hate guns."

"You might hate guns, but you love causing trouble. Besides, you wouldn't do anything yourself, that's not your style. You like to whisper things in someone's ear and let them do your dirty work for you."

Heather shifted and raised her chin even higher. "I don't know what you're talking about, but I did warn you bad things would happen if you ignored me."

"So innocent people had to pay the price?" Her heart raced, but she forced herself to speak calmly. If she made Heather angry, she'd never get the answers she searched for.

"They weren't innocent. They were both druggies. He was a bum who lived under the freeway. She came into our house to shoot up. She dressed awful and acted like a tramp. Mama wouldn't have liked them at all."

Two people? That must be what Detective Campbell was trying to keep secret. It was worse than she thought. Her stomach clenched and bile started up her throat. "How dare you use Mama to justify something like this?"

Jillian couldn't sit still. She popped up and paced in front of the bench, her heart hammering. "You told me kids were using our old house to do drugs, so I had the police run them out. That girl wasn't bothering you anymore."

"I couldn't stand her." Heather's face contorted in anger. "She was cheap and tacky and went in my room and made fun of my trophies."

"So you killed her?" Jillian's head reeled, and she had

to grab the edge of the table for support. She was losing the battle to keep her voice under control.

"Stop saying that. I didn't kill her. I couldn't kill anyone. I just don't like druggies and sometimes bad things happen to them."

"Look, I'll go by the house and if there's anything of yours, I'll put it in storage where it'll be safe. If bums or druggies start using the house again, tell me, and I'll take care of it. But you can't hurt people just because you don't like the way they dress."

"I never said I hurt them. Besides, how am I supposed to tell you if you won't talk to me? I like my things where they are. I don't want you to move them." Heather crossed her arms and turned her head away.

"I'm sure you'll find a way to get a message to me. You always have."

Heather was never going to admit anything, and maybe she was better off not knowing. The hints Heather had dropped today were almost more than she could handle.

"I've got to go back to work. Try not to do anything else that sends the police to my door." Like anything she said would stop Heather from doing exactly what she wanted.

"You think you're so important because you have a job. You're no better than I am."

If I'm not, I might as well give up now. You've tried for years to take over my body. Maybe I should let you have it. You couldn't cause any more harm with it than you have the way you are now. Jillian picked up her car keys and started toward the parking lot. "Goodbye, Heather," she said over her shoulder.

She didn't start shaking until she was back at the store.

Billy didn't like it when Jillian left the store. When she went upstairs and left him in charge, he knew he was helping her, giving her time to rest. He liked the feeling of responsibility, but felt safe because she was close by if a problem came up. When she left the store entirely, he began to get nervous. What if something happened he couldn't handle? Plenty of rough characters came into the store, and Jillian was the only one who could manage them. He paced, constantly watching the front window and chewing on his lower lip.

The tension left his shoulders when her car pulled into the lot. After several minutes, she still hadn't gotten out and Billy started to gnaw on his thumbnail. Don't let it be as bad as last time. He didn't know what happened when she went to the park, but she always came back upset.

He'd followed her once, locking the store and putting up the "Closed" sign. He got close enough to hear her voice, but not to understand her words. She sounded angry, but who was she angry with? He hadn't seen anyone else. They must have been hiding in the woods.

If he knew who it was, maybe he could help.

When she finally came in, he looked up casually. "Hey, J. R., everything okay?"

"Sure. I'm going to run upstairs for a minute, but I'll be right back. Everything okay here?"

"Fine. No problems. Take your time." He wanted to help, but he felt so useless. And after everything she'd done for him.

He'd have to go to the park himself. Maybe once he got there, he could figure out what to do. Shit, if he couldn't handle some of the customers, how was he going to manage someone who frightened Jillian?

Chapter 4

Adam didn't make it back to the office until late afternoon. He'd planned it that way. He didn't want to call Records until after Mai left for the day. It made life simpler.

"Could you get me everything you have on Jillian Rose Whitmeyer, a white female, approximately five ten or eleven, early thirties, brown and brown. Also, how do I find out who was working the front desk on a certain date?"

"I can get that information for you." The voice on the other end of the line was smooth and pleasant. Adam didn't know who it was, but it wasn't Mai, and that's all that counted. He rattled off the date and time.

He had the information on the desk sergeant in less than half-an-hour. The info on Jillian took a bit longer. Both reports were unsettling. The desk sergeant on duty was Calvin Marshall, a man he'd known and disliked for twelve years or more.

The sheet on Jillian was even more disturbing. Not for what it said, but for what it didn't say. Large chunks of time were missing or unaccounted for. Her schooling was confusing at best, and her work history wasn't exactly stellar. In his experience that meant drugs, with or without a record.

Disappointment surged through him. If she was into drugs, then she now had two tie-ins with this case. He sighed and leaned back in his chair. Not the news he'd been hoping for. First things first. Follow the gun, and then worry about the next step.

At least he had an excuse to put off confronting Sergeant Marshall. It was time to go home and give Rover his shot.

With Rover fed, dinner in the microwave, and a beer in hand, Adam sat on the back deck watching the last of the sunset. Someone in the neighborhood was grilling outside and the aroma drifted across the grass like morning fog. He loved the old house and The Heights area where he'd grown up. When founded in the 1890's, The Heights was considered a streetcar suburb. Now in the heart of north-central Houston, minutes from everything the city had to offer, it still managed to retain its small town feel.

The house was a run-down Craftsman he'd picked up for a song before the area began its gentrification. He'd done most of the remodeling himself, only hiring out jobs too big or too complicated to do on his own. He'd fought for the house in the divorce but later learned his ex-wife didn't want it. She'd only used it for leverage.

The feeling of calm and satisfaction he got from being surrounded by things he'd built himself meant more to him than the stock certificates and savings she'd demanded. Three years later, he'd paid off all her debts and was solvent again. If he never heard the Home Shopping Network again or saw another UPS truck pull up in front of his house, it would be fine with him.

The squirrels had been at his bird feeder again. No matter what he tried, it never took them more than a few hours to get the better of him. If he couldn't out-think an animal that was just a rat with a bushy tail, how could he hope to out-think Calvin Marshall, who was basically a rat with a badge and thirty-plus years experience?

Marshall hadn't been his training officer, but they'd crossed paths plenty in those days. Marshall cut every corner he could find and bent every rule until it called uncle. Adam never saw him actually break one, but that didn't mean he hadn't done it. With eighteen months to go until he had his thirty, Marshall made desk sergeant. Then he surprised everyone by refusing to retire.

"What do I have to go home to?" he'd said. "You guys are my family. I'll stay here another couple of years and keep an eye on you. See that you don't get into trouble." It sounded fishy then and downright stinky now. If Marshall had something going on, the whole department would smell. Hard Luck would want to report it to Internal Affairs for investigation, but if they found something, the entire force would suffer. Adam couldn't let that happen.

The microwave dinged, and he headed inside to his beef enchilada dinner. Rover, finished with his own meal, came over to inspect Adam's.

"What's up with you, cat? You used to at least pretend to keep the squirrels off the feeder. If I'm gonna spend this much on your medication, you've gotta to do your part."

He reached over to scratch the cat behind his ear. "Squirrels are bad enough, but if I find a rat in my garage, you'll be out on your fat, furry keister. I don't care how old and sick you are."

Rover twitched his tail but didn't answer.

Adam took his dinner and a fresh beer out to the deck. He thought about Marshall for as long as he could stand it. Then he thought about Jillian for a while.

He went to bed with a smile, and a warm feeling that went all the way down.

The apartment was dark. The moon shining through the open curtains provided the only light. Jillian sat at her dresser, hairbrush in hand, not moving. The thought of Detective Campbell's soft eyes and unruly hair made her smile, but only for a moment. How much should she tell?

She knew from painful experience what would happen if she said too much.

Had her attempt to declare her independence from Heather resulted in the deaths of two people? Or did the fact that they were drug addicts put them in harm's way? Heather hadn't admitted to anything, so it might be a coincidence.

She slammed her hands on the dresser and the brush split with a loud crack. Even if she told everything she knew, even if someone actually believed her, what good would it do? No one could do anything about it.

That wasn't completely true. She couldn't change the past, but she might be able to prevent anything else from happening by giving in to all Heather's demands. But at what cost to herself? Besides, Heather wasn't trustworthy. Whatever she agreed to now, Heather would always demand more later, until Jillian had nothing left to give, and Heather completely took over. Who knew how much damage Heather could do once she had a solid body? Jillian was at a loss as to what she should do, and there wasn't a soul she could talk to about it.

"No way, Heather," she finally said, as if saying it aloud gave it more force. "Do your worst. I'm not giving in this time. I'm not talking to you or sharing my life with you. You're on your own." If she could out-last her, maybe Heather would finally give up and move on to the next realm, whatever that was.

Exhausted, she went to bed and tried to convince herself she was doing the right thing, the best thing for everybody.

Billy couldn't check out the park during the day. He was needed at the store. That didn't mean he couldn't check it out at night. He was certain someone was blackmailing Jillian. Probably about her past. But she talked about it with anyone who was interested, so how she could be blackmailed?

Maybe someone from the Mafia was threatening her, trying to make her sell guns illegally. He'd seen that in a movie once.

His apartment was in Conroe, a small town about fifteen minutes north of Jillian's on I-45, but across the county line. It was another five minutes to the park, and he got there about ten o'clock.

"Hello." His voice cracked, so he started again. "Hello, is anybody there?" His heart hammered so loud he wasn't sure he could hear an answer.

If only he were smarter, braver, he might know what to do. She'd done so much to help him. She was the only person willing to give him a second chance. Without her encouragement, he'd have slipped back into his old life by now. He had to help her, even if the park did scare him at night.

There weren't any lights around and he'd forgotten his flashlight so he'd left his headlights on. They lit up the path, but made the rest of the park even darker. Now he couldn't see anything. Another bonehead mistake.

He sat on the table where he'd watched her talking to someone he couldn't see, unsure what to do next. A twig snapped nearby, and he almost wet his pants. The mosquitoes swarmed over him in an instant. Why hadn't he thought to bring repellent? He was so dumb.

The gun dug into his thigh. Shifting his weight, he pulled it out of his pocket and carefully set it on the table beside him. Now he could reach it quicker. He'd never be allowed a concealed weapon permit, but Jillian had insisted he take the course anyway, so he'd know what he was talking about with the customers. It was a tough course, but he could have passed it with Jillian's coaching. He called her J. R. at work, that was more professional, but he refused to call her J. R. in private.

She couldn't sell him a gun, not with his record. Conroe

might be Houston's ugly stepsister, but he knew where to find things. One drag down Main Street, and he could score anything he wanted. He wasn't about to sit in the park unarmed. Blackmailers, drug dealers, or Mafia thugs could be anywhere.

The air moved against his face, and for a moment the stench of rotting leaves and garbage was replaced by something heavy and sweet. He sat up straight and glanced around. No one was there. He was always imagining things. Maybe he was the problem. Jillian spent so much time correcting his mistakes she didn't have time to take care of her own problems. He hadn't thought of that before. Without him around, she'd be better off.

He shook off the thought and called out again. "Is anyone here? I want to talk to you." No one answered. The crickets stopped for a moment, but started again as soon as his voice faded away.

Of course no one was there. What did he think, that Mafia hit men just hung around the park waiting for someone to show up? This wasn't going to tell him how to help Jillian.

"You are an idiot, Billy. What makes you think you could solve a problem Jillian can't solve?" The voice in his head started again. "You know the one thing you can do to help her most. That's why you came out here, isn't it?"

He clamped his hands over his ears, trying to shut out the voice. "That's not it. I'm going to find the people who're hurting her."

"You're the only one who's hurting her, and you know it." The voice was everywhere. Closing his ears didn't help. "Every time she leaves you alone, you screw up and it costs her time and money." The voice sounded a little like Jillian, only meaner.

Suddenly Billy remembered the mistake he'd made with the cash register that afternoon. It took Jillian a long time to straighten it out. At least he hadn't lost any money.

Last time he got mixed up on the change, it cost her $20. He tried to pay her back out of his salary, but she wouldn't take it. Instead she got angry with the customer who tricked him.

She practically threw the guy out. "You ought to be ashamed of yourself, pulling a stunt like that in my store. You're not welcome here anymore. Take your business elsewhere. I don't care how much you spent last year, I won't be around someone I can't trust." Instead of costing her $20, he cost her a steady customer. Still, it was nice of her to say she trusted him.

He was her biggest problem. That's why she'd come to the park, because she was upset with him and didn't want to show it. There wasn't any blackmailer.

"You're so stupid, you don't even know when you're being stupid," the voice said. "Why don't you do everybody a favor and quit taking up room on the planet? You know sooner or later you'll go back to doing drugs. You've already come close several times. Think how disappointed she'll be then."

The voice was right. He was stupid. His mother had told him so almost every day of his life until she'd finally given up and kicked him out. Now she seldom spoke to him at all, and if she did, it was more likely about Jillian.

"I don't know why that woman puts up with you," his mother told him. "You're just another one of her pity projects. She thinks if she does enough good deeds, she can overcome her past and get into heaven. Not likely."

A mosquito landed on Billy's nose. He didn't have the heart to slap it.

Chapter 5

Friday was Jillian's day to open the store. She'd slept soundly once she made her decision and woke feeling better than she expected. After a quick shower and a bowl of cereal, she made her bed and switched on the dishwasher. As soon as she got downstairs, she put the first pot of coffee on to brew. By 10:00 a.m., everything had been dusted, swept, turned on, booted up, unlocked, and generally made ready for the day.

She chuckled at the thought of Billy trying to clean. He could leave more fingerprints than he wiped off and took twice as long to do it. He wasn't due in until 11:00, so she didn't start looking for him till 11:30. Even then, she was only irritated, not worried.

At 12:00, she called his apartment. She was relieved when he didn't answer. It meant he was on his way. By 1:00, she was mad. She wanted to go upstairs and fix a sandwich, but there were customers in the store and she couldn't leave. To make matters worse, she needed to use the bathroom, big time.

Business picked up, and she didn't have time to think about food or anything else, although she did leave a message on her Little Sister's cell phone. She wouldn't be able to make the volleyball game.

Jillian glanced up when the door opened at 2:15. She grinned as two deputy sheriffs entered. "Larry, Mike, I've never been so glad to see you guys in my life. Help yourself to coffee. You know where it is." She waved in the direction of the pot as she took a step toward the bathroom. The lunchtime rush had passed and even Larry ought to be able to stand in an empty store for three minutes without causing any damage.

They didn't move, so she studied them. Her heart started pounding when she saw their serious expressions.

Mike's words sent a chill up her spine. "We need to talk to you about Billy."

"Ah, shit." She leaned her head back and looked at the ceiling. "What kind of trouble has he gotten into this time? Please, please, guys. Take it as easy on him as you can. I honestly don't believe he's back on drugs. I keep a close eye on him, and I think I'd know."

"It's not that." Larry shifted his substantial weight from one foot to the other.

"When was the last time you saw him?" As senior officer, Mike took over the questioning.

"Close of business yesterday. Just like any other day. What's going on?"

"He was found dead this morning. It looks like suicide. Was he depressed? Had he been acting strangely?"

Jillian's legs turned to rubber and she grabbed the counter for support. Her heart, which had been racing a moment before, now stopped cold. "I don't know. He's always a little depressed, but no more than usual. Are you sure it was suicide, because he's sort of frail. I always worried that the drugs had ruined his liver or kidneys. Could it be from natural causes?"

Mike ignored her question. "Did anything happen yesterday? Anything that might have upset him?"

"He screwed up the cash register, but I didn't make a fuss. It happens too often to get mad." She tried to remember what she'd said. He took every little thing to heart. She had to watch each word. A moan built up in her throat, but she forced it back.

"Wait a minute. Wait a minute. Y'all are Harris County.

Billy's apartment is in Conroe. That's Montgomery County. What are you doing here?"

"He wasn't in his apartment. He was at that pocket park about a mile from here. The one with two picnic tables and a small hiking trail. We wouldn't have found him for days if Mike hadn't spotted the buzzards." Mike elbowed Larry, but Larry didn't take the hint. He kept talking. "Another few hours and it would have been a mess. His head was mostly gone as it was."

Tears began building behind her eyes, but she refused to let them fall. She wouldn't cry in front of that fat fool.

"Do you know if he had a gun? Did you sell him one, or did he take one from the store?" Mike took his hat off and wiped a sleeve across his bald head.

"Of course I didn't sell him one, or lend him one, or give him one. He's got a record and he's a recovering drug addict. I suppose he could have taken one without my knowledge, but I don't think so. What kind was it?" Her voice rose with each word.

"It was a beat-up old Saturday Night Special, all rusty and falling apart."

"I don't carry that type of gun, and you know it." How dare they come into her store and make accusations like that?

She slammed her hands on the counter, jarring the glass. Two handprints faded slowly. She remembered her earlier complaints about Billy and realized he'd never be there to clean the glass again. She could feel her heart break into little pieces.

"I know you don't, but we had to ask. Check your inventory and let us know if anything's missing." Mike's eyes were sad and his shoulders slumped, but he didn't move any closer.

"Okay, I will." The words were hoarse. Something had happened to her voice. "Would you flip the sign to 'Closed' on your way out?"

As soon as the two deputies left, Jillian's legs buckled and she sank to the floor. With the deputies gone, there was no reason to hold back the tears.

Her sister, her mother, her father, Billy. Each death took a hole out of her soul until soon there wouldn't be anything left. At least this time, she didn't have to worry about Heather's involvement.

Heather might retaliate against anyone she thought had ignored or insulted her, but she didn't even know Billy . . . did she?

After a day spent doing paperwork and checking out leads on three homicides, Adam was running late. Three-fifteen. He hoped Jillian hadn't already left for her ball game. The "Closed" sign was on the door, but it was unlocked so he pushed it open. He didn't see anyone as he crossed toward the back of the store, but a whiff of burnt coffee put him on high alert.

Should he go up to her apartment and knock on the door? He didn't want to surprise her if she was changing clothes.

Of course that's what he wanted. Otherwise he wouldn't have thought of it.

He stopped abruptly when he saw her sitting on the floor, unsure what his eyes were telling him. Her face was ashen and she'd obviously been crying.

"Jillian? Jillian, what happened?" He knelt beside her and ran his hands down her back and arms. He was looking for injuries, but he didn't fail to notice the softness of her skin.

"Billy, are you here?" His words echoed, telling him the store was empty.

"He's not going to answer." Her voice was so soft he wasn't sure if he heard it or imagined it.

"Did you have a robbery? Did someone hurt you?"

She shook her head so slightly he almost missed it.

He cupped her chin gently with one hand and lifted it until he could look into her eyes. His voice was low and soft. "You have to talk to me. I can't help you if I don't know what's wrong."

"Billy's gone. He killed himself this morning. Or maybe it was last night, I don't know."

"Did he OD?" He bit off the words, angry with himself for disregarding his own rules and trusting a reformed addict simply because Jillian appeared to.

"No. He shot himself at a park about a mile from here."

Shit. That put her uncomfortably close to another mysterious death. He wasn't even finished investigating the last two, and now he'd have to look into this one.

If Hard Luck thought he had too many open cases now, wait till he heard about this. No point trying to keep it from him. Hard Luck didn't get where he was without knowing everything that went on in his department. Something was about to hit the fan, and it wouldn't be roses.

"Come on. Let's get you upstairs. You can't sit here on the floor all day." He pulled her up and she started slowly for the stairs, almost shuffling. He poured them each a cup of coffee and followed.

The coffee was over-brewed and bitter, but Adam had drunk worse. He sat both cups on the table and Jillian sipped hers absently. She never raised her eyes from the old Formica.

It was start and stop, but eventually he got all the information, including the names of the investigating officers. He'd call them later and check out the facts, but he couldn't see how it involved her in any way. Just another tragic accident.

"I keep going over and over things. I was so sure it would be okay. Was it my ego? Did trying to help Billy myself instead of sending him to a professional cause this?"

He'd heard the same thing from the families of every suicide he investigated. Finally she started to pull herself together. He glanced at his watch—almost five o'clock. He didn't realize they'd talked so long. "Go wash your face. Do whatever you have to do. We need to get moving," he said.

"I'm not going anywhere." She looked down at herself as if her body were a pair of shoes she wasn't sure she wanted to put on.

"Yes, you are. I have to be somewhere in an hour, and I'm not leaving you alone." He wasn't sure if she agreed or if she didn't have the strength to argue, but she stood and headed for the back room.

When she reappeared, her hair was freshly spiked, her face washed, and she had on a simple black shirt. Not a tank top. She led the way through her apartment, then closed and locked the door. In the store, she switched off most of the lights and set the alarm.

Once in the car, she faced him. "Now will you tell me where we're going?"

"We're having dinner with a friend of mine and his mother."

"You can't just bring an extra person to dinner. Don't you have any manners?"

"Not many." He knew the rules all right—his father's belt had made sure of that—he just chose not to worry about them anymore. "She won't mind. She always cooks enough for an army."

"I don't care. You have to warn her. I won't just show up."

Adam called Ruben and let him know an extra person was coming. He didn't give any details.

He liked the idea of Ruben wondering what was going on.

Chapter 6

Jillian remained silent on the drive to Ruben's, but she seemed calm. Adam didn't know what to think of her. He still hadn't questioned her about the two murders, and now he wouldn't be able to for a while. He needed to as soon as possible. Tonight he'd have to be satisfied with learning more about her.

Ruben's mother lived in the same small, frame house where she'd raised her family. It was in a Hispanic neighborhood where light, music, kids, and delicious aromas spilled out onto the street through open doors.

As they reached the first step, Jillian inhaled deeply. "I didn't know I was hungry until this minute."

"You'd better be hungry. You don't want to insult Mamacita by not eating."

The screen door flew open as they stepped onto the porch. Ruben stood in the doorway, blocking most of the light. He wasn't fat, far from it, but he was big. His shoulders brushed both sides of the doorframe. A quarter inch of light showed at the top of his head. He slapped Adam on the back with a blow that would have flattened a lesser man.

"'Bout time you got here. That woman's driving me crazy. She wants me to eat twenty-four hours a day. She thinks I need to build up my strength."

He spotted Jillian and came to an abrupt halt. "Well, well, well. What do we have here? How do you do, ma'am? Ruben Marquez, at your service." He gave a courtly bow. "Now if this useless tub-of-lard gives you any trouble, you just let me know and I'll straighten him out."

Adam smiled. Surprising Ruben wasn't easy. "Don't pay any attention to him. He's my partner, skylarking on sick leave while I do all the work. Ruben, this is Jillian Whitmeyer." He paused, unsure how to describe her. Saying 'a suspect in my latest case,' seemed a poor choice. "A friend of mine."

"That's interesting, because I'm almost certain she wasn't a friend of yours when I got sick last week."

Jillian stepped into the living room, and Ruben gave her a thorough once-over as the light hit her. His eyes grew big and a grin spread across his face. "Mamacita, come in here. You need to meet Adam's new friend."

Mrs. Marquez bustled in, wiping her hands on a dishtowel. She was beaming from ear to ear. As tiny as Ruben was large, she had graying hair pulled into a tight knot at the back of her head. When she got a good look at Jillian, she froze in place and her face fell. Almost immediately she put on a polite smile. "How do you do, my dear? Any friend of Adam's is a friend of ours."

Adam wasn't worried. If Mamacita could warm to a no-good degenerate like himself, she'd warm to Jillian. Spiky hair, tattoos, and all.

Jillian looked overwhelmed. "Oh, we're not really friends." Adam's brows shot up. She didn't know what they were any more than he did. "I mean, we're friends but...I had a bad day, a friend of mine died, and Detective Campbell was kind enough to worry that I shouldn't be left alone."

Mrs. Marquez's smile warmed, but only a little. "Of course you shouldn't be alone. Bad news needs friends to share it with. Adam is always thinking of others." She gave him a look that was indecipherable.

Mrs. Marquez marched to the open door and looked out, as if she saw something standing on the steps. Finally she closed the door with a solid thump.

"Come, come, let's eat. Dinner is ready." Mrs. Marquez

led the way into the dining room, and a table that groaned under the weight of food.

Ruben placed a huge hand on Adam's shoulder, holding him back. "Where did she come from? How did you ever find such a beautiful, sexy, and completely inappropriate looking woman? She looks like a biker. Please tell me she rides a Hog."

"I don't know. I haven't seen one. But she does have a tat."

It didn't seem possible, but Ruben's grin got even bigger. "Where is it? Will Mamacita see it?"

"Not with that blouse on. But there's one thing even better." Adam hurried on before Ruben asked how he knew what was under her blouse. "She owns a gun store."

Ruben leaned his head back, looking at the ceiling. He closed his eyes and put his hands together. "Thank you, Lord," he said. When he looked back at Adam, his grin returned. "Never in the history of the world has one man made such a sacrifice for a friend. I will remember this forever. No matter what I do from now on, no matter who I bring home, anything less than a hooker and I'm golden. She'll never complain about my girlfriends again."

Adam waited for a growl to build in the back of his throat, but surprisingly, nothing came. What was wrong with him tonight? He was too young to start mellowing.

"After dinner we need to talk," Adam said. "I have a problem."

"You mean in addition to the fact that you just brought a gun-toting, tattooed biker chick into Mamacita's house? I can't wait to hear it." Ruben limped into the dining room and sat heavily, as if the short trek exhausted him.

Mrs. Marquez began serving the plates, but stopped when she reached Jillian's. "You're not allergic to peanuts, are you?"

"No, Ma'am," said Jillian.

"These days you have to ask. Everyone's allergic to everything. You can't make a good chicken *mole* without peanut butter."

"Don't worry. I don't have any allergies, and I eat everything. I love chicken *mole*. My mouth started watering when I stepped in the door. You didn't make the sauce yourself, did you?"

Mrs. Marquez sniffed as if the idea of buying sauce in a jar wasn't worth answering. She continued putting generous helpings of food on each plate, but when she reached Ruben's, she filled it to overflowing. "Was this a surprise, your friend's death, or had he been sick?"

"It was quite a shock, although maybe it shouldn't have been. He was a recovering drug addict so you always know something could happen, but he'd been working for me for two years and was doing well. I never expected him to kill himself."

"Suicide. Such a sin." Mrs. Marquez crossed herself quickly. "How could you hire a man like that? It would be so dangerous."

"He wasn't dangerous, just sad and broken. It's hard for recovering addicts to find a job and without a job, they can't get better."

This was Adam's chance to get an insight into her thinking. "Still, you said it was difficult to know for sure what one might do."

"I know that. Do I look like a pushover?"

Even Ruben stopped eating to smile at that comment.

"I didn't take my eyes off him at first. I found him an apartment in Conroe, close to his mother. I thought she would help, but I was wrong. She threw him out of the house at sixteen, when he first started using. She held herself up as a pillar of the church, but cut him off and hardly spoke to him again." Jillian's tone made clear her opinion of a mother who would renounce a troubled child.

"I never let him have any money," Jillian added. "I paid his rent, his utilities, bought his food, and his clothes. For six months the only cash he had was a few quarters for laundry."

The room was silent, except for the sound of cutlery on dishes and music coming through the open windows. Mrs. Marquez looked somewhat mollified. "How did you know what to do?" she asked.

"I understood exactly what he was going through. I was pretty heavy into the drug scene myself at one time." Her chin tilted upward.

Adam nodded to himself. That explained a lot. It also put her on his Do Not Trust list.

"When I told my father I wanted to get clean, it was the hardest thing I'd ever done. He put down his glass, sobered up—at least temporarily—and took care of me until I got myself straightened out. It was probably the last time in his life he was completely sober, but it didn't matter. He came through for me when I needed him. I couldn't have done it alone." Jillian's voice cracked, but she kept going.

"It's been seven years now, and I always try to help anyone I can. I never make a secret of my past. Someone might see me and think, 'If she can do it, maybe I can do it.' But that doesn't make me a fool. To work for me, Billy had to prove himself every day."

Seven years was a long time to be clean. Maybe Jillian did deserve a second chance.

"What type of business do you own?" Ruben's face was the picture of innocence.

"Jillian is the famous J. R. of J. R.'s Guns and Firing Range out I-45," Adam said, glaring at Ruben. Mamacita's eyes grew big.

Ruben actually put his fork down for a moment. "I know that place. It had a bad reputation at one time, years ago, but lately it's come back strong. It's supposed to be one of the nicest places in the county."

Jillian flashed him a smile. "Thanks, I appreciate the vote of confidence. It's been hard. My father was the original J. R. He opened it before I was born, but he'd let it run down pretty bad by the time I started managing it. I had to get tough fast to deal with that clientele and get it back on its feet. Before he died, I completely remodeled it and put in an apartment for myself upstairs."

Adam sat back and watched as Mamacita and Ruben warmed to Jillian.

"My biggest aim is for gun safety. I can't keep anyone from buying a gun without getting some type of gun safe, but I price them so I don't make any profit, and then I can shame the customers into buying one."

The rest of the meal Jillian entertained everyone with stories of minor disasters at the store and Billy's problems counting change. "He was an ace at mopping floors, and he could make the bathroom sparkle, but cleaning smudges off the glass display cases was beyond him. He would rub and rub, using half a bottle of Windex and a full roll of paper towels, and they would look worse when he finished than when he started."

"My Julio was like that," Mamacita said. "He could rake leaves until not a twig was left, or mend the screens perfectly, but give him a job inside the house, and it wasn't worth the effort. If he washed the dishes, the floor, counter, and walls were so wet it looked as if the faucet sprang a leak and sprayed the room. I suppose we all have certain talents and should recognize them."

"Did you let him get off dishwashing duty?" Jillian asked.

"Oh no. I just made sure he wiped everything up when he finished. We might have talents, but we still have to learn to do the things we don't enjoy as much."

As she talked, Adam saw Jillian relax and even smile

slightly.

When they finished the flan and pushed back from the table, he glanced at Ruben. "Let me help you up the stairs so you can get ready for bed."

Ruben made a big show of looking at his watch. "When did you become so helpful?"

Chapter 7

Jillian and Mamacita were still chatting as Adam helped Ruben climb the stairs. Their voices floated up from the dining room, and he couldn't help eavesdropping.

"I'm in awe you made that sauce from scratch. I've tried it several times, but it always lacked something." Jillian's voice reflected the strain she'd been under, and Adam knew he didn't have much time to talk to Ruben.

"Did you use peanut butter?" Mamacita asked. "Some people don't. Everybody worries what's in their food."

"I didn't the first time and it was too runny, but I used it the second time. Then the consistency was right, but it still had a bitter or sharp flavor." Jillian gathered the glasses as Mrs. Marquez stacked the plates.

"I'll tell you my secret. Use just one or two Hersey's Kisses. Not too much, you don't want it sweet tasting."

"I would never have thought of that. I can see how that would take the bitterness out without being enough to change the flavor."

Ruben stopped halfway up the stairs. "I can't believe this. You bring over a woman who's everything Mamacita disapproves of and instead of having a heart attack, Mamacita is divulging her secret family recipes." He leaned forward and lowered his voice. "You don't understand. Those recipes are never shared. Even the daughters-in-law don't know them."

"I think it's the women you bring home Mamacita disapproves of, not what they do for a living." Adam pulled on Ruben's arm. "Come on. Let's get you to your room. I have something important I need to talk to you about."

"It better be important. I'm only allowed up and down the stairs once a day, and I usually like to wait till at least dark before I go to bed."

Ruben's room hadn't changed since high school. His half was decorated with the football trophies he won first as a defensive lineman at Milby High School and later as a Texas Tech Red Raider. His brother's half was full of science fair projects and certificates.

Adam couldn't help smiling. The room he'd shared with his brother had been full of toy cars on his side and toy soldiers on his brother's half.

Ruben sat on one bed and Adam sat on the other, facing him, knees almost touching. He reminded Ruben of their cold case concerning the teenage girl, then brought him up-to-date on his new case—the transient found under the bridge. He described the gun next to the body and his belief that the man's friend, and the only witness, was most likely the shooter. Ruben nodded, still listening.

"Now we get to the interesting part. Ballistics came out a match for the two shootings."

"Any sign the two vics knew each other?" Even at half-speed, Ruben was ahead of any partner he'd worked with in his twelve years on the force.

"They were both high, as was my prime suspect. But I won't know if it's the same stuff for a day or two. Longer if Mai can find a way of keeping the reports from me."

Ruben's expression clearly indicated he'd said *I told you so* enough times that it didn't need repeating.

"I think the second vic might have been the dealer," Adam added quickly, before Ruben could comment.

"What about the gun? Where'd he get it? That might tell you something. Can you trace it?"

"Oh, I can trace it all right. I can trace it all the way back to Jillian's father."

"Madre de Dios. You do have a problem."

"Just wait, because that isn't even the biggest complication."

"I don't think I want to hear this." Ruben chewed his thumb-nail.

"When J. R., Sr. died, Jillian took the gun, which was the same one her sister accidentally shot herself with and her mother committed suicide with, to Travis Street Headquarters and told them to destroy it."

Ruben groaned. "So she says. How long have you known her? Two days? Okay, she's sexy as all get out, and she has a smile that goes right through you, although you might have to be careful not to put your eye out on one of those hair spikes. I know you've been on a long dry spell, but don't get foolish about this. I hope you've learned not to let your dick do your thinking for you."

Adam grimaced. He liked Ruben, a lot, but. . . "Hey, you worry about your dick, and I'll worry about mine."

Ruben held up his hand. "Fine, but does she have any proof she turned the gun in?"

"She has proof. She kept the receipt. And we're not to the best part yet."

Ruben didn't speak, he just held out his hands, palm up, as if to say, *What else could there possibly be?*

"I checked the schedule. The desk sergeant on duty was Calvin Marshall."

"Who've you talked to about this?" Ruben's eyes narrowed to slits.

"No one. I drove out to question Jillian this afternoon, but when I got there she was in shock because her friend died. Which, by the way, ties her to another unnatural death." Shit, he hated to say that out loud.

"You have to question her. I don't care how upset she is."

"I know." This kept getting worse and worse.

"You can't question Marshall or tell Hard Luck until you have every lead followed and every fact checked seven ways from Sunday."

"I want to check everything I can first thing Monday morning. I need to learn more about the probable shooter, Eddie Coleman. Remember him?"

Ruben rubbed his chin. "I never knew Eddie to be violent."

"That's the only reason I was still working the case. He's locked up on other charges, so I haven't worried about him till now. Then on Tuesday I plan to question Jillian further. You got any suggestions?"

"Watch your back. Document everything. This could get ugly. I never dreamed I'd be happy I was laid up. Don't forget, Marshall has a reputation for retaliating against anyone who crosses him."

Adam ran a hand through his hair. He'd heard about Marshall's reputation and had no desire to cross him, but he wouldn't be frightened off the case.

When he got back downstairs, Adam found Mamacita showing Jillian pictures of her children and grandchildren. Jillian was holding Ruben's Police Academy graduation portrait.

"Now Vincente, he's my youngest, he's at MIT on full scholarship."

"You have a lovely family, Mrs. Marquez. You should be very proud." Jillian replaced the photo of Ruben amid the others on the crowded mantel.

"You must call me Mamacita. All Ruben's friends do. Make Adam bring you back soon. Not working is hard on Ruben."

Adam took Jillian's elbow and led her toward the door. They made their goodbyes and started for the car. Jillian was quiet for most of the ride, which was fine with him. Hell, he was still trying to digest the fact that she'd had a drug problem.

She twisted as much as the seat belt allowed and smiled at him. "Thank you for making me join you tonight. I didn't think I could be around people, but it was exactly what I needed. I can see that Ruben's lucky to have a friend like you."

"You were what Ruben needed to take his mind off his troubles."

Jillian laughed, and he realized how much he liked the sound. "With Mamacita watching over him like a Yucatan Raven, I don't see how Ruben could get into trouble," she said.

"You'd be surprised how much he manages." He smiled, remembering past episodes, but he didn't know her well enough yet to share examples. Besides, he didn't fare too well in the stories either.

"What about you? Who's in your life that you can turn to during bad times?"

She was silent long enough that he wondered what she was hiding.

"Billy was," she finally answered.

When they reached the store, he escorted her to the bottom of an outside flight of stairs he hadn't noticed before. He couldn't decide what to do with his hands, so he jammed them in his pockets. When she reached the top, he headed back to the car.

"Adam?"

He swung around to face her. It was the first time she'd called him by name, and he realized he liked it, liked her. Too bad she was still a suspect in his investigation.

"Did you know I'm a good cook?"

"Well, I'm not surprised. I heard you talking to Mamacita." He took his hands out of his pockets, but then jammed them back in again.

"Saturday is my busy day. With Billy gone it's going to be a madhouse. I'm closed on Sundays. In the morning I do the laundry and grocery shopping. In the evening I like to cook. Nothing fancy."

She took a step down, closer to him. "I think the Rockets are playing the Lakers. There're only a few games left this season so it should be exciting. It's a young team and they're still hungry. Playing the Lakers should bring out the best in them. What do you say? Are you up for it?"

"Home cooked food and a ball game? I can't think of anything nicer."

"Good. I'll see you around six." She stepped back onto the deck and disappeared around the corner.

Now what? Would he be on duty or off? He could picture Hard Luck's face if he put in for four hours of overtime for eating dinner with Jillian and watching a ballgame. Yet her admission to prior drug use was disturbing.

It certainly wasn't the first time a woman had asked him out, but whenever it happened he became suspicious. He usually discovered she has some ulterior motive.

He'd never so much as fixed a parking ticket, no matter where the woman had her hands when she asked, and he didn't plan to start now. One step down that road was one step too many and had led to the downfall of many a good cop.

Still, he had to wonder, what had Jillian been up to that she needed his help to fix?

Chapter 8

Determined to take advantage of the perfect spring Saturday morning, Adam took his coffee and newspaper onto the deck and vowed to spend as much of the day as possible outdoors. He had plenty of chores inside, but he'd save them for the heat of August. Before settling into his favorite chair, he leaned his elbows on the deck railing and took a deep breath. The air was heavy with the scent of flowers, although his beds were mostly shrubs. Mrs. Daniels' roses must be blooming, or was it her carnations? Odd, he'd never noticed the aroma before, but it was strong today. Hopefully, Rover wouldn't decide to use her flowerbeds for his litter box. He'd hear about it if the old cat set a paw in her yard.

A woodpecker hung awkwardly on the bird feeder, fishing for a sunflower seed. Once he found a seed, he flew to the nearest tree, lodged it in the bark, and cracked it open. The bird then circled back to the feeder and started the process again. A lot of work for one seed. Like digging through stacks of paperwork to find one fact that didn't fit.

As he pushed off from the railing, Adam heard a resounding crack. A section of the deck railing broke away, falling to the ground and taking him with it. A loud fluttering of wings filled the air as birds scattered in all directions. Then it was completely silent.

His neighbor called from the other side of the fence. "You okay over there, Adam?" He lay still for a moment before tentatively moving his arms and legs. Finally he stood and looked around. Nothing broken but his damn deck. How the hell did that happen? He'd built it himself and knew it was solid.

The deck was only a foot off the ground, and he had fallen into a freshly mulched flowerbed. "I'm fine," he called back. "The only thing injured was my pride."

The rest of the day involved hammering, sawing, and multiple trips to the lumber store. He didn't know why the railing had broken, so he replaced the entire length. By evening he was tired and sore, but that rail wouldn't break again, no matter what crashed into it. Of course, he'd thought that about the last one.

On Sunday he slept late, then went to the store. He was low on cat food and couldn't remember how much bread or milk was left, so he got some of each. His usual seven boxes of frozen dinners went into the cart. He thought about his evening with Jillian and put one of the boxes back. Was it a date? A thank you? He wouldn't have picked her as the type to play games or have ulterior motives, but he'd been fooled before. Better keep his eyes open, just in case. Either way, it was an excellent opportunity to get a better read on her. Besides, he never liked to pass up a good meal.

He allowed himself forty-five minutes for the drive to Jillian's. If he was running late, he could always use the siren to make up time. He inhaled deeply and thought of spice and flowers. A hostess gift. How could he have forgotten? The one mannerly rule his mother had drummed into him that he actually followed.

But what would be appropriate? His usual, roses, felt wrong. He seemed to smell them everywhere he went lately and for some reason he found it unpleasant. She didn't seem like the fancy wine type, so what was left? He'd finally decided on a six-pack of beer when he noticed a convenience store on the left. There might not be another one before he reached her place. No traffic was approaching, so he made a quick left toward the parking lot. A pick-up truck came out of nowhere and blew past him, horn blaring, and missed his bumper by inches. He was still breathing hard when he went inside.

"That's a tricky corner," the clerk said. "I've seen three bad accidents since I started working here. I think that sign blocks the view. You're lucky you weren't hurt."

"Yeah, that's me, lucky." He sat down the six-pack and wiped his palms on his pant legs.

By the time he reached Jillian's, he had other things on his mind and the near accident was forgotten.

The aroma of roasting meat was immediately noticeable as he stepped from his car. He stood for a moment, glancing from the front door to the stairs.

"Come on up. I decided to cook outside. It's too nice a day to stay in." Jillian waved from the top of the stairs, holding an extra long spatula in one hand. She was wearing shorts, sandals, and a racer-back tank. He'd never seen legs that long and inviting.

Adam's eyes immediately found the rose tattoo on her shoulder blade. The overwhelming need to know if she had another somewhere on her body returned. The fact that she wasn't wearing a bra didn't escape his notice either. He was a trained investigator after all. *Keep your head on straight and your dick under control. This is a working evening.*

The stairs led to a deck that circled the back of the apartment. It held two comfortable lawn chairs, a small table, and a late model grill. She obviously used this area often, but who was her usual guest? "I didn't notice this when I was here before. You have a great view."

"I have to close the curtains during the day to keep the heat out. You should've seen the view before that last hurricane came right over my head. I spent every weekend for six months clearing out dead trees and brush."

"Did you have much damage?" Adam looked out over a large cleared area with a gazebo surrounded by heavy woods.

"Only if you call no electricity for sixteen days damage. It was more of an annoyance than a problem because I have a generator for the store. Man, a few days without lights takes us right back to the Stone Age. I had my busiest month ever. People worried they needed some protection, sitting in the dark. What about you, did you have any damage?"

"I only had three days without lights and even then I could charge my cell phone at the station. We were plenty busy though. People aren't at their best when they've been promised ice and water at a certain location only to find it all gone after they waited in line for a couple of hours."

Adam prowled around the deck, gently shaking the railing. It looked good, but so had his. Until it fell for no apparent reason.

After a few minutes, Jillian asked, "Does it meet with your approval?" A soft smile played around the edges of her mouth.

He acknowledged the smile sheepishly, but started examining the deck more thoroughly. "I had a little trouble with my deck yesterday. The rail broke unexpectedly. It wasn't a big deal, it's only a foot off the ground, but this could be dangerous for you."

Jillian gazed out at the wooded area behind her property. For an instant, Adam thought she was giving the finger to someone at the edge of the woods, but she was only brushing away a fly.

He completed his circuit of the deck and nodded to Jillian. "This looks nice and solid. Whoever you got to put this up, they did a great job."

"They? There was no they. There was just me and Billy."

His face must have registered shock, because Jillian started laughing. "I had a professional put in the support columns and the stairs, but I did the rest. Billy tried, but bless his heart, he was only good for carrying supplies up the stairs and holding things while I did the nailing."

No wonder her arms looked so toned. That was a lot of work. No one who was still using drugs would be capable of the work involved in clearing all that brush and putting up such a professional looking deck.

"Let's go in. I think everything's ready."

Jillian had grilled stuffed pork chops with fresh asparagus and made a spicy cinnamon baked-apple dish. She served the plates and sat them on the old Formica table. A green salad with several types of lettuce Adam couldn't identify was already waiting. The salad had walnuts, cranberries, and a raspberry vinaigrette dressing. Adam inhaled ravenously as he sat down. She opened two of the beers he brought and they each took one, clinking them together and smiling.

Adam still wasn't sure what the dinner meant, and he hated the feeling of not being in control of the way a case was progressing, but he was there, so he might as well eat.

"This is a treat for me. I don't get home cooking very often." Adam waited for Jillian to start before he began eating. He hadn't forgotten all his manners.

"You don't cook for yourself?"

"Oh, I make a killer pot of chili and at least twice a summer I'll fix a brisket that cooks all day and lasts all week."

"I started cooking when I was about twelve. Until then we lived off of peanut butter sandwiches and grilled cheese. Even when my mother was alive, it wasn't much different. She had better things to think about than cooking."

"What kept her busy?" He paused to look at Jillian. He didn't want to shovel food in his mouth the way he did at home, but the meal was so delicious he had trouble slowing down.

"She was a pageant queen. Actually, she was Miss

Texas at one time and second runner-up to Miss America. That meant she was an authority, and she made a fairly good business out of training young women to compete in pageants. Later, she set her sights on the Little Miss pageants and my sister Heather was her protégée." There was a slight edge of distaste when she mentioned pageants.

"Heather ate it up and won all kinds of trophies. Then Mother was really an expert and our house was filled with little girls learning to parade, sing, dance, and smile for the camera."

"What about you? Didn't you compete?" He took a sip of his beer. Even the asparagus was delicious.

"No. I was a chubby little kid. I'd rather play outside than play dress up. After Heather died, Mother directed her attention to me, but I wasn't very cooperative. She finally taught me a song and got me all dressed up, but I decided to show her."

"What'd you do?" He paused, his fork halfway to his mouth.

"I got up on stage, folded my arms across my chest, turned my back on the audience, and just stood there in my little ruffled cowgirl outfit while the music played."

He tried to hold in the laughter, but it burst through. "I can see you now. I think maybe you haven't changed all that much."

Jillian laughed and shook her head at the same time. "It really wasn't funny. It ruined her career. No one wanted to hire a teacher who couldn't control her own daughter."

One pork chop remained on the platter. Being on the job didn't mean he couldn't enjoy the meal. He was about to split it in half when Jillian reached over. She forked it onto his plate and asked, "What about your family? Do you see them often?"

"My dad was a mechanic during Vietnam. He always

believed that following orders was what kept him alive. When he had a heart attack about two years ago, they retired to the hill country. You wouldn't believe how his personality did a one-eighty. After years of insisting everyone adhere to a strict set of rules, he and Mom now spend their days fishing and playing golf and taking each day as it comes. They're both happier than I've even seen them."

"How did you manage, growing up in a house full of rules? I can't imagine it because I grew up without any at all. When Heather was alive, my mother ignored me. After Heather's death, I ignored my mother. I'd show her, right? Then Mother died, and Dad went to pieces, leaving me to finish raising myself."

"You may find this hard to believe, but I had a tendency to rebel. Although I am now willing to admit a few of those rules might have been for my own good. And now, here I am, in a job that punishes people for breaking rules."

When Jillian rolled her eyes and laughed, it was like opening a window to let fresh air and light into a room that had been closed and dark for too long. When the people he worked with placed bets on how long it took to make him growl, it was a sure sign he growled more often than he laughed.

"My little brother, on the other hand, thrived in a tightly structured existence and he went straight into the army. I call him the Little General, but he's a Captain. He's stationed in Alaska now. He loves it. He married a local and they have a kid on the way. I went up for a week last year. We fished and hiked. It was really nice, but it was summer. I don't know about winter. My guess is he'll probably stay there."

They finished eating, and he helped Jillian clear the plates off the table and stack them in the sink. His mother had never left a dish in the sink in her life.

"I think it's time for the game to start. Let's go in the other room and get comfortable." Jillian yanked the curtains closed with a solid snap.

He settled into a sofa that fit his body perfectly as Jillian clicked on the TV. She commented on the plays and on the players often enough to keep the conversation going but not enough to be a distraction. He was surprised how much he was enjoying her company.

"How did you get so interested in basketball?" Some women liked baseball or football, but he hadn't met many that truly enjoyed basketball.

"I played a little in high school. Not well enough to do anything with it, but I always liked it. Wish I could find some type of adult league. We had one here for a while, but there wasn't enough interest to keep it going. I'd like to get back into it. What about you? Did you play any sports?"

"Baseball. I had a partial scholarship to Southwest Texas in San Marcos. I had to supplement it with work so they got me a job with campus security."

He sat his beer down, being careful to place it on a coaster, and twisted to face her. "I told my family I liked the idea of helping people, but I sometimes wonder if I felt important, strutting around in my uniform." He stopped, surprised at himself for revealing something so personal.

"Anyway, when I graduated, I went to the police academy. I still pitch on the inter-squad team."

Adam relaxed and enjoyed the game until half-time, when Jillian dished them each a bowl of Bluebell Homemade Vanilla ice cream topped with fresh strawberries. They ate sitting on the sofa. "You can't beat Homemade Vanilla ice cream," Jillian said. "Unless maybe it's Butter Pecan."

"Or Rocky Road." He finished the last bite, almost licking the bowl.

Jillian stacked the bowls in the kitchen with the rest of the dishes. When she slipped back onto the sofa, she was much closer to him. "Well, I guess that's it then," she said. "I like basketball, you like baseball. I like Butter Pecan, you like Rocky Road. There doesn't seem much point in going on."

"Maybe if we keep trying, we can find an activity we both enjoy," he said.

Jillian kicked off her shoes and pulled her feet under her, then settled back on the sofa and leaned against his arm. *Well, I guess that answers that question. Or did it?* Damn, he hated not being in control.

When the game finished, Jillian stood. "It occurs to me I've been a poor host. I never gave you a tour of the apartment."

Adam glanced around. He could see every room from where he was sitting. A slow smile spread across his face. Well, he wasn't actually on duty. More like keeping his eyes open on his own time. He was satisfied she wasn't a psycho vigilante.

He grabbed the remote and quickly clicked off the TV as he reached for her hand. They started for the one room he hadn't been into yet. The bedroom was as neat as the rest of the house, yet still managed to look lived in. He saw a pair of sandals in one corner and a shirt over the back of a chair. The top of the dresser was cluttered. It had a feminine feel, but not overpoweringly so.

No teddy bears, dolls, or excessive pillows filled the bed. Good, he hated those things. They always got in the way at the wrong time.

When they stepped inside the door, she swung around to face him, putting her arms around his neck. He immediately pulled her closer, his breath heavier with each passing second. Why had he let himself be brainwashed into believing that a tiny, doll-like woman was the ideal? He didn't have to bend over double to kiss Jillian, and her body remained pressed against his in all the right places.

Her tank slipped easily over her head in a move he'd been thinking about since he first stepped onto her deck. He was already aware she wasn't wearing a bra. She unbuttoned his shirt, pushing it aside, and the sensation of her breasts brushing against his chest while their hands roamed over bare skin sent a surge of pleasure through his body. His tongue found hers and he drank her in greedily. It was agony to break away long enough to carry her to the bed.

Within a few minutes, much to his delight, he'd discovered her second tattoo, exactly where he hoped it would be. He smiled to discover it was as smooth and silky as the rest of her body. It even tasted a little like cinnamon-apple, although that could have something to do with the aroma in her apartment.

He would have to get her to his house and see what it tasted like there. If it was beer and cat litter, he needed to invest in one of those scented candles he saw advertised.

For now, he was going to enjoy being with a woman who seemed to want him and had asked for nothing in return. If there were consequences, he'd face them later.

The sky was still dark when Adam rose on one elbow and nuzzled Jillian's ear. "You're going to hate me, but I have to go." He nibbled her shoulder and felt himself come awake again.

She turned to face him, sleepy-eyed. "Go? Can't you leave for work from here?"

How bad would it be if Rover missed one round of medication? He lifted the sheet and gazed at her body. Damn he wanted to stay longer, but if he didn't leave soon, he wouldn't be able to stand up. "No. I have to give my cat a shot."

Her eyes took on a hard look. "That must be the truth. No one would come up with such a lame excuse if it wasn't."

"There's a history of diabetes in my family so I've always been careful what I eat. I never expected Rover to be the one to come down with it."

"You have a cat named Rover?"

"He was the terror of the neighborhood when he decided to adopt me seven years ago. Bigger than most dogs and twice as mean. He still hasn't forgiven me for having him fixed."

"Okay, if you have to go. But Adam, come prepared next time. Bring the damn cat with you."

A grin filled Adam's face as he drove home through the darkness. She'd said next time.

Chapter 9

The sun was up, but it was still early when Jillian woke. She'd noticed evenings were lasting longer, but it was the first time she realized that mornings were beginning to come earlier also. She stretched one leg over to the other side of the bed. It was already cold. The pillow was a lump beside her. She pulled it close and buried her face deep in its softness. The fragrance of Adam's aftershave lingered and that made her smile. Remembering the night before made her smile even more. It couldn't continue for long, she knew that. But damn if she wasn't going to enjoy it while it lasted.

She pulled on her shorts and tank and started looking for her running shoes. The air was early-morning cool when she stepped outside. From her front door to the I-45 feeder road was two and a half miles. That was a nice five mile run with no traffic at this time of the morning. She did a few stretches and started with a slow jog. By the time she was out of the parking lot and onto the road, she was ready to pick up speed.

She had reached the feeder road and started back when Heather joined her. "I didn't think you liked exercise," Jillian said through gritted teeth. The number of places she was safe from Heather's interference was shrinking. Soon she wouldn't be able to leave the store at all.

"I don't, but you said I should find a way if I wanted to talk to you. Besides, I needed an excuse to wear this outfit."

Jillian glanced to the side and ran her eyes up and down. Heather wore a maroon velour warm-up suit with a glittery pink T-shirt that exactly matched the stripe down the side of the pants. "It looks good on me, don't you think?"

"Quite the outfit, I'll admit. It might be more appropriate for drinking lattes in December than running in April."

"It's not like I have to worry about sweating or anything. You should see yourself. Your face is all red and splotchy. Those awful clothes probably stink. The only good thing is the sweat makes those silly spikes fall out of your hair."

Jillian ignored the comments on her appearance, Heather had already ridden that horse into the ground, and it wasn't like her sweat was any worse than the overpowering perfume Heather always wore. "Maybe you can be any age or shape you choose, but we mortals have to do it the hard way. Besides, I thought you wanted me to keep fit as part of your Master Plan."

"I don't have any idea what you're talking about." Heather looked away. "Anyway, I came to ask you about last night. You said you wanted to keep the police from your door, then you went and invited one in."

"So now you stand at the edge of the woods and spy on me?"

Heather gave an exaggerated sigh, ignoring Jillian's question. "Well, what's done is done. Tell me all about it. I want every juicy detail."

"Sorry, some things are personal."

"I know it was personal. I hope it was very personal. That's why I want you to tell me about it. Is he as big everywhere as he is in the arms and shoulders? I've heard that's important."

Jillian tried to keep the satisfied smile off her face, but settled for turning her head. Heather didn't notice and kept talking. "You should have seen him hammering on that deck rail without a shirt on. Come on, give. It's the only fun I have."

"Forget it. I'm not talking to you after what you did to Adam and to Billy." Jillian was breathing hard, but Heather didn't have a hair out of place.

"You blame me for everything that happens. His deck was only a foot off the ground. I didn't hurt him. And how could I have done anything to Billy? That's absurd."

"Don't play games with me. I'm on to you. You can drop the innocent act." If Heather hadn't bothered to deny crashing Adam's deck, maybe she was telling the truth about not hurting Billy.

"Well, if you won't talk to me, I guess I'll have to make my own fun. Just don't complain if you don't like what happens."

"Stay out of my life. You have the whole world to torment. Leave me alone."

They reached the edge of the parking lot and Heather stopped running, but Jillian continued without looking back.

Pretending Heather wasn't worth a glance over her shoulder.

Despite little actual sleep, Adam was at work early Monday morning. His first stop was the police department gym, although he had to admit, he'd managed a fairly substantial workout the night before. He pushed the door open and groaned. Not his favorite part of the day. Gyms were the same the world over—clanging barbells and stale sweat. He didn't run to keep his physique or lift weights so he'd look buff without his shirt. He considered working out part of his job.

Early in his career, a suspect decided he didn't want to be arrested and escaped by overpowering Adam and then outrunning him. He'd be damned if he ever let that happen again. Not on his watch. Not when lives depended on it.

Once in his office, he plodded relentlessly through the piles of paperwork that had accumulated since he'd been working on the Dewitt homicide. It helped to keep his mind off that damned gun. Like a cat with nine lives, it kept showing up every time he turned around. Much as he wanted to, he couldn't continue with Jillian until he'd scratched her name off the suspect list.

Ruben was right. He needed to be certain before he started tossing out accusations. He had a plan, but it was hell to wait for the right time.

At mid-morning, he pushed back from his desk and ambled into the break room for a cup of coffee. Calvin Marshall was holding court, describing how he had single-handedly protected the city of Houston from bad guys, big and small, when he was younger. Just the sound of Marshall's voice made Adam's skin prickle.

He carried his coffee out of the squad room and down to the main lobby. A young rookie was filling in at the desk while Marshall enjoyed his break.

"Do you have any of those forms for turning in a gun to be destroyed? One of my neighbors is an elderly widow, and she wants to get rid of her husband's gun. I promised to bring her a form and take care of it for her. She doesn't drive." He lied to criminals every day, but doing it to a fellow officer made him squirm.

The rookie dug through a drawer until he found a yellow form and handed it to Adam.

"Is this the right one? I thought I remembered the forms were pink." Adam pushed his glasses up on his nose and studied the sheet.

"Not since I've been here. Sergeant Marshall re-did some of the forms about two or three years ago. Trying to make things more efficient, I guess. There's a few of the old ones in one of these drawers. Want me to look for them?"

Adam shook his head with a laugh. "No way. I wouldn't want to get on the wrong side of The Scarecrow by messing up his precious forms." With his luck, Marshall would walk in, and then he and the kid would both be up shit creek.

The rookie grinned and nodded, but looked around quickly as if to make sure Marshall hadn't seen him.

Smart kid. No use pissing off someone higher up. Even he needed to remember that.

Adam spent the rest of the morning rereading the murder book on his teenage hooker homicide. He and Ruben had been investigating the prostitution angle, but she'd been high when she died. Drugs would give her a definite tie-in with Eddie and Manny Dewitt.

By afternoon he had reports from the ME, the lab, and from Records. Even Mai could hold-up paperwork only so long. He drove over to the jail to re-interview his suspect, Eddie Coleman. Eddie was a frail man, whose years of drug use and irregular meals had taken their toll, and his skin had a sickly pallor. His hair and eyes were the color of dirt, and he peered at the world through a perpetual squint. If he had ever owned a pair of glasses, they were long lost.

"It's all here." Adam held a manila folder by one corner and tapped it on the table. "Ballistics connects the gun to both crimes. You can confess now, and I'll do everything I can to help you. I've got a lot of leeway on what charges are made. Or you can try your luck at trial, but I promise the DA will throw everything she can think of at you."

"I didn't have nothing to do with that young girl." Once he started, Eddie talked faster and faster. Spittle flew from his mouth and ran down his chin. "That was all on Manny. All I did was let him have the car. It's half his anyway. I don't know what came over him. It was supposed to be a straight forward buy. He'd sold to her before with no problems, but this time he claimed he knew she was trying to cheat him. He went crazy."

"I can accept that. A business deal gone bad. But Manny wasn't the violent type. What happened? Why didn't he walk away?"

Eddie wiped his chin on his sleeve. "I don't know. I think it was the gun. He'd never carried one before and it changed him. After that he wasn't the same. He was sure everyone was out to get him. He checked out of the dump we'd been staying in and started living under the freeway. When I went to look for him, he was furious. Said I was leading them to him. Thought I was one of them, whoever 'they' were."

Adam sighed and shifted in his chair. "What'd he do?"

"He charged at me, swinging his fists, but we were both so high not much happened. When the gun fell out of his pocket, he went for it, but I grabbed it first. I don't know what he'd a done if he got hold of it before me."

"So you had the gun. Did you have to shoot?"

Eddie dropped his head into his hands. Tears streaked down his face. "That's the part I don't understand. He was my best friend. We'd watched each other's back for three years. But a voice kept repeating, over and over, 'You have to shoot him. He'll kill you if he gets the chance.' It was as clear as you talking to me now. I don't think I'll ever get over it."

Bingo. Once they broke and confessed, it was just a matter of tying up loose ends. "I'll do what I can to help you, Eddie, but I have to know where he got the gun." Adam bent forward, his eyes on Eddie's face until Eddie broke away and looked down at the table.

"There's an old guy—tall, skinny, bald—looks like a scarecrow. They call him Cal. He sometimes sells things out of the trunk of his car."

Shit! Shit! Shit! Shit! Calvin Marshall to a T. Now he had to do something about it. No excuses. Adam sat back with a heavy sigh.

"Okay, Eddie. I'll call the guard to take you back to your

cell. Don't talk about this to anyone. Do you understand? No one. I'll take care of this for you, but you have to be willing to testify. I'll come by tomorrow with a photo line-up."

Eddie shuffled back. He looked so defeated Adam didn't know if he could hold up for another day.

On the way back to the station, Adam stopped at a drug store and bought a large box of chocolate candy. Should he buy a second box and give one to Jillian? No, she didn't care for chocolate. She was the vanilla and cinnamon type. Maybe flowers. This must be a good year for them. He smelled them everywhere he went.

When he reached the squad room, he saw his boss standing in the door. Hard Luck motioned him into his office.

"What have you got, Campbell? Are you making any progress?" He was a skinny man with a hawk nose and a pinched face that got even tighter when he concentrated.

Adam stood in the door and held the box of candy out of sight. "We've got the perp in the Manny Dewitt case in custody. We haven't filed charges yet because he's offering information on another case. Give me a few days and I might be able to clear up the teenage hooker case also."

"Good, I like that. A two-fer. You've got two days. Wrap it up." Hard Luck nodded vigorously, like a bobble-head doll.

"I need to make a photo line-up with skinny, bald guys. Do you know if we have any pictures of Sergeant Marshall when he's not in uniform?" If lying to a rookie caused him to squirm, deceiving his boss made him downright antsy.

"I don't think so, but you ought to be able to find plenty of guys that match that description."

Shit, he'd have to get one on his own, giving Marshall another chance to spot him snooping around.

Hard Luck's eyes narrowed as he studied Adam. "What

about your other cases. Anything happening on them?"

"We got some good prints in the pawn shop homicide. We matched them to a Mexican national. Word is he's gone back home to Mama. He's got a pregnant girlfriend who's due in a couple of months. I've interviewed her, and she's pissed he deserted her in that condition. She's only fifteen. She found out he has two other kids by two different women and was seeing a third while they were dating."

Adam shifted slightly, leaning against the doorjamb. The hand holding the candy was starting to sweat. If he lost his grip and dropped the chocolates, Hard Luck would know he was up to something.

"When our guy got mixed up in this business and left town, she finally saw him for what he is. She'll let me know when he's back in town. Her mama's even madder than she is. If the girl doesn't call me, Mama will."

"Anything on the gang shooting?" Hard Luck put his feet on the desk and clasped his hands behind his scrawny neck.

"That one's a little tougher. They don't like to rat. I have some money spread around on the street. Sooner or later, somebody'll let me know, either for cash or to cover their ass. It's a waiting game for now."

"Don't let it wait too long."

"Yes, sir." Adam backed out and headed for his desk, where he worked until well after shift change. When the room emptied, he picked up the candy and headed for the property department, recently moved from Goliad to its new location on Washington Avenue.

Doris, a chubby, middle-aged woman, ruled the night property department with an iron-hand hidden inside a velvet glove. With gray hair and a round face, she looked like everybody's idea of a favorite grandmother. Anyone fooled by her appearance was in for a big surprise. She glanced up from a steamy romance novel when the echo of his footsteps reached her. A pair of lavender framed reading glasses were perched on the end of her nose, and she looked over them as she studied him carefully. A slow smile spread across her face, accentuating the wrinkles around her eyes.

"Adam Campbell, you old dog. What are you doing coming down here after hours with a box of chocolates? You must want something illegal or immoral. One is out of the question and the other you wouldn't have to bribe me for. Didn't you learn your lesson with Mai?"

"Hey, Doris. I wouldn't ask you to do anything illegal, and the other would be worth much more than a box of chocolates. Besides, I'm not sure I'm man enough for you."

"That's not the story I heard. Mai said you were quite the stud. That was when you were still dating. Now the things she says aren't as flattering. If Hard Luck ever finds out what happened on his desk, you'll be out on the street."

Adam was speechless, trying to decide whether he was more flattered or embarrassed. "I hope I can count on you to see he never finds out." He'd just as soon Jillian didn't hear about it either. Somehow he didn't think she would approve.

Doris grinned, knowing she had flustered him. "What about that big partner of yours? When's he coming back? He looks like he could handle three women at a time without breaking a sweat."

"Knowing Ruben, he probably has. He'll be back at the end of the month."

"Good." She rubbed her hands together. "He'll still be in a weakened condition and I could grab him when he's not looking."

"If you do, hold on tight. You might be in for the ride of your life."

"That's the plan. An old lady has to have a dream. Now, what are you trying to bribe me to do with those chocolates?" She pointed to the box he was still holding.

He presented them to her with a flourish.

"I need to copy some records. I don't need the originals. They can stay here where it's safe. But I don't want anyone to know I have them. Can you do that for me?"

"I can make copies and misfile the records, but only until the shit starts raining down. I won't tell anyone, but if they find out some other way, you're on your own."

"That's all I'm asking. Don't advertise it. Give me a couple of days to see what I can find."

"Look fast. These chocolates won't last long."

Chapter 10

Jillian hated that Heather now felt free to interrupt her morning jog, but she had learned two important things. Heather admitted sabotaging Adam's deck, but denied harming Billy. If Heather were telling the truth, she needed to be careful pursuing a relationship with Adam, but she could safely hire someone to help at the store.

The address and phone number of the battered women's shelter were a deep dark secret, but Jillian had been one of their sponsors for years, so she had both. The woman who answered the phone knew Jillian and was happy to help.

"We do have a woman staying here who's worked in a retail store. She's familiar with inventory and working a cash register, but I doubt she knows anything about firearms. That might be a lot to learn."

"If she has experience with a cash register, I can teach her the rest."

"There's one other problem," the counselor admitted. "She has an infant, and we can't baby-sit while she works."

"That's okay. She can bring the baby with her while we decide if she's right for the job. Most of my customers are your everyday, ordinary people, but a few can be downright scary. If she's just come out of a bad situation, she might not be comfortable working here."

Cara arrived shortly after noon. She was quiet and timid at first, but she had no trouble learning to work the cash register. When she saw how well Cara cleaned the glass cases, Jillian felt a tug of guilt at her heart. She missed Billy so much, yet it was a relief to have help that was competent.

The baby sat in her car seat behind the counter and napped or sucked on a pacifier, seldom making a sound. Jillian had never been around babies in her life, and they frightened her more that Heather did.

Fortunately, none of what she called her *hard cores* came in that day.

With each skill Cara mastered, she seemed to grow a little taller. By the end of the day, she actually looked Jillian in the eyes and smiled. "Do you have a brochure or something I can take home tonight and study? There's so much to remember."

Jillian handed her a stack of pamphlets. "These are some of my biggest sellers. You can study these, but you won't be able to memorize everything. Try to learn how things are arranged in the store, then you can find the type of firearm you're looking for. The model numbers are shown beside each one. It seems like a lot at first, but you'll get the hang of it."

After Cara left, Jillian leaned against the wall and closed her eyes. She hadn't realized how much stress she'd been dealing with. She barely made it up the stairs. The depression she'd experienced off and on since Billy's death followed her every step. The empty apartment didn't help, but at least she had some leftovers for supper and a ballgame on TV.

Memories of her night with Adam still kept her warm. Tomorrow would be easier than today, and the next day easier still.

Adam didn't reach Ruben's until after nine. He hesitated before knocking, but the lights were on and the TV was playing. Mamacita frowned when she saw him.

"Don't you be wearing out my Ruben," she said. "He's supposed to be resting. You wouldn't be coming here this late if you didn't have problems." She stepped aside and let him in.

He could see Ruben in the den, eating popcorn and watching a documentary. "Hi, Ruben. Thought I'd see if you needed any help getting up the stairs to bed."

Ruben grabbed a last handful of popcorn and stood.

"Another night I have to go to bed before the news? I guess that folder under your arm is just for fun. If it isn't full of porn, I'm gonna be mad."

As they started up the stairs, Ruben gripped the banister with one hand and put the other on Adam's shoulder, the weight nearly buckling Adam's knees. If Ruben had fallen, he could easily have crushed Adam. They sat again on opposite beds, knees almost touching. Adam held the folder for a minute, saying nothing.

"What have you got? I know it's not good."

Adam handed him the folder. "This is a record of everything turned in to the front desk over the last five years. Guns, cash, drugs, any found items. I need you to see if you can find a pattern. I'm not telling you what I'm looking for. Just see if you notice anything unusual. It's the kind of thing you're good at, and hopefully I haven't led you in any one direction. Besides, it'll keep you from being bored."

"Okay, I'll look. I've got a pretty good idea what you're thinking, but I'll try not to let that influence me. Call me tomorrow. We don't want to let this drag out. What about Jillian? Have you finished clearing her yet?"

"I'll take care of that tomorrow." Adam raked his hands through his hair, willing Ruben to change the subject.

"Good, because you can't trust a woman who'll cover herself with tattoos. How many does she have anyway? The more she has, the more you should worry."

"Come off it. She only has the two. The rose on her shoulder and the little . . ." Adam stopped abruptly. Son of a bitch, that Ruben was devious. He couldn't believe he'd fallen for the same trap he'd set for dozens of witnesses.

Ruben slammed his hand on his knee. "Adam, you fuck. Are you terminally stupid? You better hope she comes up squeaky clean. Otherwise you're gonna need hip-boots to wade through the shit you'll be in."

"I said I'd handle it, and I will." He jumped up, causing the papers to scatter, then stormed down the stairs.

Mamacita was waiting by the door. She was still frowning, but she handed Adam a warm, tinfoil wrapped package. The aroma immediately reminded him he hadn't eaten since morning. He hesitated a minute. "Any chance I could have something to drink?"

She rolled her eyes and went back to the kitchen. When she returned, she had a bottle of red soda and a handful of napkins.

Adam didn't go straight home. He drove by Marshall's house and parked down the street. The red soda was too sweet for his taste, but the homemade tamales were worth the mess he made. When the lights went out at Marshall's, he waited another half hour, then went home to give Rover his shot.

The next morning, Adam was parked in the same spot. It must have been garbage day, because twenty minutes later Marshall pulled his cans out to the curb. Adam pushed his glasses to the top of his head and used the telephoto lens on his digital camera to get several good shots.

As he snapped the last picture, Marshall put his hands on his hips and stared at Adam's car. Adam sunk as low in the seat as possible and held his breath. Had he been spotted? If Marshall confronted him, what could he possibly say? Several minutes passed while he waited for a tap on the glass.

When he eased his head up to peer out the window, the street was empty. Nerves overtook him and he peeled rubber down the block.

He stopped at the nearest CVS and played with the photo printer until he had what he needed, two full-face and two in profile. One of each in color and in black and white.

Rover's shot had been late the night before, and Adam had left early that morning, so he stopped by his house to take care of the cat before heading into town.

"I'm going to have to get this wrapped up fast, old boy. I can't keep making special trips home for you." *And I can't call Jillian till I've cleared her name.*

Rover didn't answer, but the look of contempt on his face said plenty.

Before going to the jail, Adam headed for the ME's office in the Joseph A. Jachimczyk Forensic Center. The six story red brick building was in the southwest part of town on Old Spanish Trail, known locally as OST. Manny's autopsy was scheduled for that morning, and while he didn't have to watch every minute of it, he wanted to be there for the end to learn anything the ME had to offer. If there was any chance the wound was self-inflicted, he wanted to know right away. Not every confession was to be believed.

After showing his badge, he signed in with the receptionist. She had hair so thin he could see her scalp between strands that were dyed the color of old rust. The skin on her face was pulled tight and painted too brightly. She might have been removed from one of the drawers in the morgue and propped up in the chair. He was tempted to poke her in the arm and see if she toppled over.

Manny Dewitt's post mortem was in the last room on the first floor. Adam winced as his shoes made a slapping sound as he strode down the corridor. The lobby may have smelled of air-conditioning and office supplies, but with each step he took, the familiar stench of death and chemicals grew stronger. As he opened the door he was enveloped in the rousing strains of the ME's favorite musical accompaniment—show tunes. This time it was *Guys and Dolls*. He saw the ME's delicate feet moving in time to the music.

"Ah, Detective Campbell, I'm almost finished, but I knew you wouldn't miss the Grand Finale." The ME turned the music down one decibel as he motioned to Adam with one gloved hand. He removed his mask when he spoke, freeing a handlebar mustache that would have been the envy of Poncho Villa.

"How's it going, Doc? You got any surprises for me?"

"Not unless you failed to notice the gunshot to his face. That was the cause of death, and it was from no more than one foot away."

"That's what I figured. Do you have anything else of interest?" Adam was accustomed to the unique aroma of the morgue and had trained himself to take shallow breaths.

The ME pointed to Manny's arms. "His tats are beautiful work. Not like the homemade prison crap I see most of the time, but I don't suppose that's of any use to you."

Adam frowned. "It's obvious any money he came across that didn't go in his arm or up his nose was used to decorate his body. That must be thousands of dollars worth of ink, and I'll bet most of it was stolen from hard-working citizens. Unfortunately, that doesn't help me find his killer."

It was hard to believe the art that so offended him on Manny's body attracted him so strongly on Jillian's.

"The tox screen won't be ready for a few days, but you might want to go to the lab and pick it up yourself. If you wait for Mai to forward it to you, the Fourth of July picnic will have come and gone. I don't suppose you'd be willing to apologize to her for whatever it is you did. This vendetta is making everyone's life miserable."

"I'm not going to grovel for something I didn't do.

She's the crazy one." Indignation flushed across Adam. He took a deep breath and immediately regretted it.

"Yes, and you knew that from the get-go, but you went ahead anyway. Now's the time to eat dirt and lick your wounds before she screws up a case. Just face the music and do it."

"Let's get back to the vic. I'm about to head for the jail to interview my suspect. Is that all you have?"

"Yes, dear boy, I'm afraid that's it. No standing ovation for this one."

Adam made his escape as the ME turned the music back up and did a quick shuffle-ball-change. He waited until he could take a deep breath without coughing before he called Ruben.

"Just as I figured, it's a homicide. Now I suppose I have to do something about Marshall."

"Who did the post?"

"Twinkle Toes."

"Ah, if Twinkle Toes says it, it must be true. Broadway's loss is our gain."

The Harris County Jail looked exactly like what it was—a place to lock away the dregs of society where law abiding citizens wouldn't have to look at them. It was a multi-storied brick building with bars on the windows and an air of desperation and despair. Breakfast was long past, but the stink of greasy food remained by the time he finally arrived.

The constant noise, the harsh lights, and the stench of unwashed bodies would have driven Adam crazy in an hour, but Eddie had spent half his life behind bars, and the familiarity was probably comforting. Eddie waltzed in, standing straighter and wearing a shit-eating grin. Icy fingers clutched at Adam's stomach.

If Eddie bailed on him, he wouldn't be able to handle Marshall on his own. He'd have to take it to Hard Luck, and the resulting scandal would destroy the careers of some good men.

"Here's the photo line-up I told you about, Eddie. Tell me if you recognize anyone." Time to see if Eddie would come through.

"Not so fast. I need some assurances. I'm the one taking all the risks. You know what can happen to someone who gets the reputation of squealing. I want immunity, and I want it in writing, signed by the DA. Besides, it was self-defense. I shouldn't be in jail at all."

"Who've you been talking to? Some jail-house lawyer? If he knew what he was talking about, why's he locked in here with you? You're not getting anything in writing. Not now, not ever. If you did, the defense could use it to destroy your testimony. I gave you my word that I'd help you. That's got to be good enough." He only had one chance to put some steel into Eddie's spine.

Eddie scratched his chin, but didn't answer.

"You know me, but in case you've forgotten, ask around. See if my word is good, but don't say why. You can talk to your court-appointed attorney. Find out what he thinks of your chances at trial. If it goes that far, I promise I'll make sure they throw everything they can find at you. See if my word's good on that, too."

Adam left the jail disgusted. He lowered his window on the way back to the station, in need of the fresh air.

Chapter 11

Tuesday was shaping up to be a better day as far as Jillian was concerned. Cara showed up on time and ready to work. A gun store was a strange place and wasn't right for everyone. Jillian understood that and had known other new hires not to show up for the second day. The firing range next door could be unnerving. Thank goodness she had a dependable manager for that.

Cara wasn't an attractive woman, skinny to the point of emaciation. Her arms and legs were lanky and didn't seem to fit her body. Like a teenager who'd just had a growth spurt. When she smiled, which wasn't often, her features fell into place and gave a hint of the woman she could become if given a chance.

She made a few mistakes as the day went on, but not many, and not the same ones twice. At lunch, Jillian left her long enough to go upstairs and make a sandwich. She sat on the deck with her feet up and relaxed. When she started back downstairs, she was more optimistic than she had been in days.

Jillian was halfway down the stairs when she heard a voice she recognized immediately. Snake-Eye was the leader of a small, but unique, group of bikers and one of her best customers. He was also the main *hard core* she had worried about Cara handling. She took a quick peek around the corner to make sure the baby was out of sight, then waited on the stairs to see how Cara managed him.

"What's J. R. doing, hiring an ignorant proletarian like you? Even that numb-nuts Billy knew how to fill an order."

"I'll be happy to fill your order, sir. It just might take me a few minutes. I'm not sure where all of these things are."

"Sir? What the fuck is this, a fancy dress ball? My name's Snake-Eye. Don't you forget it."

Snake-Eye was glaring at Cara. While he had gotten his name from one milky-white eye, it wasn't his most notable feature. That was probably his aroma; dirt, sweat, every meal he had eaten in the last week, and every joint he had smoked. It was possible his mouth had never seen a toothbrush, and the grime beneath his fingernails was so thick it deserved its own zip code.

He dressed entirely in black, summer or winter. He wore a black leather jacket with half its fringe missing, black boots, black leather pants, and black T-shirt advertising J. R.'s Guns that he hadn't changed since Jillian gave it to him at Christmas. His speech pattern could only be called unique.

Cara was staring intently at a dirty, crumpled piece of paper. Jillian had seen Snake-Eye's writing before and knew Cara was never going to decipher it. She stepped into the store and took the list from Cara.

"This is quite a list you have here. Didn't we agree you'd call ahead so I could have things ready for you?"

"Me and the boys was out cavorting and wasn't near a phone." He nodded toward his two lieutenants waiting by the door. Mouse, the smaller one, was picking his nose. T-Bone was smiling at Jillian, showing a large gap of missing teeth.

She pointed to the cell phone on his belt. "What about that one?"

"Well, I didn't recall your number."

She picked one of her cards off the counter and handed it to him. "I'll be happy to program it into your cell for you if you want me to."

"Are you gonna' sell us the goods or not?"

"Sure I'm going to sell them to you, but you know it

takes a while to get it organized. Why don't y'all head up to the IHop on the feeder road and I'll have everything ready by the time you get back." Snake-Eye's weakness for pancakes was well known.

After they left, Jillian had pangs of sympathy for the manager of the IHop, but he should be used to the men by now. They stopped by at least twice a week.

Cara started in immediately. "I'm sorry. I couldn't read the list, and I wasn't comfortable leaving them alone in the store while I asked you."

"You're right. They should never be left alone in the store. They shouldn't even have only one person watching them. Don't hesitate to call me if I'm upstairs. I can be down in a flash. You can call Gordon to come over from the firing range if you can't get me."

"What is all this stuff he wants? It looks like a lot." She tried to smooth the crumpled paper.

"Snake-Eye inherited a small piece of land way back in the boonies, no neighbors, and no prying eyes. He and his guys live in an old bunkhouse and indulge in their favorite pastime—shooting things. They drive around and shoot things while riding motorcycles, they throw things in the air and shoot them, and they shoot at targets hidden in the woods. They'll shoot a turtle in the lake, a bird flying by, or a lizard on a tree. It's a wonder they haven't shot each other. It makes them profitable customers, but not necessarily trustworthy ones."

"That explains the list. This is enough ammunition for a big city police force." Cara ran her finger down the list. "He wants clay targets, paper targets, speed loaders, and other stuff I can't figure out. How's he going to pay for all this?"

"With cash. Don't take anything else, and look at the bills closely. Larry from the Sheriff's Department thinks he grows pot, but he's been raided twice that I know of and they didn't find anything. If he does, he must sell to dealers. The lack of hygiene alone would put off even the most desperate pot-head." Jillian started for the storeroom and Cara followed her.

"That sounds logical. They're too recognizable to try armed robbery. I can imagine the description now, 'The tall one had one white eye and brown teeth. I can't describe the teeth on the fat one because most of them were missing. The short one was all twitchy and jumpy. Together they smelled like three skunks had a fight to the death and their bodies rotted in the sun for several days.'"

By the time the three men returned, their purchases were neatly stacked by the front door. Cara kept an eye on Mouse and T-Bone while they loaded everything into the back of a rusty pick-up truck. Jillian rang up the sale.

As Snake-Eye started for the door, she called to him. "Next time, treat my employees with a little more courtesy. Otherwise I'll ban you from the store entirely. If that happens, you'll have to go all the way into Houston to buy your supplies, so besides the time and gas, you'll have to pay city prices. Not to mention the fact someone new wouldn't understand you and might question the extent of your purchases."

Snake-Eye gave Jillian a mock salute. "You can't blame a guy for his faults," he said. He turned to Cara and tipped an imaginary hat. "Ma'am, it's been an adventure."

The instant the truck cleared the parking lot, Cara started cleaning the display cases Mouse and T-Bone had been leaning on. "Do you think we should open the door? We could try to air this place out a little. How long do you think it'll be before they come back? Maybe we could have some air-freshener ready."

Jillian smiled. Cara was going to work out just fine. About time she had some reliable help. After spending the night with Adam, she realized how much of life she was missing.

She was through hiding in her apartment to avoid Heather.

Chapter 12

Rush hour was still more than two hours away when Adam started north on I-45, but the level of traffic was already beginning to increase. He reached J. R.'s about 3:00. He'd avoided calling Jillian since the night they'd spent together because she was still a suspect. The upcoming encounter would be hell, but he couldn't clear her until he questioned her. He couldn't put it off any longer. He had to have the answers to close the case.

The front door was propped open and a woman he'd never seen before was mopping the floor.

"Careful, the floor's still wet," she said.

Jillian looked up from some papers. A big grin spread across her face. He felt like a rat. He was about to do something that would hurt Jillian deeply, and he'd give his left nut to avoid it.

"Hi there. I didn't expect to see you today. Have you met Cara?" She indicated the woman mopping the floor. "Cara, this is Adam Campbell."

Adam nodded toward the woman. "Nice to meet you, Cara."

As he turned to face Jillian, he kept his eyes steady. He found it difficult to keep his cop face on, considering the things they had done on Sunday night. This time her tank top was yellow, but he kept picturing her without it.

He spoke in a low voice, his palms resting on the cold glass of the counter top. "Could we talk in private? This is an official visit. I need to ask you some questions."

The grin faded and Jillian's eyes bored into his. "We'll

have to go into the storeroom. Cara's new, and I can't leave her alone yet." With that, she spun on her heels and marched into the back room, trailing indignation like perfume.

Adam followed her through the door and came to a sudden halt. There was a small desk with a computer, and several file-cabinets off to one side. The rest of the room appeared to be well-organized storage shelves. These weren't the things that surprised him.

Behind the door, in a quiet corner away from view, was a white baby crib. A mobile was turning over it and playing a nursery rhyme he couldn't place. Pinned to the wall next to the crib was a blanket covered with bright, geometric figures. In the crib, a baby sucked contentedly on a pacifier.

Jillian stepped over to the desk and switched off the baby monitor. When she looked at him again, Adam couldn't read her expression, but he was sure it didn't bode well for him.

"Well, this is the last thing I would have expected to find in your storeroom. Still picking up strays, I see." He needed to buy some time while he recovered from the surprise.

"Can you believe her father didn't want her?" Jillian's eyes blazed, but at least her anger wasn't directed at him. "He beat Cara so badly she came two weeks early. You look at this and think I'm a softy. Taking in people that need help. What you don't see is that it's good business practice. I needed someone right away. If I went through an agency, I'd be interviewing people for weeks. With one call to the women's shelter, a counselor I know and trust recommended Cara and she started that afternoon. She's qualified, she needs the job, and she's grateful for the chance."

"I can understand that part, but what about the baby?"

The mobile stopped, and Jillian wound it again. "Cara doesn't have any money. She can't pay for a sitter until she's worked long enough for a paycheck, and she can't work without a sitter. It's like a hamster running in a wheel. She didn't have any way out unless someone was willing to stop and let her off."

Jillian smiled at the baby. "This little angel isn't any trouble. She can stay here during the day until her mom is more settled. It's in my best interest for Cara to get on her feet. Then she'll be a more dependable employee. She won't be trying to juggle learning a new job, finding a place to live, and asking people to look after the baby for free as a favor. Money doesn't solve your problems, but lack of it can certainly add new ones."

"You're right. I didn't look at it from a business standpoint. It's obvious I've never had to think about things like that."

"Now, what was it you needed?" Jillian sat at the desk and glared at him, ice crystals forming in her voice.

"I'm sorry, but there are questions I need answered. It's what I came for on Friday, but never got around to asking. I've got to get them settled before we can move on. I hope you understand."

"I understand. I don't like it, but I understand. There's just one thing, ask everything you need to on this trip. Don't leave anything out. I don't want you coming back in your detective mode. If you do, I'll think that's the way you want it to be between us."

He nodded. That's all he'd hoped for. "I understand. I'd hate to blow this before we had a chance." He flipped a page in his notebook and handed it to her. "I need to know where you were on these two dates."

"So now I'm a suspect in two murder cases? I'm surprised you weren't in fear for your life while you were busy frisking me Sunday night. Maybe that's your way of performing a strip search. No wonder you cut out early. You were afraid to fall asleep around me."

"Please. You know that's not true. I never suspected you." *Well, maybe for a few minutes.* "Still don't. But I have to clear you before I can close the book on anyone else. Before you and I can take the next step."

She sighed and looked at the dates. "The first one's easy. It was last Monday." She slid a calendar toward her. "Billy opened so he left early, about three. That means I stayed to close." She opened the file-cabinet and pulled out a thick folder.

"Here's Billy's time sheet. You can see when he signed out. I closed at six. Then I had a concealed handgun permit class from six to eight."

He must have look skeptical, because she pointed to a certificate on the wall. "I'm a certified instructor, have been for several years. It was the second class. We meet two hours a week for six weeks. This one is for women only. The class is over at eight, but we tend to stay around and talk for a while."

She found another list in the file-cabinet. "Here's a list of the students. This lady, Lydia Cox,"—she pointed to a name halfway down the list—"needed to buy a small gun safe, so I opened the store. I think I can find the receipt." She looked in another file and handed it to him. "It shows the time."

Adam took off his glasses and cleaned them before studying the receipt. Near the top was a time stamp, which read 8:32 P.M. It would take a minute or two for her to sign it and get the package, then another couple of minutes to reach her car. Good, that should be easy to check.

"What about the second date? It's back in December, so it might be a little more difficult. Do you have anything on it?" He had trouble standing so close to her while maintaining a professional demeanor.

When she looked at the date, she let out a short bark of a laugh. "As a matter of fact, I think I have that one covered as well." She opened a drawer and pulled out last year's calendar. "Billy closed the store that day, but Gordon left the firing range at three. I worked the firing range until it closed at six." She thumbed through the time sheets and gave him Billy's and Gordon's.

"It was a customer's birthday, and his friends rented the firing range for the evening from eight till midnight. A party company delivered a tank of helium right at six, and then I had to get over to The Woodlands before the bakery closed at seven. There's this tiny bakery that advertises it will make a cake in any design you want." She wrote the name and address in his notebook. "They'll remember me. I doubt they get many calls for a cake in the shape of an AK-47. I had to hurry back to get everything set up."

She scribbled another address in the notebook. "This is Snake-Eye. His real name is Marion DeShaun, but don't ever call him that. He and his friends have a place in the country, down a long dirt road. They don't have a phone, but I've got his cell number."

She added it to the list in Adam's notebook. "It would be best if you just called him. They don't like visitors, and will know immediately if you start down that road."

Adam put his palms on the desk and leaned forward, his voice almost as cold as Jillian's. "I've been a police officer almost half my life. I'm used to interviewing people who aren't too happy about it. Are you insinuating I'm not up to the job?"

He took a slow breath. What right did he have to be irritated with her for questioning his competence when he was questioning her innocence? A little touch of guilt rearing its head?

"No, but these guys are weirder than shit, so be careful. They hate cops with a pure passion. Keep your hands in sight and don't make any sudden moves. You don't want them to think you're pulling anything sneaky." She smiled and it softened her words.

"Did Billy or Gordon help you with either the party or the lesson?" Billy couldn't be a witness, but this Gordon guy could, and the more witnesses, the better.

Jillian shook her head and closed the file drawer. "Gordon's in school at night and he takes off as soon as possible. Billy doesn't like the firing range. To tell the truth, I think he's afraid of guns, and I know he's afraid of Snake-Eye. That's why it shocked me so when he shot himself. Drugs I could understand, but never a gun."

She still spoke of Billy in the present tense, Adam noticed. "This may sound crazy, but do you think he was afraid of guns because he felt drawn to them? Like he was trying to resist the pull of what finally happened."

Jillian looked up, her eyes big. "That's it. That's what's been floating around in the back of my mind that I couldn't put into words. Do you think working here made it worse?"

"No. I think working here helped keep it at bay. Until it couldn't anymore."

Chapter 13

Lydia Cox wouldn't be home until after six, and Adam wanted to interview her first. If her story checked out, it changed the intensity of the interview with Snake-Eye. It was a little early for supper, but he'd learned the hard way to eat and relieve himself whenever he had the chance. Once things got moving, he might not have another opportunity.

He stopped at the first place he saw, an IHop on the feeder road. The windows were open and one section was closed off with a "Wet Floor" sign. What was with all the cleaning today? Weren't businesses supposed to clean after they close? Of course, IHop specialized in pancakes, so the floor might always be sticky. They probably had to mop several times a day.

"Black coffee, please," he told the waitress as he settled into a booth. By the time the coffee had arrived, he knew Snake-Eye's birthday matched the date of the party and that he had been questioned about numerous offenses, but never charged. His only record was a minor traffic violation and one ticket for disturbing the peace. The party company remembered delivering the helium tank and three dozen black balloons to J. R.'s. They'd never delivered to a firing range before.

"My driver's still talking about it," the owner said. "He'd been setting up Christmas themed birthday parties all week. When he pulled into the parking lot of the gun store, he called me to see if he had the wrong address. Said he'd like to be a fly on the wall at that party. I've got the time and date stamp right here on the ticket, so there's no question."

When his food came, Adam put away his phone and concentrated on the meal. Now it was time to look for the bakery. Maybe he could get some type of pastry for tomorrow's breakfast while he was there. Or a pie. He wasn't big on cake, but he loved pie.

The Woodlands wasn't far from J. R.'s in miles, but it was on another planet in atmosphere. The residential community had deeply wooded lots and deed restrictions that prohibited signage. He always managed to get lost on streets that had similar names. It was nice if you lived there, but tough if you were looking for someplace. His GPS kept telling him to turn right onto streets that only went left. The woman's voice said, "Recalculating" so many times Adam wanted to strangle her. When she said, "Take the next legal U-turn" for the third time, he growled at the machine.

"Lady, I'm a police officer, I can U-turn any damn place I please." What was going on? The GPS had never given him problems before, and where was his nice Australian lady? This one sounded like someone's idea of a southern belle. He could almost smell the Magnolia blossoms.

When the next set of instructions nearly ran him into a ditch, he switched off the GPS and tossed it to the back seat.

He finally found the bakery hidden in a small shopping center completely camouflaged by towering trees. How did these stores stay in business, hidden away from view? Most stores tried to catch your eye, and even then, half of them failed. The aroma enveloped him the minute he opened the door, and he had to rethink his bias against cake.

"Good afternoon, sir." A chubby, smiling woman stood behind the counter, smudges of flour on her face. "May I help you?"

"I understand you bake specialty cakes." As he looked around, he saw a cake shaped like a racecar and another like a clown. The woman placed the finishing touches on a cake shaped like a gift, complete with ribbons, bows, and a to/

from nametag.

"I certainly do. What did you have in mind?"

He pulled out his badge. "This would have been several months ago, but you might remember the cake. It was shaped like a gun. An AK-47. Do you have any record of that?"

"I remember it. It's hard to make gray icing. Let me look in the back, and I can get you the exact date. It was around Christmas, I know, because we were busy making trees and Santas, and all of the sudden I had to come up with a gun. It seemed so alien."

While the woman checked her records, he browsed the goodies. There weren't any pies, but there were cookies of all types. He decided to splurge and get a dozen of the Chocolate Brownie Cookies.

"Here we are." The woman held out an order form. "It was December 23rd. Ordered by J. R. Whitmeyer. She picked it up about six-forty-five. I remember because it was getting close to closing and I didn't want to be stuck with it. An attractive woman, but she didn't fit in any better than the cake. My other customers were wearing reindeer sweaters and jingle-bell earrings. She was all in black with spiky hair. I actually kind of liked the hair, wished I had enough nerve to try it."

Perfect. Paperwork was always better than someone's word. If the other interviews went this well, he'd have Jillian cleared by the time he got home. Could he stop by her place on the way? No, that would be pushing his luck, but he could sure call her.

He studied the form, then looked back at the woman. "Is there any way you can make a copy of this?"

"Sure." She took the paper and was back immediately with a copy.

"I just need one more thing."

"The Brownie Cookies?"

"How'd you know?"

"Your eyes were drooling. I've never met a man who could resist those cookies."

Jillian sent Cara home fifteen minutes early. Business was slow, and she was still upset over Adam's visit. She needed to get out of the store.

After shutting off the lights and setting the alarm, she went out the back door to her car. She had ridden a Harley for several years, but traded it in for a used Volvo after her father was killed. The noise of the Harley had kept Heather away, but seeing her father's body made safety a bigger concern.

Two blocks down the feeder road was a large drug store. After only a day and a half, Jillian realized baby Megan needed a better receptacle for dirty diapers than the office trashcan she'd been using. It not only needed to be taller and lined with a disposable plastic bag, but a tight-fitting lid was essential. Some type of pre-moistened wipe would also be a good idea. Paper towels weren't working out so well.

How could babies require so much gear? In movies, people put them in an empty dresser drawer and wrapped a dishcloth around them. Of course, in movies aliens rode back to their spaceship on flying bicycles, and Bruce Willis saved the world single-handedly.

Cara's suggestion of an air freshener was a good idea, so that was the first thing she grabbed when she reached to store. When she had everything on her list, she snagged a carton of O.J. and a small container of ice cream. She managed to get all her purchases into the back seat of her car, thankful once again she no longer rode a Harley.

She had just pulled out of the drug store when Heather spoke up.

"I wish you'd get a convertible. Don't you want to see and be seen?" Heather glanced at Jillian. "Of course, it might muss your beautiful hair."

Jillian ignored the hair comment. She only wore that style to aggravate Heather. "After seeing Daddy, how could you want a convertible?" She patted the dashboard. "Safety is more important."

"Haven't you figured out there's never any guarantee of safety? Daddy should have taught you that."

"He taught me you can avoid dangerous things. Like drinking and driving."

"Daddy could drink and drive with no problem. He'd been doing it for twenty years."

They were stopped at a red light. Jillian froze. Icy fingers crawled down her spine. She let the light cycle through to red again. Cars swerved past, blowing their horns. "Are you saying Daddy's accident wasn't caused by drinking? Did the two of you have a fight that night?"

She held her breath, waiting to see if Heather took the bait. Heather had brought up the subject, so she might be willing to talk. *If she does, am I strong enough to accept the answer?*

"Sometimes you are so ridiculous. How could I have a fight with anyone but you? You're the only one who sees me."

"I'm the only one who sees you, but you've told me that other people can hear you. I'll rephrase my question. Were you angry with him for some reason that night?"

Heather sat quietly while the light changed to green for the second time. "It was the night of the Miss America Pageant, but Daddy had the TV on a ball game. I kept telling him to change the channel, but he wouldn't do it."

"You could have watched it somewhere else. You could have gone into any home in the country. You could have gone to Atlantic City, or Las Vegas, or wherever they have it now." She kept her voice neutral, but a rope was wrapped around her chest and someone was pulling it tighter and tighter.

"I wanted to watch it at home with Daddy. We'd always done that, it was a family tradition. We did it even when he didn't know I was there. He would make popcorn, and we would watch it together. I know he could hear me telling him to change the channel. I know he could, even if he didn't want to admit it. He'd been drinking. People can hear me if they've been drinking. Daddy always knew I was there, even if he tried to pretend he didn't."

The light turned green for the third time, and Jillian pulled across the intersection and began to accelerate. "So what did you say to him that night?"

"I told him he was selfish and mean, and that he had forgotten all about me. I said he never really loved me."

The speedometer moved from forty to fifty and Jillian began to weave in and out of traffic.

A frown line creased Heather's flawless forehead. "Jillie, what are you doing? Slow down."

"I'm doing the same thing both our parents did to get away from you once and for all. Are you worried I'll mess up this body so you can't drive me out and take it over?"

"That's just your imagination. How could I do a thing like that?"

The speedometer edged to sixty as Jillian flew through a yellow light. "I don't know how, but you've been trying for years. You almost succeeded several times. I can remember what you said to me. 'Let go, Jillie. You won't have to worry about things any more. I'll take care of it for you.' What exactly did you say to Mother that caused her to check out?" She didn't need to control her voice any longer.

"I was just a kid. I was lonely and unhappy. I wanted her to join me so we'd be together."

Jillian increased pressure on the accelerator as the needle inched past sixty-five. "That didn't work out so well, did it? She went someplace else. Why don't you join her if you're lonesome? You could cross over."

"Cross over. Cross over." Heather reverted to the sing-song voice she used when aggravated. "You watch too much TV. You don't even know what that means. There is no crossing over. This is all there is. Don't you think Mother would have joined me if she could? You'll find out some day. And you won't like it much either."

By seventy she was weaving through traffic. The same cars that had honked to let her know she wasn't moving now let her know she was moving too fast. She barely noticed them. Heather's words were all she could hear. "Well, you weren't a kid for Daddy or Billy. You weren't a kid for whatever it is you did to two people recently. Kids don't go into other people's bedrooms and watch, making comments and causing trouble."

"What do you want me to do? I have to watch. I can't do it myself. I never got to have a life of my own. You saw to that. No guy ever kissed me or touched me. That's the only way I can experience it. I want to know what it's like. You used to tell me all about it, but you won't anymore." Heather shrugged. "I get angry when other people are enjoying something I can't have."

At least she was finally admitting to things she had always denied. *Are you happy now you that know for sure? Does it make you feel any better? No? Well it's all you're going to get.*

The car was edging up to eighty, still on the feeder road.

"What do you want from me? I promise I won't do things like that anymore."

"Like your promises are worth anything." She was approaching the end of the road and aimed the car at a bridge abutment. "What I want is to not have to deal with you ever again. Otherwise, there won't be enough left of this body for you to use."

The seat next to Jillian was suddenly empty, only Heather's perfume remained. She turned the wheel quickly, taking the U-turn lane on two wheels. The northbound traffic was much heavier with commuters returning home from work. By the time Jillian reached her street, the rope around her chest had started to loosen.

"I knew you wouldn't do it," Heather said from the back seat. Then she was gone before they reached the store parking lot.

Jillian dropped the baby things at the foot of the stairs and trudged up to her apartment. She put the O.J. in the refrigerator and sat at the table with the carton of ice cream. It was runny, but she ate it anyway.

Anything to keep her mind off what she'd learned from Heather.

Chapter 14

Adam glanced at his notes. Everything depended on Lydia Cox's recollection of the time line. The one Jillian had given him was too close, too tight. If he was going to clear her name, there had to be no possible way she could make it from her place to the Montrose overpass in time to shoot Manny.

By six o'clock, Adam was parked outside the Cox home, waiting for her to return from work.

The neighborhood was nondescript, with modest homes five to ten years old. Most of the homes were well kept. He wasn't sure how long the husband had been gone, but the house already showed signs of neglect. The yard had been mowed, but not that week. No fertilizer had been put out, and the flowerbeds hadn't been weeded. Buttercups and tiny onion flowers were springing up in the grass. Christmas lights had been taken down, but left in a tangle on the edge of the porch. Stray toys were discarded and forgotten, forming a blockade in front of the garage.

At ten after, she pulled up. A jumble of kids spilled from the car and ran screaming for the front door. He gave her five minutes to get settled and rang the bell.

Mrs. Cox looked frazzled when she answered the door. Five minutes might not have been enough time. She had kicked off her shoes and un-tucked her blouse, but otherwise was still dressed for work. A drink was already clutched in her hand. Backpacks and tennis shoes dotted the entry hall. She might once have been an attractive woman, but her hair was too blond, her nails too long and red, and her breasts too large and pointed. He was certain none of those things were natural.

Tired, droopy eyes suddenly opened in surprise when he produced his badge.

"I'm Detective Adam Campbell, ma'am. May I speak to you for a moment?"

"Why? Is something wrong? Has something happened? It's not Danny, is it? The kids' father?"

"No, ma'am. I just need to verify some facts on a case. It won't take but a few minutes. May I come in?"

"Sure, sure, if you can stand the noise." She turned and pushed through a cluttered room where three young boys were running around a sofa hitting each other with long Nerf swim noodles while a TV played cartoons.

He and his brother had fought, sure, but never in the house and never in front of their parents. If they had, his father's belt would have set them straight.

Adam wasn't sure he could concentrate with all the commotion, but she led him out to the patio and closed the glass doors. Three well-used plastic chairs sat around a stained, glass-topped table. He sat in one and Lydia sat in another and propped her feet in the third. She swirled amber liquid in her glass, the ice cubes making a tinkling noise. Assorted swim toys floated in the pool. Others had sunk to the bottom and lay abandoned.

"It's getting warm out here." She pulled off her jacket. Her blouse was frillier and more revealing than he'd realized. "Why don't you take off your coat and get comfortable. I'll mix you a drink."

"Thank you, ma'am, but I'll have to pass on the drink. I'm on duty. And I probably shouldn't take my coat off. I'm wearing my service weapon and wouldn't want to frighten your boys."

"The Spawn-From-Hell? It might do them good to see a real policeman with a gun. Lord knows, I can't control them."

Why didn't that surprise him? "I was wondering if you could tell me where you were Monday evening, a week ago?"

"It's my one evening to myself. Danny takes the kids, and I go to a class. I'm trying to get my concealed weapon permit. Since Danny left, I'm here alone. Having a gun makes me feel safer."

"Could you tell me what time you left the class?"

She leaned forward, her breasts pressing against the thin fabric of her blouse. Adam struggled to keep his eyes on her face. His mind told him he wasn't interested in such an obvious phony, but other parts of his body hadn't gotten the message.

"Class is over at eight, but it's all women alone, so we tend to stand around and talk about our problems. J. R. had fussed at me in class because I didn't have a safe place to store my weapon. She's a real stickler for safety. She said three boys and a gun was a tragedy waiting to happen."

Good for Jillian. "She's right about that. I've seen it too many times. No matter how well you think you've hidden it or how many times you've told them not to touch it, one day they'll find it and then something bad will happen, as sure as night follows day."

She twisted uncomfortably on her chair. "I know, but with my schedule I never could get there when the store was open. Anyway, that Monday night she unlocked the store for me and I bought a small gun safe. She and one of the other women helped me load it in the car. That was probably eight-thirty."

"Did you leave immediately?" So far everything jived with Jillian's story.

"The other woman did. I talked to J. R. for just a minute about where I should put the safe, and then she went back inside. She watched until I started the car and pulled out. As soon as she thought I was gone, she turned off some of the outside lights, leaving only the security lights on."

"You said she thought you were gone. You didn't leave?" He held his breath. The right answer could clear Jillian, but the wrong one would cause a shit-load of trouble.

"I stopped at the edge of the parking lot. It's very dark on that road, and I don't like to talk on the phone and drive. I wanted to call Danny and let him know I bought the safe. It was expensive, and I decided he should help me pay for it. I also needed him to unload it for me. We had a good old argument about that."

He had his notebook out, jotting notes as she spoke. "Did you see her leave during this time?"

"No. She couldn't have left. The only way out would have been past me, and I would have seen it."

"About what time was that?"

"I can probably tell you exactly what time it was." She went into the house and brought out her cell phone. The noise level rose immediately as she opened the door, then dropped again as it closed.

She flipped the phone open and began to scroll down until she reached Monday night. "Here, you can see where I called D. Cox at eight-thirty-seven. It says we talked for six minutes. Even then, she couldn't have left for several minutes. As I said, the road is totally dark, and I would have seen headlights if she'd pulled out of the parking lot before I turned on the feeder road. And that has to be two miles, at least." A gloating tone crept into her voice. "What's J. R. supposed to have done?"

God bless cell phones and their call logs. "Oh, she hasn't done anything. I just needed to confirm how late the store was occupied. Thanks so much for your help."

"It's getting late. Surely you're about ready to quit for the night. Why don't you stick around and we'll order a pizza and you can tell the boys what happens to kids that don't mind their mother."

He had no desire to play scared straight. "Thanks, but I have several more calls to make." He saw a gate at the side of the house and made a break for it. He couldn't face going through the den with that gang of boisterous children and the stench of unwashed feet.

Relief flooded him as he hurried to the car. Verifiable times, exactly what he'd been hoping for. He started the engine, but didn't move.

Shit, the timing was still close. How long would it take to drive to Manny's home-under-the-bridge?

The spring days were getting longer and enough light remained that Adam felt comfortable heading for Snake-Eye's place. He followed Jillian's instructions and found the dirt road leading back into the woods. Shadows made it much darker, and Adam wondered if he should wait till morning. He was anxious to finish, so he kept driving. He couldn't delay any longer.

The road twisted around and was full of potholes, but he noticed they were all the same size and alternated from the right side of the road to the left. Anyone familiar with the road and on a motorcycle could easily avoid them.

He was too busy fighting potholes to look for cameras or alarms, but it was obvious some warning had been issued. When he reached the cabin, a man he recognized instantly as Snake-Eye stood in the clearing with his arms crossed, an old-fashioned western style quick-draw holster complete with six-shooter at his side.

Adam tried to park the car at an angle so the dash-cam would have a view of the area, but that wasn't likely to protect him. If Snake-Eye decided to shoot him, that film would never see the light of day.

He pushed out of the car slowly and looked around.

The shack was so decrepit and full of bullet holes Adam considered it amazing it hadn't fallen under the weight of an enormous satellite dish. Shadows told him men were hiding on either side of the cabin. The hairs on the back of his neck warned of another, concealed in the woods behind him.

"This is private property. You're trespassing." Snake-Eye stood with his arms loosely at his sides, his gun in easy reach.

Adam opened his coat with two fingers of his left hand and reached slowly for his badge, although with the camera, radio equipment, and tax-exempt license on the city-owned Taurus, there was no doubt who he was.

"No need to reach for anything, copper. Unless it's a warrant."

Copper? How much TV did this guy watch? At least the satellite dish was earning its keep. He suddenly noticed how quiet it was. Not a bird or even a cricket could be heard. It was evening. At least the frogs should be starting up in the woods. Was nothing left alive in this corner of the universe? Was he next? He tried to swallow, but his mouth was dry.

"Cat got your tongue, copper?"

If he stayed cool, he just might live to regret this mistake. He spoke calmly and tried to ignore the knots in his stomach.

"I can go back and get a warrant if you insist. If I do, it won't be just me. There'll be at least a dozen men searching this place. It'll take several days, and you won't be allowed back until they're finished. I only need to ask you a few questions about your birthday, and then I'll be on my way. I understand you were born on December twenty-third. Is that correct?"

Snake-Eye let out a sound like a small animal being strangled. "You can bring a multitude of hosts and search this place with the finest hairbrush and you won't find a crumb, but yeah, I was a fucking Christmas miracle. What's it to you?"

"I was hoping you could tell me how you celebrated your birthday."

Snake-Eye laughed again, and the sound sent a chill down Adam's spine. It was the type of sound that came from someone who kicked puppies or stole a kid's ice cream.

When Snake-Eye made a motion as if he were pushing the air down, the men hiding in the shadows lowered their guns and a wave of relief eased the knots in Adam's gut. "You're shit out of luck, copper. I'm alibied up to my gonads."

Did Snake-Eye know what gonads were? That was only halfway up and not the best alibi in the world. "Great. So what were you doing?"

"The guys threw me a party at J. R.'s Guns and Firing Range. We was there till midnight. You can ask J. R. She never left and saw me the whole time. If J. R. says something, you can take it to the AMT. It's solid gold dust."

"That sounds kind of fun. What'd y'all do?"

"Oh, she had contests set up with prizes. She gave us all one of these shirts first thing so we looked like a club. She served a cake out in her backyard. It was fun, but J. R., she has all these rules, and she writes them with a rock. No alcohol while you're shooting, ya have to wear ear covers. That kind of thing. Anyway, she's a concrete citizen, she'll vouchify I was there."

Snake-Eye folded his arms across his chest and glared at Adam. Not easy with only one good eye, but he managed.

"What about Billy or Gordon? Did they help with the party?"

The dying animal sound returned and seemed to come from Snake-Eye. "Naw. Gordon thinks he has some kind of a high-forehead. His nose is always in the clouds with all them books and stuff. When quitting time comes, he's off like a rocket. Too good for the rest of us."

"Did you see Billy?"

"That little turd-for-brains? He didn't have nothing to do with the firing range, or with us. He was such a coward he was afraid of my shadow. The only thing he was good for was packing and carrying. In fact, I couldn't conceive it when he shot hisself. I figure he was looking at the gun and his hand started shaking so bad it went off."

Snake-Eye shifted on his feet, seeming lost in thought. "I don't need nobody but J. R. She's stand-up people."

Even in the shade, Adam could feel the sweat trickling down the back of his neck. Trying to stand still with his hands in view while keeping an eye on three hidden figures was taking its toll. "It's always best if there's more than one. That way no one can say they were coerced or paid off."

This time the strangled animal noise echoed through the clearing. "J. R.'s tough as an old boot. Nobody's gonna co-whatever her. As for a pay-off, sure as shit follows day, she'd have the cops called before you got the money out of yer pocket. I'm not sure she even has a heart. The only exception's when she sees somebody trying to do better for themselves. She'll give 'em a hand up. Even then, they have to prove themselves or out they go."

"Excellent, that's all I needed." He'd have to disagree with Snake-Eye on that one. It sounded like Jillian had enough heart to fill a ballroom.

"Good. Then get back up on your horse and drive on out of here."

Adam turned the car around slowly and eased his way down the pot-holed road. His glasses fogged up as soon as the air-conditioning hit them, but he didn't bother to clean them. When he reached the turnoff, he stopped and leaned against the steering wheel. His head was swimming and he wasn't sure why. Was it the odor? Even from ten feet away, he was sure Jillian hadn't given Snake-Eye and his friends those shirts so they could look like a club. Was it the sight of the bullet-ridden house and those poor assassinated trees, their bullet holes weeping sap like blood?

It might have been Snake-Eye's mixed metaphors, malapropos, or spoonerisms, but whatever you called them, his speech disabilities were more than Adam could handle. He'd figured out that the finest hairbrush was a fine-tooth comb, and that the ATM was take it to the bank. If she wrote it with a rock, it was probably written in stone. The multitude of hosts might have been some type of Christmas reference, but some of the others were beyond him. He would likely wake up in the middle of the night saying: Oh, that's what he meant. As he'd driven away, he had seen Snake-Eye in the rear view mirror, making the one finger salute. He didn't need to think about it to know what he meant by that.

No, he admitted, none of those things were what was bothering him. It was his own foolishness at not calling for backup and putting himself in such a dangerous situation just to prove to Jillian how macho he was. Even if he had been wearing his vest, it wouldn't have been enough protection with all those guns aimed at him.

He could picture the defense attorney using two hands to hold up a bag full of bullets. "This bag was taken from trees on the north side of the house. This bag was taken from trees on the south side of the house, and this bag is from the house itself. Now, can you tell me which, out of all these bullets, were the seven that passed through Detective Campbell's body?"

A trial wouldn't be necessary because they'd never find his body. Metal detectors would be useless over bullet saturated ground, and a cadaver-sniffing dog would run straight to Snake-Eye, refusing any command to leave.

He'd been beat-up, shot at, and run off the road, but he knew in his heart, this was the closest he'd ever come to death. He needed to tell Ruben about Snake-Eye and his friends, but he hated to admit what a fool he'd been.

Chapter 15

With a Starbucks coffee in one hand and a Brownie Cookie in the other, Adam felt better. He reached the entrance to Jillian's parking lot at 8:20; what his mother would have called "good dark." He stared longingly at Jillian's apartment. Could she see him? If she knew what he was doing, it would be the final nail in their relationship.

Sitting in the car with the windows open, he was beginning to get warm. Summer was coming. Should he switch to iced coffee? Hell no, that was a sissy drink.

He took off his suit coat and tie, but left his shoulder holster on. He was on duty, after all. By this time of night, the holster felt like a corset. It would be almost unbearable by August. He ought to give some consideration to buying that expensive holster Jillian recommended. That or lose five pounds. He looked at the half empty box of cookies.

Not tonight.

After finishing the Brownie Cookie and taking a few more sips of coffee, he fished out his notebook and began making a list. The fact that Jillian had the party written on her calendar didn't prove it actually took place. The DMV and Snake-Eye both agreed that he was born on the twenty-third. The helium deliveryman and the bakery lady confirmed the arrangements for that date. That was enough to prove the party took place when Jillian said it did, but not enough to prove she didn't slip out before it started.

Now, to make a time-line for December 23, the day of the teenage hooker shooting.

6:03. The deliveryman had a time-stamped receipt for

the tank and balloons. Figure ten minutes minimum to set it up and show Jillian how to use it. Then load the dolly back on the truck and take off.

6:45. Pick up the cake. It was a good twenty minutes from Jillian's to the bakery. Even if the bakery lady was ten minutes off, that still left Jillian enough time to reach the run-down apartment complex where the teenager was shot. Tension knotted in his shoulders. He knew Jillian didn't have anything to do with it, but proving that was harder than he'd hoped.

7:45. The time of the shooting was confirmed by several calls to 911. No one saw Jillian or her car, but they did see an aging behemoth, complete with distinctive rust spots, that matched the one driven by Eddie Coleman. That didn't mean they couldn't both have been there.

8:00. The party starts. Jillian is there and the range is decorated with balloons and streamers. A table is set up with prizes and the cake is ready to serve. Not even A. J. Foyt or Danica Patrick could've made it back to the store and been inside waiting in fifteen minutes. Certainly not Jillian in a used Volvo with a birthday cake sliding around on the back seat.

If only someone had seen or talked to Jillian between 6:45 and 8:00, but it was obvious she was getting ready for the party. She couldn't have prepared earlier because the helium and balloons didn't arrive until 6:00 and she left immediately for the bakery. An aggressive DA might claim that Billy had come back to do the decorating, but with no way to question him now, Adam couldn't prove it one way or the other.

Snake-Eye wouldn't make much of a witness on the stand, but he verified everything Jillian said. He might have been at the bottom of his class in grammar and personal hygiene, but the entrance road and warning system leading to his cabin, along with his ability to read people, showed he had a unique intelligence and a specific set of skills. Anyone who took him for a fool did so at their own peril.

Adam's stomach knotted and his chest clutched tighter. Concrete proof was just out of reach.

He'd leave the hooker case for now and work on the shooting of Manny Dewitt. If he could prove Jillian's innocence on that case, the missing hour became less important. Eddy had hinted that he was responsible, but he hadn't been willing to sign a confession. Even if he had, confessions got thrown out. He wouldn't be satisfied until he'd nailed this case down from every direction.

Thanks to her cell phone log, he knew exactly what time Lydia Cox pulled out of Jillian's parking lot. What he didn't know was how long it took to reach the Montrose overpass.

Adam turned the engine on at 8:35, raised the windows, and fastened his seat belt. The air-conditioning in his city issue Taurus was temperamental at best and a dent in the right front fender pinpointed where he had blocked a suspect intent on fleeing. He could turn the car in and ask for a new one, but his replacement might be worse. Better to stick with the devil he knew.

At 8:43 exactly he pulled onto the street. When he reached the I-45 feeder road, he checked his rearview mirror. Lydia Cox was right. Headlights in the parking lot or on the road would be clearly visible. The feeder was one way north, and he took it two blocks until he reached the first U-turn to put him on the freeway headed into town.

He kept checking his rearview mirror. The sensation of being followed had pricked at the back of his neck all day. It had disappeared when he parked in front of Jillian's, but now returned with a vengeance. The cloying scent he'd noticed several time lately enveloped him. Hadn't he read somewhere that strange aromas were a precursor to migraines? He'd never had one himself, but his mother suffered from them, and they were supposed to run in families.

Quit being paranoid. The motor pool had probably sprayed too much air freshener when he'd taken the car in to have the AC checked. There was nothing wrong with him that six or seven uninterrupted hours in the sack wouldn't take care of, although he'd willingly forego an hour or two of sleep if Jillian was in the sack with him.

Rush hour traffic coming out of town had finished and traffic into town was almost non-existent. It was Tuesday instead of Monday, so if the times came anywhere near close, he would have to check if any of the mega-churches or high schools had events letting out. He decided to try ten miles over the limit. That would have been risky for her, but he didn't want anyone to come back later and say she might have driven faster.

At 8:57, the time the squad car reported seeing Eddie bent over Manny's body, he was still several miles from the overpass. The shooting would have been at least five minutes earlier if Eddie was going to run to the body after the shooter had pulled out of sight.

Adam stopped and sighed. He rubbed his hand over his face, thinking about Rover's shot. "Sorry, old buddy," he said. "Dinner's going to be late again tonight." Finally he turned the car around and headed back to Jillian's. This time he would try fifteen miles over the limit.

Even with the increased speed and less traffic, he still couldn't make it by 8:57. Add two or three minutes at the front because Lydia Cox hadn't seen any headlights and two or three minutes at the end for the car to get away and there was no way Jillian could have been anywhere near the spot. Not even if it was just a drive-by and she shot through the window and tossed the gun at the body, something that was impossible because Manny's body was on the passenger side.

The pressure in his gut eased. One down and one to go.

He drove to the apartment complex where the first shooting took place. Noting the time carefully, he started back to Jillian's. Late at night, with no traffic whatsoever, and running one light, it took him twenty-seven minutes. At 7:45, with only one shopping day till Christmas, he couldn't have made it to the party in fifteen minutes using lights and siren.

Adam started for home, almost dizzy with relief. Rover would be pissed, but Adam could sleep soundly. Tomorrow he would start on the second part of the puzzle. Time to find out what really happened.

Two days hadn't improved the smell or sounds of the county jail. Adam met with Eddie and his court-appointed attorney in the same room, sitting on the same hard chair and leaning on the same scarred table he had leaned on a hundred times over the years. Eddie tried to look confident, but he'd lost the shit-eating grin so Adam knew he had done his homework. He leaned his head back and squinted at Adam. Either the florescent lights hurt Eddie's eyes or he couldn't see three feet across the table, but it hurt Adam's neck to watch him.

The attorney was tall and awkward with big ears and small, round, rimless glasses. He was so young he still had acne, and so new the sheen still gleamed on his law-school-graduation-briefcase. Normally Adam would have considered that a plus, but this was one time he not only wanted his I's dotted and his T's crossed, he wanted all the commas and semi-colons in place. He needed both Eddie and his attorney to understand what was at stake.

Adam faced the attorney. "Let me point out a few things. Eddie's been here long enough that I'm sure he already knows. Our state legislature, in its infinite wisdom, has decided to crack down hard on DUI's. Sounds like a good thing, right? Wrong. The courts and jail are so crowded that instead of the usual three days credit for one day served it's now seven for one. It'll probably go even higher because all the drunks in the county have figured out they can do a twenty-one day sentence in a long three day weekend and that's much better than two years probation."

Eddie nodded, but his attorney didn't say a word.

"If Eddie agrees to turn State's Evidence, his sentence will start immediately and he can begin racking up those days. He can have three years credit by September when the legislature reconvenes, and rumor has it they'll propose deferred adjudication for first time offenders. When that happens, jail credit will drop back down."

The young attorney tried to puff out his chest, but he didn't have much of one so it was slightly comical. "This was clearly a case of self-defense. My client shouldn't have to spend one day in jail."

Adam drummed his fingers on the table. "You can certainly argue it that way for the jury. The fact that he put Manny's cash and drugs in his pocket before he allegedly checked to see if he was breathing might be something of a problem. Even if he managed to walk on that one, he faces Murder One for driving Manny to the other shooting."

The attorney started sputtering. Adam held up his hands, palms out. "Doesn't matter who pulled the trigger, he's still on the hook for it. Especially with Manny not around to take the fall."

"But my client wasn't driving, Manny Dewitt was."

"If Eddie lent the car for a criminal venture, he's still in trouble. However, I can produce several people who'll swear Eddie never lent his car for any reason. Manny didn't even have a driver's license." Adam sat back and waited. He knew what was coming and was prepared, but he still held his breath.

"Mr. Dewitt was part owner of the car and had his own

key. My client wasn't aware he'd taken it. Besides, do you think lack of a driver's license would bother a criminal like Mr. Dewitt?"

"No, but it would bother Eddie. If Manny got stopped for any reason, they wouldn't have to find the gun or drugs, the car would be impounded. It would cost Eddie a small fortune to get it back." Adam's eyes held Eddie's.

"That's bullshit," the too-young lawyer spouted.

"I know Eddie knows this because that's what he told a guy who wanted to go to the social security office to get his disability payments straightened out. As you can see, Eddie, I've done my homework, too. I've been over every scrap of evidence with a fine-tooth comb." He almost said the finest hairbrush, but stopped himself in time. Snake-Eye's speech patterns were hard to forget.

"If my client helps you on this other case, I'll expect him to skate on everything else." The young attorney hovered over his yellow legal pad, Mont Blanc pen at the ready.

"That's not going to happen. Eddie's facing too many other charges." Adam didn't trust Eddie to show up if he got out before he was needed to testify. "I can see that he stays here, racking up the days, instead of being sent to the state pen. He'll probably get three to five. He can take care of three or four before he's transferred. I have one last string I can pull once you get to Huntsville. There's an experimental drug treatment program starting in the fall. It's based on a program they've been using in New Jersey with good results. How old are you, Eddie?'

"Forty-two." His head was down, his voice barely audible.

"Without any help from me, you'll get anywhere from fifteen years to the death penalty. It won't matter, because fifteen years would be a life sentence for you. In the outside world, forty-two isn't that old. Your folks are still alive, and I understand you have a sister. If you got yourself clean, and

I told them you'd turned your life around, they'd take you back. You could be home in time for Christmas."

Eddie looked at his attorney and gave an almost imperceptible nod. Adam wasn't sure if the attorney was relieved not to have to take this dog to trial, or disappointed to settle his first big case out of court.

Adam tugged out his file. "Okay, let's get this started. Tell me if one of these men sold the gun to Manny."

Eddie squinted so hard Adam worried he wouldn't be able to bring the pictures into focus. If his eyesight was that bad, he wouldn't be able to put him on the stand. Adam wasn't planning to take this to trial so that was a problem he could worry about another day. As Adam turned over each photo, the table wobbled slightly, as it always had.

"That's him," Eddie said without any hesitation.

Calvin Marshall's face glared out from under Eddie's finger.

Chapter 16

With the jail interview out of the way, Adam was torn. He could head over to Ruben's and get there in time for lunch, or he could eat out, make some phone calls, and end up at Ruben's closer to suppertime. It was a tough call, but he decided to eat first. Now he had to decide between Kim Son's and The Cleburne Cafeteria.

At twelve-thirty, Kim Son's would be packed with attorneys, both corporate and trial. That might ruin his appetite. Besides, The Cleburne Cafeteria had a plate of French Spaghetti with his name on it.

He turned the car toward Bissonnet and enjoyed his lunch without worrying about being interrupted by someone seeking information on a case.

Full and happy, Adam pushed his plate back and patted his stomach. The business types were all back at their offices and the seniors hadn't arrived yet for the early bird specials. His booth in a back corner of the nearly empty restaurant made a perfect temporary work station.

His first call was to the DA's office. He had spoken to one of the assistant DA's earlier, and now could let her know Eddie had agreed to cooperate. They had dated a few times immediately after his divorce, and while it hadn't worked out, they were still friends and respected each other's opinions.

Next he called Hard Luck and let him know that two cases were officially closed. Hard Luck had never known about Jillian and how close she came to being the prime suspect, but Adam had, and it sent chills dancing down his spine. Finally he checked his own messages.

The lab had called to report that the ecstasy in Manny and the teenager came from the same contaminated batch. It could explain the paranoia they both experienced. He called the Assistant DA back and let her know about the contaminated X and the possibility it could account for the two vics' violent actions. It would make Eddie's deal an easier sell to her boss, the District Attorney.

The DA was a hands-on administrator. It wasn't that she didn't trust or listen to her staff, more that she didn't want to be caught off-guard by a reporter sticking a microphone in her face and asking why one defendant got a plea deal and another didn't, so any facts backing a recommendation were useful.

The two closed cases should keep Hard Luck off his ass for a while, but he needed time to deal with Marshall. And that was something Hard Luck could never know about.

The waitress filled Adam's glass of tea for the third time, and he sat for a minute, staring at his phone. Finally he punched in Jillian's number. A woman he assumed was Cara answered.

"May I speak to Jillian, please?" he asked.

There was a moment of silence on the other end. "J. R., I think this call's for you."

Jillian's voice echoed in the distance. "You think it's for me?"

"Well, he asked for 'Jillian.' Is that you?"

"Oh." Even across a room and over a phone line, Jillian didn't sound welcoming.

She picked up the phone, but didn't say anything.

"Are you speaking to me?" he finally asked.

"Barely. I am glad to know you're still alive."

"That's nice to hear."

"It wasn't you I was worried about. I didn't want to lose my best customer if Snake-Eye went to jail. Does this mean I'm cleared?"

"You're clean as a whitewall tire."

Jillian laughed, and it sounded like music to Adam. "I can tell you've been talking to Snake-Eye."

"I think he totally corrupted my ability to speak the English language." He paused, not certain how to progress. "What would happen if I came over tonight? Would you let me in, or am I banished forever?"

"I had to postpone Monday's class when Billy died so I'm teaching it tonight. It lasts till eight, remember?"

"Perfect. I'll be over at eight-thirty. I don't want to embarrass you in front of the ladies."

"It's too late for that, although I understand you were a hit with Lydia Cox."

"I think those boys are little Snake-Eyes-in-training."

"Now you know why I insisted she buy the gun safe."

"I'm not sure even that's enough to keep that trio out of anything they want in to. They don't have access to power tools, do they?"

Jillian was quiet. "I'll ask her tonight if their father took the tools with him."

Adam's last errand couldn't be handled over the phone. He needed to notify the mother of Manny's teenage victim that her daughter's case had been solved. She worked at a large dry cleaning plant. The type of place small local cleaners used to outsource their work. The building was huge and reeked of chemicals. Adam worried about his lungs, even just entering long enough for an interview. It did drown out the sticky, sweet smell that had been stuck in his nose all day, something he recognized, but couldn't put his finger on.

The front desk clerk sent him to the rear, where he found her working a large steam press that turned the area into a sauna. She had lost weight since he last saw her, but it didn't improve her doughy looks.

"Mrs. Fletcher? May I speak to you for a moment? We have some news on Maryellen's case."

She hesitated briefly, but kept working. "It's been so long I thought you was finished with us. I never s'pected to see you again."

"I would never quit on an open case. When I'm in the old folk's home, I'll still be making calls from my rocker. We found the person responsible for Maryellen's death."

"Have you got him locked up?"

"No, ma'am. He was killed by another drug dealer, but there's not any doubt he was the one responsible. Do you want me to drive out to the trailer and tell Maryellen's step-father?"

She slammed down the lid to the pressing machine, shooting a cloud of steam into air already so thick and heavy he could hardly breathe. "No point in that. He took off two months ago. Only fair. I run Maryellen off when he started paying more attention to her than to me, and he left when I started thinking more about her than about him. You might be wrong on who's responsible for her death. I guess I figure in there somewheres. Least now I won't have to testify at trial, and I can rest knowing he won't be able to hurt nobody else, may he rot in hell."

The machine beeped as she raised the lid. Adam looked around the plant with its noise and odors and heat. He wondered if she wasn't the one in hell.

Adam pulled up in front of Ruben's at 4:30. Perfect timing. Fifteen minutes of pleasantries with Mamacita, an hour and a quarter to work out a plan with Ruben, and it would be time for dinner. Mamacita couldn't avoid inviting him to join them, no matter how angry she was.

Ruben tried to look irritated at the intrusion, but his eyes expressed an excitement that had been missing since the day

Adam had driven him, moaning in pain, to the emergency room. They had been in the middle of interrogating a suspect.

Some partners had standing roles as either good cop or bad cop, but Adam and Ruben alternated. Even if it was only acting, always playing the bad cop could change your perspective if you did it too often. It had been Ruben's turn to play good cop, a role he excelled in despite his size. The detective playing bad cop could duck out from time to time during an interview and let another cop take his place, but not the one playing good cop. Building trust was a complicated affair and had to be done slowly.

Looking back, he realized Ruben had tried to rush the process, but he hadn't noticed it at the time. Ruben never said a word until after the suspect had confessed and signed a statement. Then he sank into a chair, his face as white as a sheet of paper and his forehead wet with perspiration. "I think you need to take me to the hospital," he said, his voice scarcely above a whisper.

By the time Adam got him to the emergency room, his appendix had already burst. Instead of back on the job in three or four days, he was still in a hospital bed, full of tubes. When the doctor eventually released him, it was with the understanding he wouldn't be alone, so Adam had driven him back to his childhood home. Mamacita still blamed Adam for her little boy's near brush with death, but Ruben had given no indication he was in distress during the interrogation.

A week later, he was improving, but nowhere near his old self. "Let's go upstairs," he said. "I have it all spread out." He made it up the stairs without leaning on Adam or holding the banister in a death grip.

"Hey, I'm sorry to interrupt your evening again." Adam had heard the TV playing when he stepped up to the door.

"Don't worry. I can't take much more of Mamacita's programs. Tonight some expert on evil spirits is explaining that if some solid form remains, they can be destroyed if you destroy their sanctuary. Next week, it'll be sprinkle holy water on them."

"I thought that was werewolves."

"No, they need silver bullets. That was last night."

"What about vampires?"

"I don't know. Ask me tomorrow. I'd kill for a ball game." The small desk Ruben used in high school was covered with papers, but they were in organized stacks. A spreadsheet was in the center. Ruben lowered himself gently into the rickety chair.

"The number of items turned into the desk held steady in the beginning of the time period you gave me. It varied some from month to month, but it averaged out to a certain amount of weapons, drugs, and valuables each month for two years. Even dividing the weapons into handguns, long guns, knives, and miscellaneous, the count was close."

Adam sat on the edge of the bed, like a little kid looking up at the teacher. "What happened then?"

"About eighteen months ago, the count began falling. At first, only antique type handguns stopped appearing. Then it was regular handguns. For the last four months, the only handguns turned in were so old and rusted they would be a danger to anyone using them. The only exception was one turned in on a Saturday while a rookie was on the desk."

"What about other things? Did the count change on them as well?"

"Funny you should ask. Long guns haven't changed. The count is exactly the same as it was two years ago. Of course, it would be difficult to stroll out with a shotgun under your arm. Switchblades, slapjacks, brass knuckles, those types of things apparently aren't being turned in anymore."

"Any drugs turned in?" Adam took the spreadsheet from Ruben's hands and studied it.

"They were the last thing to start disappearing. About

six months ago, narcotics fell off the grid. Other types of drugs, heart meds, diabetics, anything someone might find in a deceased relative's house and not know what to do with, still come in regularly."

"I don't suppose we've seen any valuables lately."

"In the last year, only two empty purses and one old beat-up billfold with three one-dollar bills have been found on the streets of Houston. Not one ring left on a wash basin, not one bracelet with a broken clasp, unless it was worth less than ten dollars."

Adam rubbed his hand over his face. "So what are we going to do about this?"

"There's no 'we.' I'm on sick leave. And I want it cleared up before I go back to work. Something like this could ruin a career. If you report it, you're in the shit. If you don't report it, you're in the shit. Hard Luck isn't even going to want to know it happened. Marshall's a well-liked guy. He brings donuts."

"I guess it's okay to commit any type of crime if you bring donuts."

"Well, murder usually requires bear claws."

He and Ruben discussed the problem for another twenty minutes without coming up with a solution. When Mamacita announced dinner, they started down the stairs. "Not a word," Ruben said, nodding toward his mother.

"How's your friend Jillian?" Mamacita asked.

"She's doing well. Thank you for having her over that night. I think it really helped her."

"I know. She called me the next day. Someone taught her good manners." She glared at him. "She's a nice girl, and I like her, but she has problems. A shadow follows her, a dark cloud."

Adam stopped eating. "Everyone she's ever cared about has died young and violently—her mother, her sister, her father, and now her good friend. I imagine she does get down occasionally, but she seems to handle it well."

"I'm not talking about grief. She carries that in a small place in her heart, and it goes everywhere with her. This is something else. I don't know what it is, but it wouldn't come into this house." She made a sign of the cross. "She's going to need your help to get away from it, Adam, and I hope you're up to the task."

He and Ruben looked at each other and rolled their eyes. When he got ready to leave, Ruben walked him to the door and stepped onto the porch.

"I don't know what Mamacita's talking about with the shadow following her bit." Ruben made quotation marks with his fingers and a spooky, horror movie sound. "But she does know people, and if she says there's something off about Jillian, then you should think twice."

"Jillian's different, I'll give you that. But maybe that's a good thing. I haven't done so well with the ones I've tried in the past. Maybe a change is what I need. Anyway, when has Mamacita approved of any woman you or I have ever dated?"

"That's true. And she's been right every time. Maybe this once you should use your big brain, instead of the little one."

Chapter 17

Adam drove home in a blue funk. He wanted to be angry at Ruben, but couldn't manage it. It was one thing to make a joke about something, or have a friend kid about it. It was something else when three or four friends told him the same thing.

His marriage should have taught him that much.

He'd met his wife when she was working as a waitress at a diner. It had to be love because she kept his coffee cup filled and made sure his eggs were just the way he liked them.

She never met a rule she wouldn't break with a smile and a wink. "Rules are for suckers. I'm sure they don't mean us. If we get in trouble, just flash your badge."

They had plenty of fun in those early days. She seemed to enjoy sex games, usually ones involving his uniform and equipment, especially the handcuffs. She sometimes wore his hat and nothing else as she danced around the room.

Shortly after they married, the games stopped. She claimed to have only then realized what the handcuffs were normally used for.

"I could catch something," she said. "Maybe AIDS, or TB." He wasn't sure what she expected to catch from the hat.

She immediately quit work and began her new hobby—spending money. It didn't seem to matter if it was Jimmy Choo shoes or a bag of crap from the dollar store, she couldn't get through a day without buying something. If she ran out of money, she began to shoplift.

"You're stingy and selfish," she screamed as she tore the house apart looking for the credit cards he'd hidden.

He suggested she see someone about her compulsion, but instead of keeping the appointment he made for her, she moved out. Within a week, he was served with divorce papers. Three months later, she was married to one of the most eligible lawyers in the city of Houston.

When he started to date Mai, a beautiful Vietnamese woman from the Records Department, several of his friends warned him she was crazy.

That's what every man says about a woman that gets away, he told himself.

She was cute and sweet, and hung on his every word. She was an expensive date—she liked to go to fancy restaurants and clubs—but it was worth the price because she enjoyed it so. Even though clubbing wasn't his thing, he relished the look of envy on other men's faces, and knew they were wondering what he had that they didn't to attract such an exotic woman. When he had to be at work early the next morning and wanted to skip the clubs, she pouted, and he gave in. Coffee and Red Bull replaced actual sleep.

Her desire to have sex in inappropriate places was exciting at first, but her constant need to be reassured she was more important to him than his job began to take a toll.

More and more of her things began to appear in his closet, and he suspected she was moving in with him, one pair of shoes at a time.

His hours were unpredictable. As a civilian employee, she should have known that. Perhaps she did, but she didn't like it. Now when he came in late, she didn't greet him with a hug and a kiss, but with tears and accusations. If he stopped for a beer with his friends on the way home, it meant an hour of recriminations.

Ruben was his partner by then, and they went to dinner at Mamacita's house several times. Mamacita was always polite, but it was obvious she didn't like Mai.

"That old lady has it in for me," Mai said every time

they left. "She keeps giving me the evil eye. I think she's trying to poison me with that spicy food." This from a woman who covered her food with Wasabi sauce like it was chocolate syrup.

Eventually, Adam began to suspect she was using him to troll for a bigger, better catch. Finally, her jealousy and temper tantrums were too much for him, and he suggested they take a break from each other. That was when he found out what crazy meant.

She called constantly, alternating between crying and screaming. His answering machine would be full when he got home in the evening. Her command of English curse words was impressive, but she still augmented them with Vietnamese. She tried to spread rumors about him at work. He wasn't the first she made claims about, so it didn't go very far.

He came home once to find her naked in his bed. She threatened to lie to the police and say he raped her, but he'd seen her car when he drove up and had asked a neighbor to come inside with him so she left without any trouble. After that, he changed his locks and installed an alarm system.

She never again did anything outright to harass him, but almost a year later, any report he needed from the Records Department was delayed or lost. Asking Ruben or another detective to get them for him didn't always work. Avoiding her was getting old.

Now he'd met Jillian, and both Ruben and Mamacita were suggesting there was something off about her. He could see through a lying witness or suspect from across a room, but was he blind about his personal life?

"Fuck you, Ruben," he called out. "Your idea of a long-term relationship is staying for breakfast." And Mamacita, what did she know about dating? She got married at sixteen to the guy who lived next door, someone she had known all her life. As for the guys in his squad: Nelson's sole requirement in a woman was that she be shorter than he was, and Steinberg had children all over town with two ex-wives and a former girlfriend. They were hardly experts.

If he wanted to smooth things over with Jillian, and he did, he needed to get his butt over to her place and start groveling.

Chapter 18

Adam hurried home to feed Rover and give him his shot. After a quick shower, he changed into casual clothes. He hated to take the time, but his visit to the dry-cleaning plant had left even his hair reeking of chemicals. He placed his service weapon in the gun safe. After a minute's hesitation, he added his backup weapon, a snub-nosed .38 he wore in an ankle holster, before locking the safe. It was a breach of protocol to go unarmed, but he had a lot to make up for.

He had parked the Taurus and planned to take his personal car, a four-year-old BMW, so there could be no question he was off the clock, but when he turned the key, nothing happened. Surprised, he tried again.

The battery was less than a year old, and he had driven the car on Sunday, so it shouldn't be down. He counted to ten, slowly, to give the car time to heal itself. His third try offered no better results. With enough time, he could have fixed it, but he didn't have any to spare so, cursing under his breath, he went back into the house and got the keys to the Taurus.

While driving to Jillian's, he chewed on his lip. He hated to admit it, but Ruben had a point. He often thought with his dick. For some reason, unstable women seemed to seek him out. Lydia Cox sprang to mind, and the realization that he would have gone out with her if he hadn't met Jillian first made him shudder.

Did he wear a sign that said: I'll put up with anything for a little nookie? He'd wasted years rebelling against his father's rules. Was he still doing it? This time he'd try to keep his eyes open. If Jillian showed any sign of becoming datezilla, he'd cut and run before things escalated. After Mai, he'd made a solemn vow to never again get involved with a crazy woman.

He was ten minutes late when he parked behind Jillian's. He took the stairs two at a time, rushing to her back door. She was sitting on the sofa with her legs tucked under her, eating a bowl of ice cream, when he knocked on the sliding glass door. He had on a grin that even he knew was idiotic.

When she stood and started for the door, she wasn't smiling, but she wasn't frowning either, and that was good enough for Adam. She nodded toward his piece-of-crap Taurus. "Am I under arrest?"

He twisted his head toward the car. "No, no. Of course not. I had to bring the cruiser. Mine wouldn't start."

"Then why exactly are you here?" She held up the empty bowl in one hand and the spoon in the other. "If it's for ice cream, you're out of luck. It's all gone. If it's for anything else,"—she tilted her head toward the bedroom—"you're still out of luck."

"That's not why I'm here. I wasn't planning on that." Not planning on it maybe, but he definitely had hopes. "I didn't like the way we left things the other day, and I wanted to come over and apologize."

"It's a long drive for something you could have done over the phone."

"You're worth the drive." Was that a slight thaw?

A mosquito landed on her arm. "You better come in and shut the door before the house fills up with bugs."

He suspected he was only a half step above the bugs in her opinion, but that was a half step better that he was before. He'd learned early that it's a lot harder to send someone away when they're already in your house than when they're still outside.

"You know it wasn't personal. I never suspected you of

anything, but I had to prove it before I could close the case on someone else."

"Not personal? Wait until you have to prove yourself to a homicide detective, then tell me it wasn't personal. It sure felt that way, especially after what we'd been doing two nights before."

"I know. But I couldn't ask you when I came by on Friday. Not after seeing how upset you were." He knew immediately he'd made a big mistake. She didn't like being reminded how vulnerable she'd been. "And on Sunday... Well, I couldn't ask you on Sunday. That was too special. I tried to make it a separate trip. An official one, not personal."

"I understand what you're saying, but you should have devised a way, and you should have done it before we slept together. That made me feel...used."

"You're right, and I apologize. I bungled it completely. Now that we've established I'm an idiot, can we move on? I'm not familiar with this part of town, but there must be someplace to get a drink, listen to some music. Would you let me take you out somewhere?"

"There's no need, I have beer." When she pulled two Shiner Bocks from the fridge, an enormous weight lifted from his shoulders. If she had bothered to buy his favorite beer, he still had a chance.

"So, other than pissing me off royally, how was your week?"

"It should have been a good one, but somehow it wasn't. I met several interesting people and closed two cases. I even got to tell a mother I found the man who murdered her daughter. That's supposed to make me feel better, but this time it didn't. After all, it's the only payoff we get in this department. We can't find a missing person or return stolen property, but we can let relatives know their loved ones have been avenged. She might not have been a good mother, but she did love her daughter, and knowing who killed her doesn't bring her back."

"It does help, though, maybe not today, but in time." Jillian put her hand on his, and the knot in his stomach began to relax. "I had reports from some of the people you met. Snake-Eye wasn't too impressed, but Lydia Cox is a big fan."

Adam laughed and shook his head. "Not even if she promised her husband would have full custody of those kids. Now, the bakery lady might be another story."

"Give me a break. She has to be ten years older than you. Probably fifteen."

"Yeah, but when I was eating those Brownie Cookies, my eyes misted over." How long had it been since he'd met someone he could tease and laugh with? "Snake-Eye, on the other hand, made my eyes mist over for other reasons entirely."

"He's a unique individual. Did you know he has an MBA from the University of Houston? He once worked in a big brokerage firm downtown. When they caught him smoking pot in the john, they kicked his ass to the curb. They didn't call the cops on him, though. That would have been bad for business."

"You've got to be shitting me."

She put her hand over her heart. "I shit you not. He may have psychological problems, but he's a certified genius."

"He is certifiable, I'll give you that."

"I'm never sure how much of what you see with him is an act. He came in here once and told me to buy some stock I never heard of. I didn't do it, of course, but I kept an eye on it sometimes and it kept going up. A few months later, he told me to sell it. When I looked the next time, it had gone down. If he ever tells me again, I'm buying it. Anyway, he and his friends may be weird, but they don't hurt anybody."

"Except those poor trees. He's hell on flora and fauna."

"That's true, but they're his trees, so I guess there's no law against it."

He settled back on the sofa and smiled. Only a few minutes and he was already comfortable and relaxed. "How's your new lady working out? Cara, was it?"

"She's doing great. I think she's going to be just fine. I still miss Billy, but I hadn't realized what a strain it was keeping an eye on him." She twisted on the sofa to face him. "Saturday's coming. What do you like to do on the weekends?"

"Ruben has a small cabin on Lake Livingston, and he keeps a boat there. We used to take it out at least once a month. It might be a while before he's ready to go out again."

"Fishing or water-skiing?"

"Fishing."

"Good. I can't stand all those boats zipping around, making so much noise. Who cooks the fish?"

Great, she wasn't a water-skier, and she didn't seem to worry about public opinion or appearances. Things were getting better and better.

She had her arm on the back of the sofa, and he put his hand on top of hers, playing with her fingers. "Well, the cabin's pretty rustic. Ruben and I built a two-burner propane cooker, and he fries the fish outside then usually dumps in some french-fries. Sometimes we put on a pot of water and boil a few ears of corn. Nothing fancy, but it tastes good with a cold beer."

"And how many people are usually eating this feast?"

The fact that she cared enough to question him was promising. "It's awfully isolated. Not many people are interested in going out there for a day of fishing."

"Fried fish, cold beer, and a day on the lake, what's not to like?"

Besides being beautiful and sexy and owning her own business, she liked to fish. If Snake-Eye was right about what she was made of, then for once in his life he had stepped into a pile of gold dust, instead of the pile he usually stepped in.

Ruben and Mamacita had it all wrong this time.

The evening ended the same way Sunday had, only better. He took his time undressing her, enjoying every inch of silky smooth skin. Nibbling and caressing his way around her body until he couldn't hold back any longer. She was open about what she wanted, and he found it exciting. He was happy to accommodate any request.

Afterwards, they took a shower together, his third of the day and by far his favorite. He had trouble deciding which he enjoyed most, applying soap to Jillian's body or letting her soap him. Either way, having their bodies sliding against each other while their lips kept them anchored was a pleasant experience. One that led them straight back to bed.

"Are you going to slip out in the middle of the night again?" she asked.

"No, I left a double helping of food for Rover and he can wait on his morning shot. I've got some comp time coming and don't have to be in till eleven. I'll have time to go by the house."

She smiled and laid her head on his chest. "Well, I guess you can teach an old cop a few new things."

In the morning, they started again, slow and languid in the soft light. He took his time, tracing the contours of her body with his lips and letting his hands follow until he was certain she was as sated as he was. They were resting contentedly, arms and legs in a tangle, when he worked up the courage to ask her a question. "Could I put my cop hat back on for a second and ask you something?"

She stiffened slightly. "What is it?"

"Do you ever take old guns in for trade? I need a used gun, not too old. It can be in working order or not, as long as it looks good. I could pay a couple of hundred bucks. Do you have anything like that?"

"Don't get anything used. I'll find you something good and get it for you at cost. It won't be much more, but it'll be dependable. You can't afford to have something that's not reliable."

"It's not for me. It's for a case. You remember the gun I came here about that first day? I think the guy you turned it in to sold it to someone else."

"And for that you get the big bucks? I knew that when you set the picture down. So, are you going to work some kind of sting on him?"

He rose on one elbow. "I'm going to try."

"In that case, I've got just the gun you need. And it won't cost you a thing. It's an old .45. I never use trade-ins, but for some reason I took this one about a year ago. I haven't done anything with it. It'll be perfect. So what's the plan?"

"It won't be anything elaborate. I'm just going to find someone to turn it in and then follow it."

"The store's going to be closed Friday for Billy's memorial. I had to set it up. His mother wouldn't have anything to do with it because he killed himself and that's a sin. Anyway, I'll go downtown Friday afternoon and turn it in."

"He might recognize you."

Jillian was sitting up in bed, her voice humming with excitement. "That won't matter. I'll say what a good job he did last time so I came back to him."

"It's too dangerous. I can't involve a civilian. If things go wrong, he might come after you." The thought of Jillian tangled up in this mess put a knot in his stomach.

"You're in this alone, aren't you? If you weren't, you wouldn't need to ask me for a gun or look for someone to turn it in. What do you plan to do once you have him?"

He hesitated. "Threaten him. Try to make him walk away. I know you won't like it, but I can't arrest him. If I did, it would be bad for the entire department. Lots of people already think cops aren't any better than crooks. If this came out, it would be a disaster for good cops everywhere."

"It wouldn't do your career any good either, would it? I have a pretty good idea what happens to cops who turn in other cops."

Adam jerked up and swung his feet off the bed. "This doesn't have anything to do with my career, and if you think it does, you don't know me. I'm thinking what it would do to the department and every good cop that works in it."

"I know that," Jillian said, her tone softer. "I mean you have to be careful. You're two steps behind me. I figured all this out before you left the first day. Only I didn't know you then, and I thought you were going to let it go entirely, maybe just try to warn him off."

"If I had my way, he'd be in jail with the other crooks, where he belongs."

She got up and wrapped the sheet around her. "You've got to use me. You can't go to Internal Affairs. They would have to make it public, and no one would forgive you for giving the department a black eye. I'm not some delicate thing you have to protect, Adam. I've been taking care of myself and doing a damn good job of it since I was twelve years old."

"Cooking and running a business, even if it is a gun store, is a world different than facing an armed criminal when he's trapped. And that's what Marshall is—a thief. I can't risk it. I won't risk you."

"I started this and I'm going to finish it. If you think I'm willing to stay back on this one, you don't know me very well, either."

He didn't answer, so she kept going. "I have the gun downstairs. Come on, I'll get it for you."

They threw their clothes on and hurried down. Jillian went straight to the storeroom and began looking in boxes for the gun. She had just found it when the front door opened. The alarm beeped twice as it was turned off.

"Who is that?" Adam whispered.

"It's Cara," Jillian said, peeking around the corner.

"I thought the store didn't open till ten."

"It doesn't, but it's her first time to open on her own, and I guess she wanted to get in early. It takes a while to get things set up, especially with the baby."

"Do you want me to hide back here? I don't want to embarrass you." They were both barefooted and had severe cases of bed head. He badly needed a shave. "We look like we just got out of bed," he whispered, and they both laughed.

"Hey, it's my store. I can do whatever I want."

Jillian stepped into the store. "Good morning, Cara. You're here early."

Cara jumped. "I'm sorry. I didn't know you were in here. Megan was up at first light. I spent an hour trying to get her back to sleep before I gave up. I didn't know how long it would take me to open, so I came on in. I hope I didn't disturb you."

"Not at all. I was just looking for something I left back here."

"Hello, Cara. It's nice to see you again." Adam came out and stood beside Jillian.

Cara jumped even higher than she had the first time. "Good morning to you, Mr... er, um, Detective..."

"Adam."

"It's nice to see you again, too, Adam."

She was wearing a large, brightly colored scarf around one shoulder and across her front. Adam had never seen anything quite like it.

"Megan was anxious to come to work," she said, patting a lump in the scarf. Just then the lump started to wiggle and let out a small cry. Cara reached in and pulled out the baby. "This thing works great. Thanks, J. R., Megan likes it because she's close to me yet I have both hands free to do things. I can even nurse her without anyone realizing it."

Adam immediately began looking around the room, trying to find someplace safe to avert his eyes. Cara chuckled. "I think I'll go in the back to feed her and put her down before I start work."

Before Cara could begin nursing Megan, Adam hurried out to his car, stepping carefully in his bare feet, to get his camera. While Cara fed the baby, he and Jillian carried the gun to the front of the store where the light was best. They placed it on a clear spot on the floor and shot pictures from every angle. They took several that showed the serial number, and he recorded it in his notebook.

"All right, you can be the one to turn in the gun, but that's all you can do. I don't want Marshall to see us together, so when you're finished, leave immediately. There's a restroom and some potted plants to the right as you come in the door. I'll be standing behind the plants. I should be able to get some good pictures without him seeing me. Hold the gun out, by the barrel, and turn your face to me. That way I can get a picture of you handing him the gun. Do you have any questions?"

"What do you want me to do after I give him the gun?"

"He can't have any idea we're in this together. When you leave, go to the Starbuck's around the corner. You can wait for me there. I won't be long."

They stood, and he handed her the gun. "I still don't like involving you." He ran his hand down her arm and looked in her eyes.

"You can't go through life protecting me. I'm not the needy type."

"I know that. If you were, I probably wouldn't be this interested."

She grinned, and he pulled her close and kissed her. Cara chose that minute to come out of the storeroom.

"Megan's down for the count," she said. Now it was her turn to look away. "We won't hear a peep from her for a couple of hours."

Jillian pulled Adam into a back corner of the storeroom and kissed him again. "How much time do we have before you need to leave for work?"

"Not enough for what I have in mind."

Chapter 19

Adam and Jillian were in the back room with their arms around each other when the front door slammed open. He lifted his head. "It's too early for customers, isn't it?" Jillian's closed shop was beginning to feel like a major department store.

"Maybe Cara went outside to get something from her car." Jillian looked toward the front of the store, but a wall was in the way.

Adam motioned for Jillian to wait as he stepped quietly to the door. He heard voices, but couldn't understand them. Kneeling down so his head was near the floor, he looked quickly around the corner, then snapped his head back.

"I can see Cara. Some man is holding her arm and pointing a gun at her."

The man was stocky and had a good start on the beer belly that would most likely define him in later years. His sandy hair was disheveled, and his face had the pasty look of someone who spent too much time indoors.

"I'll bet it's her husband, Trevor. She's gone to a lot of trouble to keep him from finding her."

Adam glanced around the storage area. "Do you have a weapon back here? There must be something with all these guns."

"I've got guns, but they're not loaded. All the ammunition is on the other side of the room and to get to it we'd have to cross in front of the door. There's a loaded gun under the counter, just below the cash register, but he'd see you if you went out there. Did you bring your weapon?"

"No, I was trying to appear innocent and trustworthy. I even left my ankle holster at home." He could kick himself for that decision. The first time in years he'd left home without a weapon and look what happened. Hard Luck had better not find out about this.

"I'll go out. It's my store. It'll seem normal." Jillian started for the door, but he grabbed her arm.

"You have to take the baby and go out the back door. Take my car and get away from here. You can call for help on my radio. Wait for me at the IHop on the feeder road."

"We discussed this. I'm not a hot-house flower. I can take care of myself. I don't need you to protect me."

"Damn it, for once will you listen to me?" He held both her shoulders. His voice was low, but intense. "I'm not trying to protect you. I'm trying to protect the baby." *Okay, I am trying to protect you, but I have enough sense not to say it out loud.* "You know as well as I do that once he starts shooting, the bullets could go anywhere. These walls aren't any protection. The baby could get hurt easily. You have to get her out of here before he realizes where she is."

"I don't want to leave you."

"Now you know how I feel about you helping bring Marshall down. You have to leave, now. I'll call you when it's safe." He kissed her quickly and handed her his keys.

She tiptoed to the crib and lifted the baby. At the door she whispered, "Be careful," before stepping outside.

Megan didn't wake when Jillian gently lifted her out of the crib or as she put her on the seat beside her. Trying to race barefoot over the gravel to Adam's car, she'd resented him for making her leave, but once in the car, she realized he was right. Megan's safety was the most important thing.

The minute she left the parking lot and turned onto the street, Heather appeared beside her. "What's happening?

What's going on? Where did you get the baby?"

"As if you didn't know. I suppose you're going to tell me you didn't have anything to do with it. You probably told that guy where to find Cara."

"I did not." Heather managed to sound insulted, a sure sign she was lying. "I don't even know who you're talking about or who this baby is. I would never do anything to hurt a kid."

"Of course you would. You have many times. Every little girl that beat you at any pageant had some type of accident. One fell and broke a leg, and Patty Zykorie ran into a glass door and has a big scar on her face." Jillian's voice began to rise.

"Maybe, but that was a long time ago."

"You messed up every one of their marriages by whispering insinuations in their ears. That hurt *their* kids, and it wasn't so long ago."

"But I would never do anything that put you in danger. You know that."

"Well, that's true at least. You don't want to mess up your only chance for a new body."

Jillian pulled to the side of the road and started pounding on the radio. "Come on! How do you turn this thing on?"

"Calm down and look at it. Your cop boyfriend does it while he's driving, so it can't be that difficult."

Finally, she saw a switch and turned it on. "Officer needs assistance. Officer needs assistance. Can anybody hear me? We need some help."

"Yes, ma'am. I can hear you. What's your location?"

"I'm at J. R.'s Guns on Weaton Road. That's just off the I-45 feeder road near the county line, a few miles south of Conroe. A white male is holding a gun on his wife. Detective Adam Campbell is also there, but I don't know if he's armed. He's the one wearing khakis and a brown print shirt. The gunman has on a ratty black T-shirt with no sleeves."

"We have a unit on the way."

"You better send an ambulance, too."

"Are you in the building, Ma'am?"

"No, I took the baby and drove away."

"Good. Don't go back until you get the all clear from the officers."

Jillian looked up and saw a rusty pick-up coming down the road in her direction. "Oh, no. Why would Snake-Eye come here at this time of the morning?"

"I told him to," Heather said. "I suggested he check to see why the cops were asking questions about you. That was before you called the police. I didn't know what was happening, only that you were in trouble."

"Well, I've got to stop him. He'll make everything worse." Jillian honked and stuck her arm out the window. When he slowed down, she put her head out. "Don't go in the store. Cara's husband is in there with a gun. Adam, Detective Campbell, is trying to get to the gun I keep under the register."

"Okay, I won't go in. I'll just pull up in front and honk. That should distract the malcontent long enough for your friend to make his move." Snake-Eye drove away before Jillian could object.

As soon as Jillian and the baby were out the door, Adam tried to smooth down his hair and button his shirt. There wasn't anything he could do about his bare feet, so he tried to slip behind the counter quickly.

"Hey, man," he said. "What's going on?"

"Who the fuck are you?" The man jerked Cara around to face him.

"I'm Adam. I work here. Who are you?"

"You work here, uh? Well, you look like you just got out of bed. What have you been doing with my wife?"

Adam looked down and saw that his shirt was buttoned crooked. "Nothing, man. I just met her five minutes ago." He tried to ease closer to the register, but Trevor had the gun pointed at him.

"That's a likely story. She's such a slut she wouldn't care how long she'd known you. Anyway, she's supposed to be working for some woman."

"J. R.'s not in yet. This is my first day, so I don't know what's going on." He face was slack, but his eyes never stopped moving as he judged the distance from his position to the gun under the register. Which could he reach quicker, the gun or Trevor?

"What's going on is this little tramp tried to run out on me and take my baby with her." Trevor slapped Cara across the face as he spoke. "Where's the kid, bitch? What have you done with my son?"

"It's not a boy, Trevor. She's a girl."

"A girl? You can't even do that right." He hit her again.

"Hey, man," Adam said. "This is crazy. The kid's not here. Who ever heard of a baby in a gun store?" He took another step closer to the register.

"Stay right there, jerk. I haven't finished with you."

"Okay, man. I'm cool. Let me open the register, and you can have whatever's inside. Then you'll have enough to take off."

"I'm not leaving without my kid."

The front door opened, but Adam didn't look up. *Shit. I told her not to come back until it was safe. Now I have two people to watch out for, three if she still has the baby.* One deep breath told him it wasn't Jillian.

"What the fuck is this, a party? Why wasn't I invited?" Snake-Eye looked around the shop. "I wouldn't mind a little fun."

"Get the fuck out of here, mister, if you want to live to see another day. This is between me and the bitch."

"Hey, I don't care what you do. I don't even blame you. The stupid bitch is too dumb to count. She shorted me on my last order. Let me pick it up, and I'll be on my way. I can't afford to let the police know I was here. What'd she do to you, anyway?"

"She tried to run off on me. Took the kid and hid out."

"Well, no wonder. She deserves anything you give her."

Cara was barely standing. Her face was bloody and one arm was hanging crooked. "It looks like you've already tuned her up pretty good. Don't know why you want her, she's all sticks and bone, but you can't let them get away with something like that."

That was all Adam needed, a third person to keep track of. Someone to get Trevor more agitated.

Trevor nodded and shook Cara's arm. "You're right. Whatever happens to her, it's her own fault. At least somebody understands."

Snake-Eye turned to Adam. "You owe me a box of .45 caliber ammo. You shorted me one box."

Adam didn't move and Snake-Eye pointed to the wall behind him. "It's right there on the shelf."

He looked at Trevor. "Don't do nothing till I'm out of here. I've got enough troubles of my own." He waited while Adam handed him the box. "Good day, all. Don't do anything I wouldn't do," he said, and gave the cackle Adam remembered from two days before.

At least they were back to two. Adam slid closer to the register.

Snake-Eye gave Trevor a salute with the box of ammo. Then, just as he passed, he pirouetted on one foot and slammed Trevor in the back of the head with the box of bullets. Trevor went down like a puppet with the strings cut.

Adam vaulted over the counter, gun in hand, but

caught his big toe on the edge of the cash register, causing shockwaves of pain to shoot up his leg before landing. He limped to Trevor's body and knocked the gun away with his injured foot. "Son of a bitch!" he yelled, hopping on one foot and trying to hold the other.

"What were you planning to do, dick-head?" Snake-Eye kicked Trevor in the ribs. "Wait for him to die of old age? Or were you going to let him keep hitting her until his arm got tired?"

Adam didn't answer, but handed Snake-Eye the pistol. "Keep this on him for a minute. And quit kicking him. I'll have to explain every bruise."

Cara had fallen when Trevor let go of her, but managed to stand again. She hobbled over to Trevor's body and kicked him on the other side. "Good. You can blame them all on me," she said, and kicked him again.

In the back room, Adam grabbed the baby blanket and started ripping it apart with his teeth. He tied Trevor's hands tightly with strips of blanket.

Snake-Eye paced nervously around Trevor's body. "There's no way I'm getting mixed up in this. I can't afford to answer any cop questions. Keep my name out of it. I didn't show up." He looked Adam up and down, taking in his disheveled appearance and lack of shoes. "Adam, huh? I guess there's no mathematics for taste."

Adam yanked the gun from Snake-Eye. "If you don't want to be involved, you better head out now. Jillian was using my radio to call for help."

He turned to Cara. The pain was such his breath came in short gasps and he held his toe off the ground. "Can you keep him out of this? You'd have to promise never to mention his name. Forget he was here. You can say you passed out and it was all over when you came to. Anything Trevor says after that blow to the head will be suspect."

Cara looked from Adam to Snake-Eye and back again.

"I'll never tell a soul exactly what happened, but I'll never forget it either."

She stared at Adam. "What about you? Can you lie to your fellow officers?"

Chapter 20

Jillian craned her neck toward the store. She'd go crazy if she didn't find out what was happening. "Heather, can you see what's going on? Is there any way you can help?"

"I'm not going in the store. You know that. And I can't see in there. I don't believe anybody's been killed, though. I think I would feel it."

Jillian's mouth was dry and her stomach rolled as she twisted one direction and then the other, trying to see anything at all. When Snake-Eye's truck appeared, she opened the door and stepped out.

He stopped long enough to give a thumbs-up. "It's all over. Everything's okay. I wasn't here. You didn't see me. I'm busy eating pancakes." He started off again, trailing dust, but stopped and yelled out the window, "I owe you for a box of shells."

As he sped off, sirens wailed in the distance. Snake-Eye whipped his truck into the side entrance of the used car lot and disappeared as the first police car flew around the corner. She waited while three squad cars and then an ambulance sped past.

Heather looked at Jillian's messy hair and wrinkled clothes. "If we're going to sit here and wait, you might as well tell me about last night. Or maybe it was this morning."

"Both. And it's none of your business." Jillian backed the car around and started to the store. Megan was still asleep.

"Bye, Heather," she said as she pulled into the parking lot.

For once, it was actually good to see her.

Adam limped behind the counter and picked up a box of shells. He gripped the box with both hands and touched it to the back of Trevor's head, getting blood on one end. He lifted the box shoulder height and dropped it on the floor, spilling bullets everywhere.

When he heard the first sirens, he faced Cara. "You were passed out, right?"

"Right. Do I have time to kick him again?"

"Better not. You're too weak and frail. You probably can't even answer questions."

Mike and Larry were the first team through the door and they had their guns drawn. He held his hands up. "I'm Detective Adam Campbell with the Houston Police Department. The man on the floor broke in here with a gun and tried to abduct this woman and her baby."

Cara started sobbing loudly. "He tried to kill me. Detective Campbell saved my life." She clung to Adam's arm.

He tried to send her a mental message—don't overdo it—but Mike and Larry seemed to eat it up.

Mike stopped suddenly, lifting his nose and narrowing his eyes. He sniffed loudly, then turned his head and sniffed the other direction, as if trying to place a familiar odor.

"What happened here?" Larry crossed toward Adam, and his feet shot out from under his bulky frame on the spilled bullets.

Adam bit back a grin as the big man tried to steady himself. "I was unarmed, so I threw a box of shells at him."

Mike and Larry looked closely at him for the first time, taking in his appearance. The back of Adam's neck grew warm, but he returned their gaze without flinching.

"Where's J. R.?" Larry hefted himself off the floor.

"She took the baby and left through the back door."

Mike kept looking at Trevor on the floor and back to the counter. "That was some throw." His voice was more skeptical than admiring.

"Adam used to play baseball in college." Jillian pushed the door open with one hip while she held the baby tightly against her chest. "I think he still pitches for the police/fireman's league."

Seeing Jillian and Megan, safe and unharmed, made Adam's knees tremble. He hadn't realized how worried he'd been. Even the throbbing in his toe seemed to diminish.

"Megan, sweetheart, are you okay?" Cara ran to Jillian and tried to take the baby out of her arms.

Jillian shook her head. "You're not in any condition to hold her yet. Let's put her back in her crib and you can watch her sleep. She didn't even wake up."

As they headed toward the back room, Adam watched Mike gave Jillian the same appraising look he had undergone a few minutes earlier. He liked the deputy's knowing gaze even less when it fell on her. A bolt of protectiveness shot down his spine and his hands balled into fists.

Jillian slipped up the stairs to her apartment. When she returned, her hair was freshly gelled, her shirt was changed, and she was wearing sandals.

She handed Adam his shoes, then pointed to his shirt and raised her eyebrows. He turned his back and quickly redid his buttons, but there no way he could get his shoe on over his swollen toe.

"That's better," she said, "but you might want to do something about your hair."

He ran a hand over his hair, but it sprang back immediately. "I think I've completely ruined your reputation."

"Well, you have, but not in the way you think." Jillian looked around the room, now filled with police, sheriff's deputies, and EMT's. "Most of the men in this room have hit on me at one time or another and been turned down. I think the going speculation is that I'm gay. A fallacy I've done my best to encourage. It makes life easier. I think you've blown my cover."

"Sorry about that." Adam grinned in spite of himself.

"That's okay," she whispered. "You're worth it."

Half an hour later, the store was beginning to empty. Trevor regained consciousness and was transported to the county jail, where a doctor would check him over. Cara and Megan left by ambulance to the nearest hospital for examination.

The EMT's tried to convince Adam to go with them and have his foot x-rayed. He refused, and they admitted the toe probably wasn't broken, but had definitely been dislocated. They put butterfly bandages on the cut, and he convinced a paramedic he'd played ball with to pop the toe back into place, making the pain he experienced when it dislocated seem like a mosquito bite.

"You sure you don't want to come in with us?" asked the young paramedic. "You need stitches on that toe, and you shouldn't be driving."

"I'll be right behind you," Adam promised. "I can catch a ride with one of these officers."

As soon as the ambulance pulled away, Adam sent Jillian upstairs to get some Super Glue. He lifted the bandages gently and covered the cut with the Super Glue, holding the edges together until it dried. After replacing the band-aids, he wrapped duct tape around the injured big toe and the one next to it, holding them in place.

Within minutes, he was sitting at Jillian's desk, his foot propped up and a bag of frozen peas on top of it. He tried to explain to his boss why he wasn't at work, but Luchak wasn't buying it. "I'll be there in a couple of hours, and you can give me all the grief you want. Right now I've got to find some aspirin and a cup of coffee."

If he didn't already have a headache, facing Hard Luck would give him one.

Adam delayed leaving as long as possible, but Jillian seemed to have everything under control.

"My only regret is that I didn't get to see Snake-Eye sucker punch Trevor. At least I saw Larry take a pratfall as I waltzed through the door. That should be good for a few laughs when I get bored." She had her hand on his chest, smoothing his collar.

"You remember everything we went over about Friday, don't you? We can call it off or postpone it if you need some time to..." Her eyes stopped him, and he remembered she didn't appreciate being treated as if she were fragile.

"We've been over it a dozen times. I know what to do. Now, get out of here so I can finish cleaning up. I've still got five bullets missing, and I don't want one of my good customers falling the way Larry did." She kissed him gently. "I'll be waiting for you in the coffee shop near your office."

He glanced over his shoulder as he limped out the door. She was already sweeping the floor.

Chapter 21

Adam ran by the house to change clothes and take care of Rover. He had one good suit, which he saved for personal use or the times he had to be in court. Other days he wore inexpensive suits or sport jackets. His one extravagance was shoes. He learned early the value of good shoes since he might spend the day going door-to-door interviewing witnesses or need to chase a suspect down a city street or through backyards and over fences.

He considered cutting the toe out of an older pair of shoes, but they were the ones he wore on rainy days or when he needed to do a grid search in an empty field. He dug in the back of his closet and found something his ex-wife had bought when they took a three day Cruise to Nowhere, steaming around the Gulf of Mexico. He'd never actually worn them, but they might work.

After stalling as long as he could, he headed for the station and all the ribbing that was coming.

He entered the squad room wearing a suit and one dress shoe. On the other foot was a sandal exposing a swollen and bloody big toe. Every person in the room stood, as he knew they would, and began applauding. Some gave catcalls or mock bows. They were all laughing.

"All rise for our newest superhero, Toe Jamb Campbell." Frank Nelson stood in the back of the room and swept his arm in Adam's direction.

"Okay, get it over with. You're all jealous because you weren't injured in the line of duty. This is a war wound and should be treated with respect." Adam limped to his desk with all the dignity he could muster.

"If that was in the line of duty, she must have been the mayor's ugly step-sister." He'd expected the ribbing from Nelson, but when Steinberg joined in, he knew it wasn't going away any time soon.

"War wound, my ass. It was more likely a booty call wound. And by the looks of that foot, if she stepped on your toe, she must have been in excess of three hundred pounds." Nelson was still in high form.

"Ya'll have it all wrong." Tenequa The Terrible was the only woman on the shift, but her language was the saltiest. At close to six feet with hair in a bleached blond buzz cut, she somehow managed to be both the most frightening presence to perps and the most comforting to children and nervous witnesses. "It's been so long for Toe Jamb, he plumb forgot how to do it properly. He's so used to putting his foot up someone's ass he forgot what went where. I tell you what, honey, I got a book explains it all. I'll bring it to you next week."

It's my own fault. I knew I shouldn't have laughed when Larry skidded across the floor on a layer of bullets. As soon as I did, he couldn't wait to get on the radio and spread tales. Now every cop in the city, in the county, knows. He could live with all the cartoons and gag gifts that would magically appear on his desk over the next few months, but if that nickname caught on, he might have to transfer to another department.

He was almost glad when he saw his boss beckon from his office door. "Campbell, let's have it. There wasn't enough crime in Central Division so you had to go out in the sticks to find more? I hope your fellow officers in the county are pleased with your work, because it'll be your hard luck if this blows back on me in any way. You may need to go to them to look for another job."

"It shouldn't cause you any trouble, Lieutenant.

Everything was by the book. There won't be any questions."
Well, part that statement was true anyway.

"Except why I have an officer on the injured list. You've screwed up my good record. Only five months till I retire, and you pull something like this? Now what am I going to do with you? I might as well send you home. You aren't fit for duty. If I find out you were diddling when you should have been working, you'll see what hard luck is."

If he was sent home, it would ruin his plans for exposing Marshall. "I don't need to take any time off, sir. I can work in the office the rest of today and tomorrow. It'll give me time to catch up on paperwork. I should be as good as new by Monday."

"Okay, Nelson and Steinberg are working a drug dealer case, and they need to trace a money trail. You can stay here and work the telephone and do some research on the computer. The dealer was alive, tied to the steering wheel with duct tape, when the car was set on fire. A good Samaritan heard him screaming and was injured trying to get him out."

"That's a shame." Adam pushed his glasses up on the bridge of his nose. "Just when you think there aren't any left, one shows up and gets hurt.

Adam liked to work the phone. He'd been told he had a reassuring voice and people tended to open up to him. The computer was something else. He hated to spend all day working on it, but at least this was real police work, not busy work.

He rolled his chair next to Nelson's desk, careful to keep his foot protected, and pulled out his notebook. "What do you need me to do?"

Frank Nelson was a small man, not more than five six, and meticulous about grooming, often brushing imaginary pieces of fluff off his suit. He had an attractive baby face and was often called "The Kid," but only behind his back. He was fond of practical jokes, which weren't always appreciated by other members of the squad.

"We have a good idea who our suspects are, thanks to the description given by our witness." Nelson scooted his chair closer, and Adam jerked his foot out of the way. "They're two brothers we've had dealings with before. About a year or so ago, their mother went missing. Her new boyfriend says she was tired of her sons freeloading and wanted to kick them out. The sons, of course, say it was the other way around. She was trying to kick the boyfriend out."

Nelson lifted a piece of lint from Adam's jacket, examined it as if it were contaminated, and dropped it in the trash, moving his chair ever closer. "Now, the boyfriend was no prize, so it could be either way, but he's still alive, and if they actually thought he did something to their mama, he wouldn't be. We never found any trace of her or her jewelry and the sons are still living in her house."

Remy Steinberg leaned forward to pick up the story. He wasn't much larger than his partner. He claimed five nine, but that probably meant five eight. He was Jewish on his father's side, Cajun on his mother's, and cowboy by choice, so he could play almost any part when interviewing. He preferred to dress in western cut suits, big belt buckles, and cowboy boots, although the boots could have been for the extra height. Adam often wondered if he was trying to hide the fact he'd been born in New Jersey. Steinberg was a perfect example of what happened when the flame was turned up too high on the melting pot that was Houston.

"Skip ahead a year and the boys, Antwoin and DeJean Avalon, are developing a reputation as up-and-coming dealers. When we got the description, the first thing we did, after moving the witness to a safe house, was get a warrant to search the boys' home. We couldn't find a thing. It was completely clean, at least in a legal sense. In actuality, it would've made a pigsty look homey. If their mama isn't already dead, the sight of that house would kill her."

Adam made notes on a legal pad and causally dropped his pen on the floor. When Nelson rolled his chair closer for the third time, Adam looked him in the eyes and didn't flinch. The roller hung on the pen and Nelson tipped forward. He grabbed the edge of the desk a nano-second before falling over.

Adam gave a slow smile.

Steinberg chuckled, but kept talking. "We'll keep following the murder, but we need you to look for someplace else they could be keeping the drugs."

An hour later, deep into research on his computer, the phone rang. He answered it without thinking. "Homicide, Campbell."

"Adam?" He didn't recognize the woman's voice.

"Yes."

"It's Lydia Cox. Did I catch you at a bad time?"

He tried not to groan audibly. "Not at all. What can I do to help you?"

"I hoped we might try again for that pizza. Danny has the kids this weekend so the house will be quiet. We could have a few drinks, get to know each other."

Getting to know Lydia Cox was the last thing he wanted. Two weeks ago he might have been desperate enough to try, but after meeting Jillian he could see the difference. Jillian was a strong, independent woman. She'd made an effort to get to know him and find out if they had interests in common, before they started a relationship.

Lydia was lonely, unhappy, and careening toward alcoholism. She didn't care anything about him. She was only trying to use him to fill an empty weekend.

He hesitated long enough before answering that she tried another direction. "It would be a big help if you could look at my new gun safe and tell me if it's what I need."

"I don't know much about them. You'd do better

listening to whatever Jillian said. She's the expert."

"Jillian? Do you mean J. R.?" She gave a short, unpleasant laugh. "So that's what's going on. Don't get your hopes too high in that direction. I think you may find she's playing for the other team." With that, she slammed the phone down so hard his ear hurt.

He spent the rest of the day at his desk. When he hobbled home, his rear ached almost as much as his foot. At least Rover was glad to see him.

After supper, he spent an hour playing with the camera. He took shots of Rover using the zoom lens and tried to remember the setting for low light. The buttons were tiny, and he wanted to be sure finding the right one was second nature. He could use his cell phone, which was smaller and talking on it would look more natural, but he needed the special settings of the digital camera to be sure there was no mistaking Marshall's face or the gun.

He would only get one chance. If he blew this, Marshall would continue to piss on the department.

Friday morning, Jillian dressed carefully for Billy's memorial service. She had plenty of black clothes, but none of them were exactly church appropriate. Fortunately, the service was going to be held at the park where Billy died.

It was more of a wake than a funeral. She'd arranged for several large coolers filled with ice and beer. Everyone would tell a story about Billy and toast his memory. He didn't have many friends, but the beer was free so plenty of people would show up.

Heather was waiting at the park wearing an over-the-top long black dress and a big hat with a veil. Jillian did a double take when she saw her. "Where in the world did you find that outfit? It looks like something from an old time movie."

"It is. I saw it on a movie poster one time, and I always wear it to funerals."

"Do you go to many funerals?"

"I used to, but not so much anymore. I like celebrity funerals. So many famous people are there. If I can make them stumble or drop something, it shows up on the news later. I used to wait at hospitals and nursing homes for someone to die. I decided if I was there just at that moment, I could see where they went, or hang on and go with them."

"I take it that didn't work." Jillian didn't like to encourage Heather, but she was fascinated. Why hadn't she known these things about her sister?

"No, they're just like me. They don't go anywhere. It's just over." Heather adjusted her hat and veil.

"How do you know they don't go anywhere? Just because you can't see them doesn't mean they didn't go. Maybe if you didn't hold on so tight, you could cross over, too."

"Shut up, Jillie. You shouldn't talk about things you don't know anything about. I've told you before. There isn't anything to cross over to. This is all there is. At least I have you. I'll bet not all of us have someone who can see them and talk to them."

"Aren't I the lucky one?" Jillian turned her back as she began setting up for the wake. Heather seemed talkative. Might as well try one more time to get the true story. "Do you think it's appropriate for you to be here since you had a hand in Billy's death?"

"Are you back on that old horse? Anyway, I knew Billy. I didn't much like him, but I knew him. I know he was a big help to you. Besides, I don't have many social occasions to go to. I don't want to pass one up."

Unbelievable. Heather was incapable of caring about anything but herself.

"This isn't a social occasion, Heather. It's a tragedy. A

nice young man who was working hard to overcome his past was killed for no reason. I'll miss him terribly. If you think my being lonely because he's gone will make me closer to you, then you've made another major miscalculation."

"You aren't that lonely. You've been spending a lot of time with that cop. I hope nothing else happens to him. Then you really would be lonely."

Jillian suddenly swung around, dropping the napkins she'd been setting out. "I swear, if you hurt him, I'll never speak to you again." The cloying scent of Heather's perfume made it difficult to think.

"Don't worry, I haven't hurt him. I've only played with him a little. A few minor inconveniences. Just enough to show you what could happen if you remain this stubborn. You probably shouldn't take up with someone in such a dangerous job. Or if you do, you should tell me all the fun details. As for not speaking to me, you've said that before, and yet here you are, speaking to me."

It was more disappointment than anger. After Heather had tried to help her yesterday, she hoped Heather had changed, grown up a little. Heather would never change. The only thing she would ever care about was getting whatever she wanted, having what she called fun.

Jillian turned her back on Heather. People were beginning to arrive.

Adam stood in front of his closet door, staring. He had seen his ex-wife do the same thing many times. He never understood. Just reach in, grab something, and put it on. How hard was that? Now he got it. He put on his brown suit, but the coat pockets were false and the camera would be too obvious if he put it in his pants pocket. He tried to slip on his good brown shoes, but that wasn't going to happen. Even if he could have forced his foot into them, he would have an obvious limp, and his entire plan depended on being inconspicuous.

He finally decided on charcoal gray pants and a navy blazer. The blazer had a sturdy pocket that held the camera with no bulge. He slid his foot gently into a pair of dark gray tennis shoes. They were tight, but he could wear them without limping and, while not as good as dress shoes, they weren't as noticeable as wearing one sandal.

Adam got to the station early and stopped by the gym before he started work. His sweats were in his locker and it only took him a minute to change. He couldn't use the treadmill, so he rode the bike for half an hour and then worked the machines. It was the first time he had worked out in several days and it allowed him to burn off some of the nervous energy he'd been feeling.

He spent the day at his desk, working the phone and the computer. He did get a few good leads for Nelson and Steinberg, which helped pass the time, but the clock seemed to move like a slug stuck in molasses. At 3:00, Jillian called to say she was on her way.

"That's perfect timing. Marshall just left the desk for his break so he should be back when you get here. Call me before you leave the car so I can get into place. This is your last chance. If you want to change your mind, I understand." He held his breath. He wanted to keep her safe, but without her help, he couldn't work the scam on Marshall.

"Not on your life. That man's greed caused a lot of heartache. We might not be able to send him to jail, but we have to do everything we can. I tried to do the right thing and he used me, so I need to be part of his comeuppance."

He couldn't have stopped Jillian if he tried, but if Marshall figured out what was going on, she would be in danger. Jillian was a civilian. He should never have put her in this position.

Chapter 22

"I'm in the parking lot. Is everything ready?"

"Okay, give me five minutes. Don't forget, stand to the side so you don't block his face." Adam lowered his voice and whispered into the receiver. His nerves were jumping worse than the time he'd faced down a stoned construction worker holding a tire iron.

He stood, stretched, and put on his coat. "I'm going on a coffee run. Does anybody want a Starbucks?"

The only person in the room was Two Times Tommy, and he was too cheap to pay for good coffee. "No, I'm fine, I'm fine. I'll stick with what I've got here, what I've got here," he said, pointing to the cup of warm brown sludge that came from the coffee machine.

Adam took the stairs down from the sixth floor and entered on the far side of the lobby. He watched until Marshall turned to talk to a group of officers starting out the door, then he slipped around the corner and stood behind some potted plants. He had time to pull the camera out of his pocket and adjust the focus before Jillian came in.

The lobby had been empty when he opened the stairway door. It filled suddenly as two elevators discharged their passengers. He'd always disliked the building at 1200 Travis. With its marble and glass façade, it reminded him of a cross between a bank building and a skyscraper, not the headquarters of the fourth largest police force in the country. Now he was thankful all the windows allowed him to watch as Jillian climbed the stairs to the front door.

With so many people in the way, would he be able to

get a clear shot of Marshall?

Two women from the Sex Crimes unit passed him on their way to the ladies' restroom. They glared at him as if he were a pervert, hanging around in front of the bathroom. That alone didn't bother him; all women from Sex Crimes glared at men. It was an unfortunate side effect of their work. If they started asking him questions, it would draw attention to him and ruin his plan.

He wished he could use the camera on his phone, but the digital camera produced clearer photos. He began frantically patting his pockets and turned into the men's room as if he'd forgotten something. When he came out seconds later, the lobby was clear, and Jillian was approaching Marshall.

She marched directly to the desk and sat a small paper sack on it. "Good afternoon. I was in here about a year ago, and you were so helpful, I wondered if I could impose on you again."

"Certainly, ma'am. What can I do for you?"

Adam clamped his jaw and drew air between his teeth. Marshall's voice, his ingratiating manner of speaking, made him cringe. Eddie Haskell in the flesh.

"A few days ago I found a friend of mine crying and playing Russian Roulette. It upset me terribly, but I was able to talk him into giving me the gun. Later, his mother and I took him to a rehab facility. I want to feel confident he never gets the gun back."

Jillian opened the sack and held the gun out by the barrel. "Could you take this and make sure it's destroyed? Then if he asks for it back, I can truthfully say it's gone." She held onto the gun and looked to the side for a moment, as if trying to compose herself.

"I'd be happy to take care of that for you. Your friend's lucky to have someone like you who cares about him." Marshall fumbled around in a lower drawer and came up with a pink form.

Adam almost dropped the camera. *Gotcha, you scum sucking pond slime.* As quickly as it came, his elation slipped away. He realized he'd been hoping there was some mistake. Catching Marshall was like cornering a skunk. Just because you had him trapped didn't mean he couldn't still spray you. And when he did, the stink would last a long time.

Jillian took several minutes filling out the form. She turned from time to time, even lifting the form slightly. Adam got several good shots of her with Marshall in the background.

Marshall took the form, separating it and keeping one copy for himself and giving one copy to Jillian. He placed the gun and his copy of the form in a lower drawer and smiled at Jillian. "You can relax now, ma'am. Everything's taken care of."

She folded her copy of the form and put it snugly in her purse. "Thank you so much for your help. I'll never forget you for this."

"You're welcome, ma'am. The HPD is always glad to help get guns off the streets of Houston."

Jillian walked out of the door just as the two women sex cops came out of the restroom. Their glare was even more intense than the first time they saw him. Adam wanted to follow them across the lobby, using them to hide his movements, but that would be riskier than crossing on his own.

Jillian found the coffee shop exactly where Adam said it would be. She stepped up to the counter and ordered herself a cinnamon latte with skim milk and no whipped cream, but hesitated before ordering Adam's. She remembered his smile when he tasted the coffee at her shop, so she ordered him a hazelnut with regular milk and whipped cream. No way was he a skim milk kind of guy. She was waiting with the two lattes when he arrived five minutes later.

They both grinned when he pulled out a chair and sat. She pushed one cup his way. Words poured out of her mouth. "I didn't think I was nervous. It was all so easy until I hit the street. That's when the shakes started."

"You're wasted in that gun shop. You should've been an actress. Meryl Streep has nothing on you. Not just the acting, either. You knew exactly where to stand and how to hold the gun and then the pink form so I could get a good shot of them."

She lifted her cup, but sat it down again immediately, too excited to drink. "Did you get some good shots?"

"I think so. I was worried at first because so many people were in the lobby. By the time you got there, they'd left."

"That's why I waited and looked around as if I didn't know where to go. Of course, the desk was only ten or twelve feet away, so I couldn't fumble around too long. Being that close to him was tough. I wanted to grab him and start shaking." She nodded toward the camera. "Let's see what you've got?"

She scooted her chair next to his while he turned on the camera and began scrolling through the pictures. Her hand rested on his thigh, and the strength she felt though the soft fabric of his slacks reassured her.

She studied each picture as he showed it to her, pointing to the ones she liked. "That's a good one. You can actually see him taking the gun from me. Did you have any trouble?"

"Two women, Sex Crimes cops, nearly arrested me for loitering in front of the restrooms, but I wagged my willy for them and they were so impressed they asked for an autograph. They're experts on the subject, you know."

Jillian leaned her head back and laughed, feeling the tension leave her body. "Well, it is world class, I'll admit, but it's what you do with it that's impressive, and that is mine alone."

She kissed him quickly. "Why don't I take the camera? I can go by the drug store and have the pictures printed before you get home."

Adam hesitated a moment, then handed it to her. "I was worried about chain of custody, but I guess that doesn't matter. We aren't going to use them in court. I have to get back to the office before I'm missed, but I'll slip out early and meet you at my house in about an hour."

After he left, Jillian sat back and drank her coffee, trying to calm down. The entire day had been stressful, but the unpleasant part was over now. She breathed deeply and the rich coffee aroma of the store did as much for her as the drink itself.

Rush hour traffic was picking up as she left downtown, but the map Adam had drawn was good and she wasn't worried about finding his house. Curious maybe, to see how he lived.

"So, now you've become a spy? An undercover cop?" Heather leaned forward, crossing her arms on the back of Jillian's seat. "Do you have any idea how dangerous that is? Are you so infatuated with him that you're willing to take risks that affect both of us? What kind of guy is he anyway, that he'd ask you to do something like this?"

Heather must be worried if she's willing to sit that close to my gun. "Keep out of this, Heather. It doesn't concern you. It only affects me. And he didn't ask me. I practically had to beg him. It's your fault anyway. If you hadn't interfered, none of this would have happened."

"I couldn't let you destroy something that belonged in our family. It was Daddy's and Granddaddy's. I don't mind you having a boyfriend, as long as it isn't serious and you're willing to include me so we can both have some fun. But if you start trying to cut me out, I'll get angry. When I get angry, bad things happen. Remember, this guy's a cop for God's sake. Be careful what you tell him. Boyfriends come and go, but I'm your sister, and I'm forever." Heather stabbed the air with a perfectly manicured nail.

"You're not forever, Heather. You're just here until you give up and go on to the next level, whatever that is. And I'm not talking to you about my love life, that's confidential. In fact, I'm not talking to you about anything, period. Now scram, I have work to do."

Jillian parked in front of a CVS close to Adam's house. She left the camera in the car and took only the memory card inside. When she had all of the photos displayed on the screen, she picked the best ones and started working. She adjusted the focus so the serial numbers were clear and easy to read on the pictures taken in her shop. The photos taken in the station were not as well lit, so she played with the contrast until it was as sharp as she could get it.

When she got to the photo showing Marshall handing her the form, she kept adjusting until the pink color was unmistakable. After printing all the photos she needed, she grabbed a six-pack of Shiner Bock, paid the clerk, and left. Adam's house was less than two blocks away.

A side gate led to the backyard, and she made herself at home on his deck. She found a comfortable chair and opened a beer. As soon as she was settled, the birds returned to the feeder, and an enormously fat ball of yellow fur came through the cat door to check her out.

Holding his cup of coffee, Adam strolled casually through the lobby. He never looked in Marshall's direction. Tommy had left, but Nelson and Steinberg had returned, so he pulled his chair close to their desks and began explaining what he had found on their case. Forty-five minutes later they were up-to-date, and he limped to the door of Hard

Luck's office.

"I'm going to take off, Lieutenant. If I don't get this shoe off soon, I may be crippled for life."

"That's your hard luck. You shouldn't be diddling during working hours. Take the shoe off and go barefooted. You promised you weren't going to take injured leave." Hard Luck took off his glasses and pinched the bridge of his nose. "Four and one half months and counting. That's how much time I have left before I have to spend my days driving around, playing golf with my wife. Your little escapade out in the country isn't going to ruin my perfect record. I'll need something to remember and be proud of while she tells me I'm using the wrong club."

"It doesn't have to be injured leave. Call it comp time for the case I took after I clocked out last week, and I won't ask for anything else."

"Then get out of here. Try to be one hundred percent by the next time I see you. If the chief comes by, I don't want to have to explain what happened to you."

Adam started for the door, but Hard Luck called him back. "Hey, Campbell, was she worth it?"

"That she was, Sir. She's worth every bit of the shit that's going to rain down on me about this."

"In that case, you're a lucky man. You can ask me, I know. This job is hard on relationships. I'm on my third wife. If you're lucky enough to find a good one, then you put up with all the shit you need to in order to keep it going, even if they talk during your back swing."

Chapter 23

Jillian sat on Adam's deck and lifted her face to the late afternoon breeze. If she stayed relatively still, the birds and squirrels continued to play around the feeder. She sipped slowly on a beer from the six-pack she picked up at the drug store. Despite the racket from squabbling blue jays and fox squirrels, it was the perfect atmosphere for reflecting. She needed to decide what she wanted to do about Adam.

In high school, she'd been too shy and chubby to attract the attention of boys. Once she started playing basketball, the weight had fallen off and the boys had started to notice her, but Heather's presence kept her too introverted to respond. In college, she discovered drugs.

She'd partied every night and slept all day. Guys swarmed around her like flies to watermelon. They were only too willing to show her how to have a good time. After the first semester, she didn't bother to register for classes again.

One morning, she woke up in a strange room and realized she had lost two days. Heather was sitting in a chair watching her.

"Promise you'll come be with me when you die," Heather said. "At the rate you're going, it won't be long, and I don't want to be alone."

She drove straight home and confronted her father, asking him to help her get clean.

She started working at the store with her dad and found it accomplished two things. She loved the work and was good at it, even better than her dad. She also discovered

Heather wouldn't come anywhere near the store. That's when she came up with the plan to build an apartment over the showroom. Unfortunately, once she was out of the house, her father gave up any pretence of staying sober, no matter how hard Jillian tried to help him.

She'd tried dating, but that caused its own set of problems. It seemed she had two choices. She could hang out in a bar and find someone for a one-night stand; have fun, but never let them get to know her. Or she could find a guy she liked and date him for a while. As long as she brought him to her place, Heather couldn't bother them too much. If the guy was a little shallow, and never tried to get too close, it could last for a while. If the guy actually cared about her and tried to know her better, she had to drop him fast.

When she waited too long, Heather would intervene. "It's time to show him what's going on or show him the door," she would say.

If Jillian didn't comply, Heather would do something unpleasant to make herself known.

The only other option was to tell him about Heather first, and when she tried that, it was a disaster. He would run like a grizzly was on his heels.

Lately, she'd stopped dating altogether and tried to find other ways to fill her life. She let Larry, the sheriff's deputy, spread rumors she was gay. It made life simpler.

Now here she was, waiting on Adam's back deck. She knew she was safe for the moment. Heather would be uncomfortable around a policeman. Unfortunately, Adam was a detective and that meant he had an inquisitive mind. He was infatuated now, but sooner or later he was going to notice the things Jillian did to keep Heather at bay and that logical mind was never going to accept the idea of something he couldn't see. It was the first time in a couple of years she'd taken a chance and opened herself up to someone and the very things that drew her to him were the things that would eventually doom the relationship.

That's life, I suppose. I'll take it one day at a time, and if Adam gets too nosy or Heather gets too jealous, I'll run for the hills.

By the time Adam reached home, his foot was throbbing. Seeing Jillian's car parked in front of his house made him forget any discomfort. He hurried around to the backyard and saw Jillian sitting in his favorite Adirondack chair, Rover asleep in her lap.

"What have you done to my attack cat? He's supposed to be protecting the yard."

"He was easily bribed with a piece of cheese cracker."

Adam scratched him under the chin. "You have no loyalty. You'd let a gang of street rowdies party in my living room if they'd give you tuna fish. You're completely useless."

He leaned over and kissed Jillian gently on the lips. "This is nice. Not coming home to an empty house and a resentful cat. Did you have trouble finding the place?"

"No, your map was easy to follow. I stopped by the drug store and printed the pictures. Wait till you see how well they turned out."

She handed him the stack of photos, and he began flipping through them. "This is a good one. You can see Marshall's face as he takes the gun. And here, in the one we took at your shop, the serial number shows up. I wasn't sure if it would."

He held up a photo of a large yellow blob. "What's this? It looks like an alien from a science fiction movie."

"That's what I thought when I saw the picture. After I met Rover, I still wasn't sure."

"Come on, let's go in. I've got to get this shoe off." He

took her hand and they went into the kitchen. "I was fine until I told Hard Luck I had to leave because my foot hurt, then it started throbbing. It must be payback for lying to my boss."

"I know how you feel. I've got to get some of these clothes off myself. Do you know I'm actually wearing a bra? It must have been invented by a man who hates women. It's completely cut off circulation to essential parts of my body."

He wiggled his eyebrows and grinned. This day might turn out all right after all. "Perhaps I can help with that. I can't have a guest in my home be uncomfortable." He pulled her through the house and into his bedroom, where they stood enjoying each other for several minutes. How could she be so soft and firm at the same time? Every inch of his body was on fire, the pain in his foot long forgotten.

He let go of her long enough to take off his jacket, and started toward a large closet on the far side of the room.

"Where do you think you're going?" She grabbed his hand and pulled him close as she tossed her purse to the far side of the bed.

"I need to put my weapons in the gun safe."

"Later." She removed his shoulder holster and dropped it beside the bed. "You promised to make me feel better. And I take promises very seriously." She unbuttoned his shirt and tossed it to the side.

She shoved him back and he fell onto the bed, laughing. When she tried to pull his pants off, they hung on his ankle holster. Within minutes, the pants and holster were in a heap at the foot of the bed, and she was massaging the indention the holster had left in his leg. "Poor baby. You look worse than I do."

"Let me check on that," he said, pulling off her blouse and unfastening her bra.

It was dark when Jillian sensed him moving around in the bed. She opened one eye. He was hiding his watch under the blanket, but the glow of the dial gave him away. "Do you have an appointment?"

"No, no." He lay back down and put his arms around her. Within a few minutes, she felt him squirming again.

"Okay, what is it? What's going on? I know you're not tired of me yet."

Adam hung his head, looking sheepish. "Would you be terribly upset if I checked on eBay? I bid on a carburetor for a '57 Chevy. They're awfully hard to find, and I've been looking for months. I was confident I bid enough I wouldn't have to worry, but now I'm wondering if I should have gone higher."

"I already knew I came behind your job and cat. Now I find out I rank behind a carburetor?"

"Wait." He grabbed his laptop from the kitchen and brought it to the bed. They sat together for five minutes while the clock ticked down and he won his bid.

His shirt was caught on the bedpost, and he tossed it to her. "Put this on, and I'll show you." He stepped into his pants and pulled them up, but left the belt undone.

"Didn't we get into trouble for this type of thing once before?" she asked as they went out the back door. They scurried across a short breezeway to the garage.

He reached in and flipped on the lights. When he hit the button, the garage door went up. "No one's going to bother us. This neighborhood shuts down at dark."

At that moment, a voice called from across the street. "Hey, Adam. Did you get the carburetor?"

"Should be here next week."

A neighbor crossed the lawn. "Oh, sorry, I didn't know you had company."

He was a slight, balding man, wearing what were

obviously his Saturday kick-around clothes: baggy plaid shorts and a golf shirt that had seen better days.

"Hey, Chester, this is my friend, Jillian. Jillian, this is Chester. He's been keeping me company while I try to bring this old gem back to life."

Jillian smiled and pulled on the hem of Adam's shirt. Letting go long enough to shake hands didn't seem like a good idea.

"Did Adam show you this beauty? He's been working on it for months. It was a total wreck when he started."

It still looked like a wreck to Jillian, but she could see he'd been working on the engine.

"He found it in a junkyard. We've spent many a Saturday driving around looking for parts. With the carburetor, he can finish this old girl. He's already got the exhaust system working. Then he'll sell it to an antique car enthusiast. They like to work on the body, but don't always have the expertise to fix the engine."

Jillian wanted to inspect it closer, but she was worried about leaning over. Finally, the neighbor went back across the street and she could look without fear of exposing herself.

The garage was a mini workshop. The walls were lined with tools and equipment. He had installed a hoist in the ceiling. Everything was neat and tidy. Even the floor was spotless.

"I've never seen a workshop this clean." She knew he liked to work with his hands, but she had no idea he was this talented.

"It's not always like this. I haven't been able to do any work lately without the carburetor, so I cleaned up and organized. With the profit I make on this car, I'm going to put in an air conditioner."

"So, you've done this before?"

"This is my most ambitious project. I told you my father was a mechanic. The only time we got along when I was young was working on cars. When he moved to the hill country, he gave me his tools. A couple of years ago, I went to a car show with a friend who's into antique cars. While we were there, one of the cars broke down, and I was able to fix it."

He ran a hand lovingly down the side of the Chevy. "Suddenly, people started calling me to help with their old cars. With each one I repair, I use the money to buy more tools or fix this place up. Did you see the Art Car Parade last year?"

"I saw parts of it on the news. I didn't see the parade." Each new thing she learned about him made her feel closer. Losing him would be hard.

"Did you see the car covered with flowers made out of bottle caps?"

She tried to remember. "Yeah, I think I saw that one. It won something, didn't it?"

"The President's Trophy, I think. Anyway, it broke down the day before the parade and the owner called me in a panic. The last time he had it repaired, the mechanic was careless and broke off some of the design. He had it towed here, and I fixed it. When I returned it, not one bottle cap was broken.

He stopped for a minute, and Jillian could tell he was proud. "It's just a hobby now. I can work as much or as little as I want to. It's nice to come out here and tinker, but it's more than that. My job can be stressful, and this is my ace in the hole. It's my Fuck You job if it gets too much and I want to quit or when I get ready to retire."

Jillian looked at him from across the hood of the car. "I didn't know you wanted to quit your job."

"I don't nine days out of ten, but knowing you have something to fall back on helps get you through that tenth day. I love my job, and I feel like I make a difference, help people. I'm proud of the department, and being a detective is an achievement. Being in homicide is the top of the heap. So I didn't mean that as a complaint. When I see a greedy, self-serving fuck-head like Marshall bring dishonor on the department, I get upset. He makes honest cops look bad and a tough job even tougher."

"He's going to get what he deserves."

Adam shook his head. "No. He's not going to get near what he deserves. It's not just HPD he's put a black mark on, it's every police department in the country. You don't think the wire services would love this story if they found out? Then the damage would impact every community. People don't like to take time to drive to a police station and fill out forms to turn in something they think might be dangerous. But they do it because it's the right thing to do, and the majority of people do the right thing."

Jillian came around the car and put her hand on his shoulder, but he continued getting more worked up. "Now someone in Des Moines or Tallahassee will stop to wonder if it's worth the trouble, if the police will just put it back on the street again. Marshall's going to get off easy, but turning him in would do more damage than I could live with."

They started back inside. Adam put his arm around her waist and the motion pulled the shirt up. Jillian noticed the breeze on her bare bottom, but didn't pull away. "Would you feel better if you took it to your Lieutenant and let him make the decision?"

"No. Ruben and I discussed it. Hard Luck's so clean, he might as well have a strip across his forehead that says Sanitized For Your Protection. If he found out ahead of time, he'd take it to IA. If he finds out later, he'll do whatever it takes to back me up. I'm satisfied I'm doing the right thing. Enough of this. Let's get dressed and I'll buy you dinner."

"If it counts for anything, I think you're doing the right thing, and it was my gun to start with. However, I can't go out to dinner with you. I'm opening the store in the morning and it's going to be a long, hard day without Cara, so I better get home."

Adam turned to face her, holding both her hands and kissing her on the forehead. "It does count for something. It counts for a lot. But I'd like it better if you'd spend the night. I wish you could stay tomorrow. It's First Saturday. They'll have an Artist's Market and street musicians. There's a shuttle to different outdoor events. I'd love to be able to show it to you. What about tomorrow night? You could come over as soon as you closed the store. I'd take you someplace nice to eat, and we could spend the day together Sunday."

A real relationship, not just a few hot nights. What would that be like? Jillian stood on tiptoes and put her arms around his neck. The shirt rode up even higher, but she didn't care. "That sounds like heaven. I'll be here as quick as I can."

The drive home was smooth, with minimal traffic, but Jillian didn't notice. Her lips and thighs still tingled, and she wore a secret half smile. Her breasts were tender as they moved inside the fabric of her dress. Heather sat in the back seat with her arms crossed over her chest and didn't say a word.

When they reached the edge of the parking lot, Heather spoke up, her voice heavy with disdain, "Don't worry about me. I'll get out here. I have plenty to do to keep me busy."

As glad as Jillian was to be rid of Heather, she had to wonder, was Heather being sarcastic or threatening?

Chapter 24

Jillian was right. Saturday was a long, hard day without any help. Cara called at noon to let Jillian know she would be back at work on Monday.

"Are you sure you'll be up to it? You can take a few more days if you need."

"No, what I need is to get back to work as soon as possible. Otherwise, I'll dwell on things, and that's not healthy. Did I thank you for taking care of Megan? That's the only way I got through it, knowing Megan was safe."

By 5:30, business was slowing down and Jillian started closing out the register. The door was locked and the lights turned off by 5:50. She ran up the stairs and changed quickly. Adam had said he wanted to take her somewhere nice, so she put on a sundress and strappy sandals. She threw some shorts and a tank into a paper sack and was pulling into his drive at 7:15. The front door opened and he stepped out before she had the motor turned off.

He came up to the car window and leaned in. "I made reservations at an Italian place, but there's Chinese and Mexican close by if you'd rather."

"Italian sounds good. If you won't make fun of the way I slurp spaghetti."

He put his hand over his heart. "I am a gentleman to the core. I would never make fun of the way a lady eats. Besides, I probably won't notice it over the noise I'll be making."

As he leaned farther into the car to kiss her, he saw the paper sack. "What's this?"

"Fresh clothes, clean underwear, hair gel, and a

toothbrush." She grinned and winked.

Laughter spilled in the window. "Didn't want to make the walk of shame tomorrow in the same clothes you came in, huh? I would have lent you a toothbrush."

Jillian raised her eyebrows. "So you keep an extra toothbrush on hand for overnight guests?"

"I went to the dentist a couple of weeks ago and he gave me one I haven't opened yet."

"Well, I do like a man with good oral hygiene."

He gave an exaggerated grin. "Look Ma, no cavities."

"I might just leave this one and the hair gel here, if that's not too presumptuous."

"Presume away. *Mi casa es su casa.*"

Jillian studied him for a moment. He looked very handsome, but then he always did. Something was different. He kept blinking. "Adam, take out those silly contact lenses and put your glasses back on. I appreciated that you got dressed up for me, but when I'm ready for you to take off your glasses, you'll know it."

Relief flooded his face as he rubbed his eyes.

They took his BMW. It was the first time she had ridden with him, and she found it pleasant to let someone else do the driving for a change. *I could get used to this. I've been taking care of myself since I was twelve years old. Maybe it wouldn't be so bad to let someone else do it occasionally.*

The restaurant was small, but obviously a popular neighborhood eating place. Mouth-watering aromas enveloped Jillian as they opened the door. The lights were dim, and candles glittered in Chianti bottles on every table.

She was trying to decide what to order when Heather spoke up. "The man brought you to a gas station for dinner?"

"It's a nice restaurant," Jillian said.

"I'm glad you like it." Adam smiled at her. "It's one of my favorites. I like the way people have converted these old gas stations and stores into restaurants and bars, preserving the old buildings, but giving them new life. That's what I consider true recycling. There're a couple of ice houses and taverns nearby we can try next time, but I like the atmosphere here."

"I like it, too. It's quaint and different."

"If you want calamari, it's one of their specialties."

"No way," Heather said. "Just get the spaghetti and meat sauce. And sit up straight. Your boobs are hanging out of that cheap dress." Heather was wearing a sequined cocktail dress appropriate for a fancy nightclub.

"I hope this dress is all right." Jillian tugged at the hem.

Adam's eyes lingered and he licked his lips. "You look beautiful," he said, and she knew he meant it.

"I think I'll go for the spinach ravioli in creamy pesto sauce." Jillian sat her menu aside.

Heather groaned. "Yuck. Is that like the stuff Mother used to serve us out of a can? And made with spinach? Come on, you can do better than that."

Adam bent forward. "Do you want to split a Caesar Salad? You can have one of your own if you want, but they're awfully big here."

"I knew he was too cheap to spring for a good meal."

Jillian smiled at Adam. "That sounds perfect. I hate to spoil my dinner by eating too much salad."

Heather turned away and sulked through the rest of the meal, only making occasional derogatory comments about Adam's table manners or bad jokes.

Jillian ignored her and savored the salty salad and creamy ravioli sauce. She let the aroma of garlic bread drown out Heather's perfume.

When the bill came, Heather spoke up again. "I hope you brought your credit card. He's about to pull the old 'I lost my wallet' trick."

Adam reached for his back pocket and his face turned blue. He looked like he was strangling on a piece of bad meat.

"Excuse me a minute," he said. Jillian could see him talking to the cashier and gesturing. After a long conversation, he left the restaurant and headed toward the car.

"What did you do?" Jillian hissed at Heather.

"Relax, it's in the car."

When he returned, his face was flushed and he had a sheen of perspiration on his forehead. He stopped at the cashier's and paid the bill before returning to the table to get Jillian. The drive back to his house was quiet, and he never mentioned the incident with his billfold.

He parked in the drive, next to Jillian's car, and they went in through the front door. She sat her purse on the sofa and began to look around. It was the first chance Jillian had to really check out his place. When she had been there the day before, they hadn't lingered in the living room. It was definitely masculine, but still managed to be stylish and well planned. The original hardwood floors had been brought back to a gleaming finish and the wood tones were carried through in the built-ins.

Rover waddled in, glad to see her, but stopped suddenly when he saw Heather. His back went up and he hissed.

"Oh crap, a stupid cat." Heather swatted at him with her foot, and he hissed again before scurrying back to the kitchen.

"I'm sorry. I don't know what's gotten into that cat. He can't have forgotten you since yesterday." He went into the kitchen and Jillian followed. She watched as he gave Rover his shot, then opened a can of gourmet cat food. Rover was still looking at Heather and hissing.

"That's the dumbest thing I've ever seen. He's giving the cat a shot? I hope it doesn't have anything contagious."

"How long has Rover had diabetes?" Jillian rested against the center island.

"The cat is named Rover? Now I've heard everything. Jillie, please, you can do better than this."

"It's been about four months since he was diagnosed. The vet says if I can keep it regulated, he should have a few more good years."

"You realize the only things he has in the refrigerator are condiments and beer. The freezer isn't much better. Frozen TV dinners. He seems to divide them equally between Mexican and Hungry Man, although there is one Healthy Choice in the back, covered with ice. I think he drinks too much. He has thirteen empty beer bottles in the trash." Heather wandered into another part of the house, investigating drawers and cabinets.

Adam took her hand and started back to the bedroom. Jillian tried to snag her purse, but it was on the far side of the sofa. Once in the room, he tossed his weapon in the gun safe and locked it before Jillian could stop him. She twisted in his arms and began to undress him slowly. Finally she stopped. "You're not wearing your backup piece?"

"We're on a date, Jillian, not a raid. It's locked in the gun safe. I wish I didn't have to wear the other one when I'm out with you, but we're considered on-duty at all times. I have to carry it. I fudged a little when I went to your place the other day. I should have carried it, but I wanted to seem like a civilian."

She began to pace. "Maybe you should get one out. Someone could try to break in and you wouldn't be able to get to it in time."

"No one's going to try to break in, sweetheart."

"That's what everyone says, until someone tries to break in." Her breath was coming in short, rapid gasps and her heart was hammering.

"The house is alarmed, and it's obvious by my car that a police officer lives here. This is a safe neighborhood. I promise you, honey, I won't let anything happen to you."

"What about the cat door? It's big enough for a teenager or a small man to squeeze through." Her palms were sweating, and she tried to wipe them on her dress.

"No, it's not. I checked that out before I put it in."

"Well, at least let me get my purse. I've got a .38 in there."

"Jillian, stop this. You are perfectly safe in my house. You weren't worried last night." He held onto her hand and wouldn't let her go to the living room after her purse, never seeming to realizing that she had surrounded the bed with guns the night before. Finally he wrapped his arms around her, and she began to calm down.

Once they were in bed and he was kissing her, Jillian tried to respond, but knew too well what was about to happen.

Heather strolled in from the bathroom. "At least he seems to be healthy. He doesn't have any medications except an ancient bottle of antibiotic that has two pills left in it. That and sports creams. He must have every brand known to man. I'll bet he smells like a winner. Oh yeah, there's one tube of hemorrhoid cream with the cap left off—half empty and dried out."

She pointed to a picture on the dresser. "Well, isn't that special?" Sarcasm dripped from her voice like venom. "He has pictures of his family on his dresser. I never would have taken him for a Mama's boy." She leaned closer and studied one of the photos. "Is that his brother? Oh my God. That mess of hair must be hereditary. Watch out or you'll end up with a litter of Don King wanabies."

Heather stood next to the bed. "I told you he was a loser. He's not even that good a lover. Sure, his arms and shoulders are big and muscular, but his ass is skinny and hairy. What in the hell is he doing to your tattoo? It looks like he's trying to lick it off. That's disgusting."

He looked up and grinned. "I can't believe how

delicious you taste, inside and out."

Heather rolled her eyes. "Oh, please, how repulsive."

Jillian ignored her and pulled him up for a kiss. "You taste pretty good yourself."

"Uh oh, here's something you're just going to love. In his bottom drawer, underneath his sweaters, is a picture of him in a suit. He's a lot younger. His hair is longer. And he's with a woman wearing a wedding dress. They're both grinning like fools. I'll bet he didn't tell you about that."

Jillian ignored her, and Heather got down on her knees for a better view. She had changed into a reveling negligee. "Come on, Jillie, please, just this one time. Let me in. It looks like fun. I want to see what it's like. I'll step out again as soon as it's over. I promise."

Adam knew Jillian was trembling, but he didn't realize immediately she was crying. "What's the matter, honey? Did I do something wrong?"

Jillian shook her head, but didn't answer.

"Are you frightened? If you really don't feel safe, I can get the guns out. I'll cover the room with guns if that's what you need to feel safe."

"It's too late. We should have done it earlier. She's already here."

He sat up and looked around. "Who's here? There's no one here except us. Even Rover stayed in the kitchen."

"Heather. She's always here, wherever I go."

"Heather, your sister? But she's dead." Alarm bells sounded in the back of his mind, but he refused to listen to them.

Jillian shook her head. "No, she's not."

Adam desperately tried to get his mind to work like a woman's. "I understand you think about her, honey. She was your sister and you loved her. Do you feel bad because things are going well for us and you think she was cheated out of a life when she died so young?"

Jillian wiped her eyes. "Not exactly."

Chapter 25

"What are you doing?" Heather yelled. A faint flush was almost visible on her pale skin. "Haven't you learned anything? You know what happens when you tell people. They'll lock you up again, and this time they'll throw away the key." She paced around the tiny room.

"Tell him he was right. You were thinking of me and how I missed out on things. Hurry, before he gets that look in his eyes like you're crazy."

Adam took a deep breath. "We've already established that I'm a little dense. You're going to have to explain this to me slowly, using small words."

Jillian tried to swallow, but it caught in her throat. She had to force the words out. "My sister Heather was killed when she was thirteen years old, but she didn't die, not exactly."

She closed her eyes. It was out. She'd said it. She ought to feel better, but she didn't.

He looked bewildered. "Jillie, honey, I don't understand what 'not exactly' means."

"Don't ever call me that," Jillian yelled, throwing a pillow across the room. "That's what she calls me."

The wire holding a large mirror over the dresser snapped and the mirror fell with a loud crash. Broken glass exploded over the room. Jillian gasped, and he threw his arm around her shoulders, pulling her face into his chest. Glass peppered his back, but he held her close until the room fell silent. Jillian's face was ashen.

Heather whirled to face Jillian. "I told you not to tell

him. Now look what you've done. You've made me angry. I can't be responsible for what happens when I get angry." Heather stalked out of the room.

"Jillian, don't worry about the glass. I'll clean it up later. This is more important. I'm sorry about the name. I didn't know you were touchy about it. I understand talking to deceased loved ones. I've seen Mamacita roll her eyes at Ruben and look up to the ceiling and say 'Hubert, do you see what your son has done?' If you were close to someone, it must feel as if they're still with you after they've gone."

God, she hated talking about this. She'd rather pull her own teeth. "I wasn't close to Heather when she was alive. She was older than me and to be honest, quite self-centered even then. I think Mama spoiled her with all the praise and attention she heaped on her at those silly pageants."

"I can still hear you," Heather called from the other room.

He shrugged his shoulders. "Maybe that's worse. Add a dose of guilt to the mix."

"Well, you might be right about that part. I did suffer from a lot of guilt about killing her, and I'm sure that made me enable her at first. But that's not what this is about. Heather's spirit never crossed over, or whatever is supposed to happen. She's still here, almost in the flesh, but not exactly. I see her as plain as you. I talk to her, and she talks to me."

Once the words started, they poured out. "Who do you think made that mirror fall?"

"A cheap wire, poorly installed, made that mirror fall. And I still say you talk to her and see her because you think about her. Lots of people do that."

Jillian could see him struggling to use logic to convince himself and her that she wasn't crazy.

"I don't think about her, except when she makes me. In fact, I do everything I can to avoid her. Do you know why I live over a gun store? Because she's deathly afraid of guns and won't come anywhere near them. She won't even come onto the parking lot of the store."

Jillian tried to control her voice. If she got too emotional, there was even less chance he'd believe her. "She doesn't like loud noise or crowds, and that's why I played basketball in high school. I used to ride a Harley, but after Daddy's accident, I switched to a car for safety's sake. At first just carrying a weapon in my purse kept her out of my car, but eventually she got used to it and now she's not afraid to ride with me, but stays in the backseat. If I put my purse in the back, she rides in the front, and that's worse."

"You always keep a weapon on you?" His face was beginning to show signs of worry.

"That's why they call it a carry permit—so you can carry it with you. There's not much point anymore, now that she's used to it."

"Jillian, honey, you've become obsessed with your sister's death. You need to talk to someone about it."

She reached over the side of the bed and picked up her dress, pulling it over her head. Might as well get this over with. He was bound to find out eventually. "The only good that does is that she disappears when they lock me up. She doesn't like it there. I pretend they've cured me and they let me out. It happened once when I was little and again when I was a teenager."

The worry lines on his face deepened. Just what every man likes to find out, that his girlfriend has been locked up in the loony bin.

"Look, I'm going to prove to you I'm not crazy. I know things I couldn't otherwise. But first, I need you to put your clothes on. I can't have this conversation while Heather is making derogatory comments about your skinny, hairy ass."

"You think my ass is hairy?"

Jillian sighed and tried not to roll her eyes. "I don't think so, Heather does. And I know it isn't skinny. It's tight and muscular." After all that was going on, he was worried she wouldn't like his ass? Heather was right about one thing, men were all babies.

Adam pulled on his pants and sat near the end of the bed. "Okay, I'm listening."

"You drink way too much beer. You have thirteen empties in the trash. You told me you watch what you eat, but apparently you just watch it go down because all you have in the freezer is Mexican and Hungry Man TV dinners. Oh, yeah, the one Healthy Choice left over from the previous administration doesn't count if you don't actually eat it."

He had that look in his eyes, but she kept going before he could say anything to stop her. "You must work out a lot because of all the different sports creams you've collected. That ancient bottle of antibiotics is probably expired by now and you're supposed to take them all, not save two for another day. And I'm going to assume your hemorrhoids are better since the tube is all dried out. This one's my favorite. You have a picture in your bottom sweater drawer of a wife you neglected to mention."

Adam's jaw dropped as he stared at her. He made several false starts before he was able to speak. "Is that what this is about? I didn't tell you I was divorced? I should have told you right away. I know that and I'm sorry. It wasn't that I was trying to hide it." He stopped and started again. "I guess I was trying to hide it because it makes me feel like a failure. I hate to load all my old baggage on you."

She reached over and squeezed his hands. "I don't care that you were married before, as long as you're not married now. I do think you should have told me, but I'm not worried about your baggage. Lord knows, I've got steamer trunks of it myself. I kind of kept a few things from you."

They sat, side by side, on the edge of the bed. Jillian could almost imagine what he was thinking. She'd been through it before whenever she tried to tell someone.

"You said you had a lot of guilt about killing her. What if I could prove to you that you didn't kill her?"

Heather came back to the door of the bedroom. "Don't listen to him, Jillie. He's trying to mess with your head."

Jillian didn't answer, so he continued. "You were unconscious, lying on the floor with a big knot on your head when your parents got home. Heather was still alive, but barely. She was able to speak to your mother before she died. She did blame you. She said you got the box out and were playing with the gun when she came into the room. She claimed she pushed you to get the gun out of your hands and it went off."

"That's almost what happened, except she's the one who took the gun out and started playing with it. She didn't usually misbehave, that was my job. Why should she? She got everything she wanted. This time she was angry. I'd been sick and she might have to miss her pageant. I think the points added up till the end of the year, so missing one was a big deal."

A tear crept down Jillian's face. "I hate that my parents spent all those years thinking I got the gun out."

He angled his head closer. "But that's not what happened, don't you see? You were unconscious, so they couldn't ask you. Then later, you didn't talk at all for several months. So they tested everything. The gun needed more pressure to pull the trigger than a six-year-old could manage, especially one who had been running a high fever with vomiting and diarrhea for two days."

"But Heather pulled on it. She was strong enough."

"No, you would have had to hold on, and you couldn't have. Even if you had used two hands, you probably couldn't have done it. And they know you didn't use two hands because you only touched the gun with your right hand. Also, you didn't touch the toggle or have any gunshot residue on you at all, but Heather did. Your fingerprints weren't on the box, either, just Heather's."

Jillian couldn't sit still, but there was glass everywhere. She threw a pillow on the floor, stood on it, reached for her shoes and shook the glass out of them. "So what exactly do they think happened?"

"Heather got the gun out and was looking at it. You came in and wanted to see it. You must have tried to pick it up and she pushed you. You fell off the bed and got a concussion. Heather heard your parents coming and tried to put the gun back in the box hurriedly. When it wouldn't go in, she jammed it and the toggle hung on something. She probably tried to force it and the gun went off. You didn't have anything to do with it. In fact, sick as you were, you should have been in the hospital, not being treated with Pepto-Bismol and chicken soup."

"All these years she's been blaming me, and I didn't have anything to do with it?" Her blood turned to ice.

"Now maybe you can let it go."

She turned back to face him. "Do you know the last thing she said to me? She leaned over me and the awful perfume she always wore filled my nose. She whispered in that mean voice she used when Mama wasn't near, 'This is all your fault. I'll make you pay for this.' And believe me, for the last twenty-six years, she's kept her promise."

Adam reached over to the nightstand and put on his glasses, but didn't answer.

"How do you know these things? Were you checking up on me?"

He took a step onto the pillow and then one closer toward the door where there wasn't any glass. "It was on the first day, when I learned you once had possession of the gun. Not after we started seeing each other. I wouldn't do a thing like that." He reached for her arm, but she pulled away.

"I can't believe Heather did that to me for all those

years." She looked around the room. Her skin felt hot, like it didn't belong to her. "Heather! Heather! Where are you, you lying scum?"

For one second, the house was totally silent, then Rover let out a horrendous screech. Jillian stood rooted to the spot, her eyes wide with fear. "Oh, no. Oh, no. Oh, no," she moaned as she ran for the kitchen, Adam immediately behind her.

The kitchen was just as they left it. Rover's food bowl and water dish were undisturbed and he was nowhere in sight, until they went behind the center island. He lay on the floor with his neck at an unnatural angle, not breathing. Adam grabbed him and started CPR, but his head hung limply.

Adam swallowed deeply several times and cleared his throat while he held the old cat gently.

"Oh, Adam, I'm so sorry. I never suspected she would do a thing like this." Her voice broke.

"Come on, Jillian. He was old and sick. He liked to sleep on the island and he fell off. That's all it is." His voice didn't sound too steady either. His head drooped so low, she couldn't see his face, and his breath was uneven.

"I'm going to head home now, Adam. But I want you to think about the things I've said. And I need you to remember something. Heather's dangerous. The things she's done to you so far—hiding your wallet, breaking your deck post, fixing your car so it wouldn't start—they were just to make you look bad in front of me. Now she's angry, and she might actually try to hurt you. She's hurt other people."

Adam opened the door to the laundry room and took out a towel. He wrapped Rover in the towel and laid him on the dryer before closing the door again. "If she's a spirit, how can she do these things?"

Jillian sighed. He was still trying to convince her with logic. "Mostly she preys on weak people—those who drink too much, do drugs, or aren't terribly bright—and whispers in their ear. Tells them how bad their life is or suggests someone is out to get them. She encouraged my mother, my father, and Billy to kill themselves. I know you think you've solved your murder cases, but her fingerprints are all over them."

He folded his arms and squared his shoulders. "I like to think I have a pretty strong character, Jillian. I'm not going to do anything foolish."

"You slept with me while I was a suspect in a couple of murders. That doesn't sound too strong."

Embarrassment flickered across his face for an instant and then was gone. "That still doesn't explain how you think she killed Rover or broke the mirror."

Her knees trembled so she went back to the living room and sat on the sofa. "She can exert some amount of force. She probably pulled on the mirror and the added weight was enough to make it fall. You can be driving along and something will make you think, 'Look at that beautiful sunset.' And while you're looking, she'll tug on the wheel and a truck will appear out of nowhere. Why were you leaning over the rail on your deck? Did something catch your eye?"

"A woodpecker. I wanted to get a better look at him."

It wasn't enough to make him believe, but at least he was talking about it.

"Animals, especially cats, seem to be more aware of her. Anything that notices her gives her more strength. She hates cats. So, yes, I think she probably had enough strength to do that to Rover."

Adam stepped into the kitchen and returned with two beers. "Okay, tell me how many fingers I'm holding behind my back."

"It doesn't work that way. Heather can't be trusted. She left after her temper tantrum, but even if she were still here, she would lie to make you doubt me. She might have lied about what I've told you already, but I don't think so. She was doing her best to make you look bad."

Jillian took her beer and kept talking. "I said weak people were more likely to notice her, but that's not always true. Very strong people are also likely to be aware of her. I think Mamacita sensed her. She's a woman of deep faith. If you can trust in angels or the Holy Ghost, then you have to be willing to accept other things."

She put her beer bottle on the coffee table untouched. "I'm going now, but I want you to promise me you'll keep an open mind and think about what I've said. And be careful. I'm afraid she'll try to get even by hurting you."

"I don't like the idea of you driving home while you're this upset. Why don't you stay the night? You can sleep in the guest room. Then in the morning you can head home or stay and we'll talk some more."

"We both have a lot of thinking to do, Adam, and we need to be alone to do it. Call me when you're ready to talk, or don't call and that will say everything I need to know."

She kissed him gently and started home. She knew Heather wasn't to be trusted, yet she'd worn blinders, hoping nothing would happen. Her throat constricted and tears pricked the backs of her eyes. Rover's death was her fault as much as Heather's. She didn't deserve to have him call.

Chapter 26

After Jillian left, Adam stayed on the sofa and drank his beer. He didn't want to think about Ruben's warning that there was something wrong with Jillian. Or his own refusal to listen. What did she have to gain by making up such an outrageous story? Was everything she'd said since they'd met a lie?

He'd come so close to having everything he didn't even know he'd wanted. Now it had all been snatched away at once. His head swirled. It was too much to take in at one time.

Too restless to sit still, he took a shovel from the backyard tool shed. He found a spot under the big fig tree where Rover often napped and began to dig. When the hole looked deep enough, he stopped. Then he remembered how large Rover had become and dug a little deeper.

In the house, he ran his hand over the old cat's fur one last time before wrapping him tightly in the towel. Fighting back tears, he cradled the bundle like a newborn child, and carried it to the fig tree. He knelt, and gently placed Rover in the hole, then filled it in, tamping it down firmly.

"Goodbye, old cat." He sighed. "You were a good friend, and I'll miss you. Wherever you are, I hope you're chasing squirrels and lady cats."

He went back inside, washed his hands, and reached for another beer. Jillian's perfume lingered in the air. It was unlike her to wear something so heavy. He appreciated that she had tried to dress up for him, but it reminded him of Mai. Maybe he could buy her something lighter. No, not much need for that now.

She was right about one thing, though. He was drinking too much beer. As he put the beer back in the fridge, he reached for the trashcan. There were three empties inside, not thirteen. So much for her first prediction.

The bedroom was unusable, and he was too tired to begin cleaning. He decided to sleep in the guestroom, although climbing the stairs had sapped the last of his strength. The bed didn't have any sheets, so he laid down on one side of the spread and pulled the other half over his legs. His exhaustion was as much mental as physical, and sleep didn't come easily. A bad end to a day that had held so much promise.

At first light, he stood in the door to his room and surveyed the damage. He reached in as far as he could, snagged his shoes, and shook them out. A piece of glass must have hung on the insole because it cut his foot when he tried to slip them on. "Wonderful," he said to the empty house. "Now I can limp on both feet."

It took several hours to clean the mess, and he knew he'd be finding slivers of glass the hard way for weeks to come. The sheets were in the washer and the spread was set out to go to the cleaners when he carried an overflowing bag of glass shards and broken picture frames to the garbage cans outside. As he took the lid off, he stopped and looked inside.

Two bags already filled the can. He lifted one in each hand and carried them inside. After spreading newspaper on the kitchen floor, he untied the bags and emptied them. The first held six beer bottles and the second held four. Adding the three from the kitchen, he had thirteen empties. He stood and stared at the bottles while his brain ran in circles. She guessed, that's all.

He re-tied the bags and returned them to the trashcan outside before going into his bathroom. Behind the tubes of sports cream was an old bottle of antibiotic with two pills remaining. "Okay," he said out loud. "But I've never had hemorrhoids in my life." The house didn't answer.

There was no need to check his sweater drawer. The picture of his ex-wife was there. Only one place left to look. He opened the freezer door and took out all the frozen dinners. In the back corner, under a sheet of ice, was an old Healthy Choice dinner. Where did that come from? He didn't remember buying it. He chipped it out of the ice and threw it away.

She didn't guess about that.

Without bothering to return the dinners to the freezer, he turned to look at the cat door. Getting down on his knees, he stuck his head through the opening. It fit, but his shoulders hung on the rim. He tried putting one arm and shoulder through and almost got stuck. He stood and studied it again, visualizing Jillian's body. *You're smaller than me, but not nearly that small.*

Next, he went outside and looked at the lock. It was old and worn, but he didn't see any signs it had been picked or forced. A key was hidden in the tool shed, but how much time would she have had to look?

When he'd left her on Friday, she was sitting in Starbucks drinking coffee. He had gone back to the office and worked forty-five minutes. If she had dropped her coffee in the trash and run like hell the minute he left, she still had to go by the drug store and print the photos. She'd obviously spent time on them. He'd been a policeman for many years and knew how to hide a key so it wasn't easily found.

In the tool shed, he moved the fertilizer spreader and looked for his extra key. It was exactly where he'd left it, covered with dirt and a few grains of fertilizer. It either hadn't been moved or she was more devious than he could have imagined. As he stood looking at the key, the contents of the tool shed began to tip in his direction. Every hoe, rake, broom and shovel fell on him, knocking him to the ground. A large pair of clippers stuck in the grass, inches from his face.

Adam's side gate squealed as it swung open and a voice called out, "Hey, neighbor, are you back here? I heard a lot of commotion and wondered what you were doing."

"Hi, Chester. I had an accident with the tool shed."

"Shit! That could have been bad." He shook the tool shed and turned back to Adam. "I think this thing's a little wobbly. Probably roots making the ground uneven. You ought to put some cement blocks under it for safety."

He helped Adam to his feet, and they piled the lawn equipment back in the shed. When Chester saw the mound of dirt under the tree, he stopped. "What've you been digging? You didn't plant something there, did you? I don't think it'll get enough sun."

"No. That's Rover. He didn't make it. I guess he's chased your dog for the last time." Adam raked a hand through his hair and stared at the grave. His chest was heavy and he seemed to have forgotten how to breathe. Some part of him had still hoped that losing Rover was just a bad dream.

"Man, I'm sorry to hear that. I liked that old cat. He didn't take shit from anyone." Chester hitched up his pants. He had undergone lap-band surgery a year before and lost almost a hundred pounds. He bought new clothes periodically, but not lately. The ones he had on looked as if he were waiting to lose more weight or gain some back.

"That's true. I think he owned me instead of the other way around." Adam struggled to keep his voice neutral.

"I'll tell Martha, but she might not be as upset as we are. She thinks her little dog hung the moon. Whenever Muffin would take out after Rover and then Rover would turn and chase her, Martha would get all upset, but I secretly rooted for the cat."

They stood, silently remembering Rover's antics. "I came over to apologize for the other night. I didn't know you had company or I'd have stayed away."

"You didn't interrupt anything. I was showing her the car."

"I hope I didn't embarrass her. She seemed a nice one. Will we be seeing more of her?"

"I don't think so," Adam said, fastening the tool shed door. "She's got a lot of problems that I'm not sure I'm ready to deal with."

"Sorry to hear that. She was a looker."

"Yeah, but you were the one doing all the looking. Say, Chester, that reminds me, I could use your opinion on something." Adam tramped back to the deck.

"What do you think of this cat door? Do you think a small person could get through it?"

Chester studied the opening, scratching his head and rocking from one foot to the other. Finally he got on his knees, putting his head through the door just as Adam had done. He even tried slipping one arm in at a time. "Maybe a little kid, like five or six. Not anyone older than that. Since we don't have any gangs of marauding five-year-olds, I wouldn't worry about it."

He helped Chester back to his feet, and Chester hesitated, scratching his head again. It was a habit Adam noticed often enough to wonder if that's what had happened to all Chester's hair.

"Listen, Adam, I'm going to say something that's way none of my business, but have you noticed how often the women you bring home have serious problems? Either you're fishing in the wrong stream or you're way too picky. If you're waiting for the perfect woman to come along, you're shit out of luck. There's no such thing. There're just women whose problems you can live with and those whose problems you can't. You could spend your whole life waiting, then look back and wonder what happened. If you like her, grab a pair of hip boots and wade in."

Chester had a point. Adam had been warned Mai was crazy when he started up with her, but he had done it anyway. Maybe the problem was with him. However, he didn't think hip boots would work with Jillian. He wasn't even sure chest-high waders would do the trick.

After Chester left, Adam went inside. The TV dinners were still sitting on the counter so he stuck them back in the freezer and started to his room to clean up. On the way, he passed the stairs to the guest bedroom and bath. He had taken several steps when he paused and turned around, heading up the stairs instead.

The guest bathroom was nearly empty. The cabinet held three sets of towels and washcloths, an extra roll of toilet paper, and a bottle of drain cleaner, nothing else. Under the sink, he found the plunger he had lost. He pulled the drawer out and didn't see anything, but angled his head to one side to look in the back corner. There sat an old, dried-out tube of hemorrhoid cream with the cap missing. Shit.

He stood, then bent and looked again as if he wasn't sure what it was. He hadn't put it there; he knew that. Could Jillian have hidden it? He poked it with one finger, but it didn't move. It had been stuck to the drawer for some time. His parents used this bathroom when they visited. Adam tried to remember if his father had complained about hemorrhoids on his last trip. Maybe, he wasn't sure.

He reached for the phone. His Sunday call was generally a couple of hours later, but his parents would assume he had plans for the evening.

"Hi, Mom, hi, Dad. How are y'all doing?" They talked for several minutes about his parents' golf game and how the fish were biting.

"Hey, Dad, how're your hemorrhoids? They still giving

you trouble?"

His mother jumped in immediately. "He'll never admit it, but they're giving him hell. If he'd lay off the spicy food and eat a few vegetables, a little fruit, he'd be better off."

"It's not spicy food, it's your mother's cooking. Anyway, I'm doing much better. What did you do all day today?"

Adam told him about the mirror falling and the mess he had to clean up.

"Were you having some kind of a wild party? No way that wire broke unless someone was swinging on it. I weighed the mirror myself and went to the hardware store for wire that was specifically made to handle that much weight. I even hung it on two bolts so it would be secure. If that wire broke, you need to call the company that made it and complain because it was defective."

His father paused. "Now, do you want to tell me what really happened?"

Chapter 27

Adam decided to approach the problem the same way he did at work—he would make a list. That always made him feel in control of the situation, and since the day he first met Jillian, control was something he felt slipping through his fingers. He sat at the kitchen table with a pen and paper. Opening the fridge for a beer, he grabbed a diet soda instead. But not because of anything Jillian had said.

The beer: Jillian could have looked in the outside cans for the empties while waiting for him, but the count would have been different on Friday afternoon than it was on Saturday night.

The frozen dinners: She didn't have a chance to look in the freezer either night, so how did she know about the Healthy Choice?

The antibiotic: She used the bathroom before she left on Friday and could have seen it then.

The hemorrhoid cream: There was no way she could have known about it unless she was in the house before he came home on Friday.

The picture of his ex-wife: Could she have looked in the drawer while his back was turned? But how did she know which drawer? Even then, she would have had to dig around under the sweaters to find it. Nope, didn't happen.

Getting in: She could have stuck her head through the cat door and looked around, but that was all. The key was well hidden and didn't appear to have been moved. If she had picked the lock, he couldn't see any signs of it. Besides, the alarm was on. So maybe she was some kind of whiz at breaking and entering and knew how to cut the wires. She would still have had to reattach them without any evidence left behind. Impossible.

He was starting to get a headache, and something was nagging at the back of his mind. It was the picture. Why did he keep going back to the picture? Because he had moved it, that's why.

When he was straightening up the house on Saturday morning, he moved the picture from his top sock drawer to his bottom sweater drawer. He wasn't trying to hide it, but it felt as if he were moving further away from that time in his life by putting it there.

If she had broken in on Friday and found it, she would have said it was in the top drawer. She said it was in the bottom drawer, where it had only been for a few hours. And she had not had any opportunity to look in that drawer on Saturday.

He was willing to admit his own ego led him to approach Snake-Eye without a vest or backup, but there was something else. A little voice had put the idea in his head. It kept telling him not to be a wuss. If Jillian could handle Snake-Eye, so could he.

Now his headache was worse.

Jillian fixed a bowl of soup, but that was all she could manage. It had been a long time since she let anyone get close to her. She and Billy had been friends, but she always kept a wall around her personal life.

She enjoyed the time she spent with Adam. It felt easy, and, except for one little thing, she'd been able to be herself. Without his help, Billy's death would have devastated her. She wanted to see more of him. However, she couldn't go on the way she had in the past. She didn't want to keep things from someone she cared about, and she didn't want to be with someone she didn't care about.

When the phone rang, she hesitated. As long as he hadn't actually called it off, there was hope.

"I was worried about you," he started right in, as if afraid she might hang up when she knew it was him. "I wanted to make sure you got home okay."

He hadn't called her honey, or sweetie, and that wasn't good, but he had called, and that was something. "I didn't have any problems. Traffic was light, and I was home in no time. What about you, did you get that mess cleaned up?"

"It took half the day. I had to sleep in the guestroom."

"What about Rover? That just breaks my heart."

"He's buried under his favorite tree. He'd been sick for a while. I knew he didn't have long. There's a question I need to ask you."

"Just one?" She laughed.

"You said. . ." He paused, and Jillian knew it was hard for him to give it enough weight to talk about. "You said Heather's fingerprints were all over my two cases. What did you mean?"

"She didn't want me to get rid of the gun. She said it belonged to our father and grandfather and I should keep it. She argued with me all the way downtown. When we got to the station, I expected her to disappear. I never guessed she would actually go into a police station, but she did, so I should have known how serious she was."

Jillian could hear him breathing on the other end of the line, so she knew he was listening. "When I gave it to Sergeant Marshall, she leaned over and started telling him it was a valuable piece of history and shouldn't be destroyed. She said it probably belonged in a museum. He didn't blink an eye. I thought he didn't hear her, some people don't. He just pulled out the form. I signed it, and left. It never occurred to me that he didn't destroy it. I don't know if she had anything to do with the rest of the stuff he stole. It might be once he had stolen something it was easy to take more."

"I suspect he'd taken kickbacks before, but I'm not sure he'd outright stolen anything. This was just one step farther down the road. What about the other two?"

Jillian sighed. She hated this. Hated talking about it, hated admitting what her life had become, especially to someone she cared about. Hated the way people looked at her if she did tell. As long as she kept it to herself, she could pretend it wasn't real. "I have to go by what she told me, and any story she told would be tailored to make her look good. I think she felt a connection to that gun and kept track of it. When your guy . . . Was his name Manny?"

"Yeah, Manny Dewitt."

"When Manny went to sell the drugs to that young girl, Heather told him she was trying to cheat him. I suspect she actually was trying to cheat him and Heather wanted to warn him. I don't know if he was high, or if the girl made a threatening move. Maybe he thought she was going to rob him. I don't know why he shot her, but Heather put him on edge, made him nervous." She held the phone tight against her ear. Adam's voice brought up more emotions that she could deal with.

"What about when Manny got shot? What did she have to do with that?"

"She told his friend Manny was dangerous and would try to shoot him. That he had to protect himself. Whether she did it for fun, to cause trouble, or because she had a responsibility to warn him, I don't know."

They spoke for another few minutes before Adam said goodnight and they both hung up. Jillian wasn't sure what he was thinking, but he talked to her about it without suggesting she was crazy, and that was the best she could hope for.

Chapter 28

Monday morning was better than Jillian had any right to expect. Adam had called the night before so she was optimistic. She managed a nice run and Heather hadn't appeared, and Cara had called to say she'd be in by late afternoon.

"Are you sure you're up to coming in? Don't rush because you think I need help."

"No. What I need is to work." Cara sounded determined. "I need the money, the experience, the distraction, and at some point, I'm going to need a good reference."

"You've got the reference if you never show your face in here again. Are you planning on quitting? I'd understand if you did."

"I think it's like riding a horse. If I don't get back there, I might not be able to do it. I'll stay until after Trevor's trial. I want to be sure I testify. Then I'm going to get a divorce, change my name, and have his parental rights revoked. After that I'm going to move to another state where he won't ever find us. I can't live my life looking over my shoulder, and I'm not going to take a risk with Megan. But all that is likely to take a year."

"You can count on me. I can't wait to testify."

When Cara finally appeared around two o'clock, Jillian wasn't sure it was a good idea. She pushed Megan's stroller with one arm, but kept the other one tight against her body in a sling. Her face was swollen and discolored.

Cara must have seen the look on Jillian's face. "I'm a good advertisement for the store. If this doesn't convince people they need protection, I don't know what will."

Megan was smiling and gurgling, as if Thursday had never happened.

Adam groaned when the alarm went off. He sat on the side of the bed and raked his hand across his chin, unable to work up enough energy to face the day. He still didn't believe Jillian. She was either one of those loopy people who thought they talked to spirits, or she was downright certifiable. Although, he would have felt better if he could work out how she did it. The fact that her story about Manny and Eddie jived was pure coincidence. She figured out what had most likely happened.

The swelling in his big toe had gone down, and he could wear regular shoes, but the cut on his other foot hurt like hell with each step. He'd gotten a small sliver of glass in one finger and it was going to remind him every time he used the computer.

He was crossing the street to his office when the hairs on the back of his neck stood up. He tried to glance behind him. Was Mai following him again? This was getting ridiculous. Suddenly a young, black kid grabbed his arm and yanked him back, causing him to fall on his rear in the middle of Main Street. A city bus blew past, inches from his face.

"You better come back down to earth, motherfucker, or you're gonna end up a greasy spot on the street. I wouldn't mind, but it would tie up traffic for hours."

When he stood, the kid saw his gun and badge and got flustered. "Sorry about that, officer."

Adam patted him on the back. "Thanks, son, I appreciate the help."

The rest of the day wasn't any better. Hard Luck still had him working the computer for Nelson and Steinberg. Each time he hit an L, his finger protested. At lunch, he went to James Coney Island and spilled chili on his tie.

By late afternoon, he was ready to report to Nelson and Steinberg. They stood over his desk while he showed them what he found. "Your two brothers have been very careful. They don't have any property in their own names, and their mother didn't own anything but the house. However, they have an elderly aunt who owns a home in Sharpstown."

"We didn't find anyone with the same name." Steinberg shook his head.

"She's a half sister. She never shared a name with their mother, and she was married so it's even harder to trace. She doesn't have any kids. Her husband was killed in the war. I don't know which one, probably the Spanish-American. Anyway, we all know what devoted family members our boys are, so I found it odd they're paying for auntie to stay in a nursing home. They haven't *visited* her, but they put her in there and pay the bills on time."

Nelson blinked in astonishment. "They're actually paying cash to keep her in a nursing home?"

"Well, it's not much of a home. It's been written up for multiple violations. I wouldn't want anyone I cared about in there. She covers most of it with her Social Security, but they chip in the rest. If she was declared indigent and put on Medicaid, the government would take her house and sell it. And that's where things get interesting."

Adam pulled the next screen up on his computer. "I can't find any record of the house being rented, and the boys haven't received any payments that I can find, yet all the utilities are turned on and in use. The boys are paying the gas and electric bills regularly."

Nelson was grinning. "Good work, Adam. This should be enough to get a warrant on the house."

At end of shift, his rear hurt as much as his finger and toe, and his day wasn't over. He lingered in the office until he was sure everyone was gone and the night shift had started.

He drove over to the property department on Washington and parked as close as possible to the ugly blue building. Doris was right where he'd left her the week before.

"What's with you?" she called as he came down the hall. "Your ass is dragging and you're limping on both feet."

"I've been working a desk all day and I'm numb."

"Well, I could take care of that for you. I could rub it till it felt better."

"Seeing you makes it feel better."

"Pooh, what fun is that? I'm more of a hands-on type of woman. I know you didn't come down here for my pretty face. Did those records help?"

"They sure did, thanks. Now I need one more thing. Was an old .45 turned in anytime since Friday afternoon?"

"No weapon of any kind has crossed these doors in well over a week."

"Are you sure? It might have been when you were off duty."

"Honey, there's a lot of things I don't know, but I know what comes in and goes out of this room, on duty or off."

"Okay, if it comes in later tonight or tomorrow, would you give me a call?" He pulled out a card with his cell phone number. If the gun didn't show up soon, he'd have to go after Marshall. He considered telling Hard Luck, but dismissed the idea. Even with Jillian and Ruben's help, he was in this alone.

She held the card up to the light and ran her thumb over the embossed lettering. "I suppose this number is for official use only?"

"The way I feel right now, you'd probably kill me."

"Yeah, but what a way to go."

After leaving the property room, Adam began to think about Mai. She'd been on his mind a lot lately. He smelled her perfume everywhere. Their problems may have started with Mai's attitude, but what if he'd said something when her actions first began to bother him instead of waiting until he couldn't stand it anymore and blowing up? Did he share some of the blame? He couldn't do anything to change that now, but it was never too late to smooth things over. The box of candy he'd bought Doris gave him an idea.

He and Mai had dated for quite a while but somehow hadn't overlapped Christmas or her birthday. In all that time, he had never bought her a real present. Sure, he'd paid for meals, concert tickets, and clubbing, but she was a woman who put a lot of store in gifts and he hadn't given her any.

He pulled in quickly to Macy's and went straight to the jewelry department. He found a diamond tennis bracelet that wasn't too expensive—the band was narrow and the diamonds were tiny—but it had plenty of sparkle and that's what mattered.

Mai's apartment was only a few blocks away. When he rang the bell, she answered immediately. "What are you doing here, Adam? I'm getting ready to go out." He could see that. She had on her favorite clubbing outfit and reeked of that perfume with the name he hated. What did she call it, Heroin? No, Opium.

"What's happened to you, Adam? You look terrible. You've let yourself go all to pieces."

He looked down. His suit and shirt were fresh from the cleaners that morning and his shoes were polished.

"Where are the contacts you bought? And you've quit going to that stylist I found you."

Adam adjusted his glasses and raked a hand through his hair, but didn't say anything.

"At least you're still wearing the Polo glasses I picked out."

Only until these silly frames break and I can buy some new ones.

"You have to leave. Someone's about to pick me up."

"This'll just take a minute, Mai. I wanted to talk to you."

"It's too late for that. After the way you treated me, I'd never take you back. I don't care how much you beg."

He wouldn't have taken her back on a dare, but he didn't tell her that. "I know that. I wouldn't ask you to. But something's been bothering me. We broke up just before your birthday."

"It was the worst birthday I ever had." Her lower lip trembled. "I sat home and cried. I didn't have anybody to take me out."

Adam doubted she spent any time crying and he knew for a fact she hadn't stayed home. She was seen using the concert tickets he had bought for that night.

"I feel bad about that. I had already bought you a present and everything. Every time I see it sitting in my drawer, I feel worse. I hope you'll let me give it to you now."

Mai's tears suddenly dried up. "You want to give me a gift? Shouldn't you give it to your new girlfriend?" she said with a pout.

She could pretend the package was a gift. He knew it was a bribe and nothing more.

"No. It's your gift. I'd never give it to someone else." The rumor mill must be working if she already knew about Jillian. He pulled the box from his coat pocket and handed it to her. When she took the cover off, her eyes lit up, just as he knew they would.

"Well, I suppose if you've had it all this time..." She held out her arm as he put the bracelet on. "That was nice of you, Adam. We'll consider this a peace offering, but now you have to go. I don't want my date to see you." She stood on tiptoes and gave him a quick kiss, pushing her tongue into his mouth as if to remind him what he was missing.

He nodded, acting too choked up to speak, and started down the stairs. *If that's all it takes to make my life run smoother, I wish I'd come up with it a year ago. Besides, I did owe her a gift.*

Insincere words and cheap trinkets weren't going to carry much weight with Jillian. He might actually have to be honest.

When he got home, he called Ruben and brought him up to date. He told him about everything, except the time he'd spent with Jillian and what she'd said. That wasn't part of the case. After Ruben's earlier warning, he didn't want to give his partner a chance to say I told you so.

"Sounds like you have everything covered. I'd have chipped in on the bracelet to get that witch off our backs. You better wait another twenty-four hours on the gun so there's no way he can say it hadn't made it to property yet." Ruben's voice was growing stronger every day.

"How did Jillian do?" he asked. "I'll bet she acted like a pro. I may have had my doubts about her early on, but she's turning out to be a keeper."

"She did a great job, real professional. Unfortunately, on a personal level, things aren't going as well."

"That's you in a nutshell. All gung ho when it's inappropriate and cold feet when things start to work out."

Ruben was never going to let up until he learned the whole story.

"It's not that. I'd love it if we could work things out. But there's a little problem. I think she might be actually, literally, crazy. She thinks her dead sister follows her around talking to her and causing trouble."

Ruben was silent for so long Adam began to worry. Finally Ruben spoke softly. "Tell me exactly what she said."

He started at the beginning and told Ruben everything. He described her pronouncements about his house and his efforts to find out how she had known those things. He told about the mirror falling and about Rover's death. Ruben asked a few questions, but let Adam tell the story in his own way.

"How does her version of Manny and Eddie's actions line up with what they had to say?"

"Well, I only have Eddie's word on what Manny said, but they line up almost exactly, even to the point of a woman's voice speaking to them. I haven't talked to Marshall, so I don't know what he'll say."

"She was worried Heather might try to hurt you. Has anything happened since she left?"

"I got a piece of glass in my foot that almost reached the bone, I cut my finger so I can barely use the computer, I was nearly impaled by a set of clippers when the contents of the tool shed fell on me, and a bus missed running over me by a millimeter. In the car on the way home, the sun reflected off a building and I wanted to turn my head, but I remembered what Jillian said and kept my eyes straight ahead. It's a good thing I did. A car changed lanes and cut right in front of me."

Laying everything out like that made Adam see how strong the coincidences were. Maybe Jillian wasn't as crazy as he thought. Forget it. If he believed her, he was the crazy one.

Ruben let the silence drag on before he started to speak. "You're not going to care for what I have to say, partner, but here goes. When I first met Jillian, I liked her, but for some reason, she worried me. Later, when Mamacita said she had a dark shadow, I knew exactly what she meant because I sensed it, too. When you grow up in a house with Mamacita, you learn to have faith in things you can't necessarily see. I'm not saying to accept everything Jillian says, not just yet, but keep an open mind. There are things in this life we're not meant to understand. And be careful. Keep your eyes on the road at all times."

"You're not actually saying you believe her?"

"No, I'm just saying don't write her off. Not yet anyway."

Chapter 29

The next two days were like trudging through molasses. Time moved so slowly, Adam thought the clock was broken. Evenings weren't any better. Without Rover to keep him company and limiting himself to only one beer a day, he was at loose ends. He wanted to call Jillian, but didn't know what they could talk about. After a few days, he phoned and asked about the store and Cara, but the conversation was strained.

The carburetor finally arrived, so he was able to work on the car in the evenings. He thought that would be his salvation until it slipped off the jack and nearly crushed him. He tried to convince himself it happened because he wasn't concentrating, but he decided to work on it another time.

When the phone rang shortly after midnight on what was technically Wednesday morning, Adam didn't know what to think. It was Yvonne Flores, the pregnant teenage girlfriend of his pawn shop murder suspect.

"You said I could call you any time if I had a problem," she said.

"Sure, Yvonne, did Hector come back?"

"Not yet, but my water broke. I might be further along than I thought."

"Okay, you better get to the hospital. I'll be there in the morning to see if Hector shows up."

"That's the problem. I don't have a car."

"Call a taxi. I'll reimburse you."

"No taxi's going to take me in this condition. And they want their money up front. What am I going to do?" She was wailing, and the fear in her voice was palpable.

He groaned. This was a part of life he wasn't prepared for. "Stay there, I'll come get you. It'll take me about half an hour. Will you be all right for that long?"

"I don't know. I never had a baby before. You better hurry."

Adam took his city issued car. He wasn't about to risk having a baby come in the backseat of his own car, and if things got dicey, he wanted to be able to use the siren.

When he reached Yvonne's apartment, she was waiting at the curb with her mother and little sister. She looked enormous. Damn right she was further along than she had told him. He put her suitcase in the trunk while they all piled into his car, then he peeled away. He watched Yvonne's face in the rear-view mirror. It was chalk white.

"How far apart are the contractions?" he asked when he saw her grimace in pain.

"About two minutes." She started sobbing. "I was going to be the first in my family to graduate from high school. I wanted to go to college and be a teacher. Now what am I going to do?"

Adam didn't know how to answer her so he turned the conversation back to more immediate concerns. "Is your doctor expecting you?"

"I don't have a doctor. My mother used to be a midwife, and she's been taking care of me. But I want the baby to be born in a hospital, so he'll be legal."

She moaned again, and Adam looked at his watch. One minute.

Her mother began yelling at him in Spanish. He had no idea what she said, but her gestures indicated he should hurry. He made an executive decision. Ben Taub Hospital was too far away. They'd have to take her at Methodist, with insurance or without, if she was this far along.

He pulled in front of the emergency room on two wheels and leaned on the horn. An orderly came out with a chair and Yvonne and her mother rushed off. Just as he was about to relax, he realized the little sister was still with him.

"Don't you want to go with your mother?"

"She told me to stay with you," the little girl said. "I'm hungry. Can I have something to eat?"

Damn, he didn't like being left with a strange child, but the two women had disappeared and he had no idea where they'd gone.

They wandered up and down deserted corridors together, looking for the cafeteria. Signs pointed one direction, but when they went that way, another sign would point back the way they came. In desperation, he decided to follow his nose and eventually found it.

The little girl, he never learned her name, wasn't kidding. She was hungry. She ate a full meal, and then asked for ice cream. He didn't want her to feel bad, so he joined her.

They killed an hour, and then went looking for the maternity ward. By the time they found it, Yvonne had delivered a baby boy. Neither she nor her mother seemed worried that the little girl had been missing for so long.

"Have you told Hector?" he asked.

At the mention of Hector's name, the mother started a long monologue, which ended with her spitting on the floor.

"I don't know where he is, but he's supposed to be in Mexico. Mama called his brother, so he'll know soon."

If Hector was hiding in town, he could be arriving any moment. If he was in Mexico, as Adam had been told, it would be a day or more. Adam was betting on an hour.

He knew he should call for backup, but he kept thinking of all the red tape that would mean. If he could just show up for work in a few hours with the case solved, it would go a long way toward smoothing out any problems he might encounter with Hard Luck if he got into trouble over Marshall.

He looked in the lounge for a comfortable chair and sat for a while with a cup of coffee. If Hector showed up, so be it. If he didn't, Adam would call for help and go home to take a bath and change clothes before starting work. He knew what Hector looked like from his mug shots, but Hector had never seen him. The brother had, though, and that could be a problem.

Twenty minutes later, he saw Hector's brother poking his head around the corner. Adam held the newspaper up so his face couldn't be seen. He had thrown on jeans, a golf shirt, and a pair of slip-on Vans, when Yvonne called. He hadn't taken the time to shave and combing his hair didn't really make that much difference anyway. He knew he didn't look like a cop. When Hector's brother saw Mrs. Flores leave the room, he signaled and Hector hurried down the corridor toward Yvonne's room.

Adam waited. It was much too dangerous to try to apprehend him in that small room with Yvonne, her sister, and the baby. He deliberated about calling for help. A security guard could be there in seconds, but Adam wouldn't know him and was hesitant to depend on someone he had never worked with. He didn't even want to use the backup piece strapped to his ankle. He had mentioned to Jillian the ease with which bullets went through walls, and in a hospital setting like this, it was much too dangerous. He would have to wait until he got Hector into a secure place or let him go and try again later. While he might be hesitant to use a gun around so many civilians, Hector wouldn't be.

When Hector stepped out of the room, Adam slipped in behind him. They walked toward the stairs, Hector unaware Adam was following him. His plan was to hold back until they were in the concrete stairwell to make his move and just hope Hector's brother wasn't waiting. As they passed the elevator, the doors opened on an empty car, and Adam took the opportunity to shove him inside. Hector stumbled, but regained his balance and stomped on Adam's foot.

Son of a bitch! How did he know? Just when that toe was almost well.

Hector threw himself backwards and smashed Adam into the elevator door. Air flew out of his lungs with a loud whoosh. Adam hung onto the handrail with one arm and wrapped the other around Hector's neck. He used his leg to keep Hector from pulling away while he tried to allow small, painful sips of air back into his lungs. As Hector worked to pull Adam's leg away, his shoe slipped off and Hector saw his toe. It was still slightly swollen and had turned a rainbow of colors.

Adam was larger than Hector, but older by almost fifteen years, while Hector was obviously in his prime and adept at street fighting. Hector grabbed the toe and started twisting. Adam let out a yelp and dropped his leg. Hector immediately drove his elbow into Adam's mid section.

Adam didn't have time to hop or limp, so he swung his sore foot at the back of Hector's knees and Hector fell to the floor, already reaching for the gun hidden under his shirt. Adam kicked again, and Hector's gun skidded across the elevator floor. A fresh jolt of pain shot up Adam's leg, but this time he didn't have enough air to manage a sound. Hector tried to reach for the gun, but Adam threw himself on his back and clamped a hand on his wrist. By the time the elevator reached the ground floor, Hector was in handcuffs and Adam was carrying one shoe, his toe bleeding again.

"You hurt me, man," Hector complained.

"Stand up and stop whining or I'll leave you alone with Yvonne's mother for five minutes. Then you'll have something to bitch about."

He called a squad car to take Hector in while he went home to change.

Hard Luck was pleased with the arrest, but unhappy that Adam was back in sandals. "When are you going to quit trying to be a cowboy and learn to call for back up? It would have been your hard luck if his brother jumped in."

"He was supposed to be in Mexico. I didn't expect to see him for a couple of days."

Half of that was true at least.

By Wednesday, Cara had settled back in at work. Her arm was obviously tender, and she favored it, but no she longer wore the sling.

"Do you feel up to watching the store for an hour while I run an errand?" Jillian asked. "If you don't, just say so, it can wait."

"Go. Run your errand. Megan and I are fine. If I have a minor problem, I'll fake it. If I have a major problem, I'll call you." She made a shooing motion with her hands.

Jillian's Little Sister, Kendra, had called the night before, asking Jillian to come to an awards ceremony at school. Any senior who won a scholarship was being recognized. Kendra's father had left when she was three, and her mother popped in and out of her life with each new boyfriend. She was staying with an aunt who made it clear Kendra's presence was an imposition. There was no doubt her family tree was irreparably broken, and Jillian was determined to give her as much support and encouragement as possible.

"I'll be there if I can, honey. I just don't know what condition Cara's going to be in or if I can leave her alone. If there's any possible way, I'll be on the front row, applauding," Jillian told her. After a ten-minute drive to the school, Jillian saw the crowded parking lot, and knew she wouldn't be able to sit on the front row. She would have to make up for it by cheering louder than anyone else.

The school was a two-story, dingy white brick that had seen better days. Overcrowding had necessitated the placement of temporary buildings, which had been located beside the old school for fifteen years. Even the parking lot needed repaving.

The halls stank of old gym clothes and teenage hormones as Jillian hurried to the auditorium. She found a seat near the front and stood to cheer as Kendra's name was read. She even made it a point to clap and cheer for any student who didn't seem to have family present.

When the ceremony was over, Kendra came out to meet her, beaming. "I knew you'd make it. Did you see my certificate?" She handed Jillian an embossed sheet of paper.

"School's over for the day. Do you think we could go to Dairy Queen for a Blizzard to celebrate? Lots of kids will be there."

Jillian's stomach suddenly growled, reminding her she hadn't eaten lunch. She pulled out her cell phone. "Let me check on things at the store."

Cara sounded insulted that Jillian would doubt her ability to cope. "There's not even anyone here now. I just sold an H&K, a holster, and three boxes of ammunition, then sent the guy over to the firing range to try it out. He'll probably come back to buy another couple of boxes of ammo when he finishes. Am I good, or what? I think I can handle things a while longer."

Jillian and Kendra spent an hour at Dairy Queen. While Kendra and the other winners compared their certificates, Jillian wolfed down a hamburger, then took her time with an ice cream cone, letting the creamy goodness melt in her mouth.

The noise was overwhelming. It was amazing what a piece of paper with some fancy writing could mean to a kid who'd never had much encouragement. Jillian couldn't have been more proud if Kendra had been her real sister.

She wished she could tell Adam about it, but she doubted she would see him again. He'd be respectful enough to call and check on her, and he might even come over to break up in person instead of over the phone, but that would likely be the last time she'd hear from him. If only she could rewind back to the day she'd told him about Heather. She could have tried harder to get him to set some guns out, or told him she wasn't feeling well and had to go home. Anything but the truth.

No, that would only have postponed things, and she had already decided—no more short-term, surface relationships. But what was the alternative? No relationships at all? Besides, she really liked Adam. She'd come closer to showing her inner self to him than to anyone else, and he had accepted her as she was. He'd even liked the things about her most people drew away from.

Coming so close to finding someone that she actually cared for and then losing him made the loneliness more acute. Well, Adam hadn't officially broken up with her yet, so maybe there was hope.

No more moping. "Come on, Kendra," she said. "It's time for me to go back to work."

Doris never called, so Adam phoned her on Wednesday night. She still didn't have the gun, but offered to let him come over and help her wait for it. "I'm sure we could find something to do to help make the time pass," she said. "A good-looking guy like you shouldn't have to wait alone."

He hung up and dialed Ruben.

"It looks like we're a go for tomorrow night. You're coming with me, aren't you?"

"I wouldn't miss it for the world. I want to see Marshall's face when he realizes you're on to him. You'll have to pick me up. Mamacita hid my car keys until the doc gives the okay."

"Tell her we're going to join some friends for a beer.

Maybe Marshall will offer us one so you won't be lying to her. I know what a piss poor job you do of that."

Ruben didn't like to admit that as a detective in the prestigious Homicide unit, he couldn't lie to his mother with a straight face.

If Tuesday and Wednesday seemed to last forever, Thursday was absolutely unending. Adam couldn't concentrate on the computer, pulling up the same information several times. Hard Luck called him in his office to talk about an old case, and he couldn't remember the particulars.

If he didn't get his head together, he was going to screw up, not only with Marshall, but his whole career.

After lunch, he carried his notebook to Nelson's desk. "What did you find when you searched the aunt's place?" Adam asked.

"We hit the mother-lode." Nelson was practically jumping with excitement, a sight that made him look even more childlike. "Guns, drugs, cash, even records. And guess what was in the bedroom? Mama's jewelry. In the backyard, the flowerbed had been dug up and looked like a grave, maybe more than one. We're waiting for the crime scene unit to let us know what's in there. They'll take all day, but we already have arrest warrants in the works. We'll be leaving in about ten minutes. Want to join us?"

Some Lieutenants would have broken up the two sets of partners, placing one of the larger men with a smaller partner. Hard Luck knew putting Ruben and Nelson together would make them both look ludicrous. That would cause them not be taken seriously. Besides, Nelson and Steinberg were well-known for their ability to appear unthreatening and dupe suspects into opening up, both in interrogation and at the front door. Many dangerous criminals had foolishly opened the door to Nelson's smiling baby face.

The warrant arrived on time, and Adam grabbed at an excuse to get out of the office. Steinberg laughed when

Adam hobbled into the van. "You'd better come in the front with us, Toe Jamb. If they get out the back window and start to run, I don't think we should count on you to give chase."

"We'll put Tommy and Tenequa in the back," Nelson said. "That way Tenequa can scare them into giving up and Tommy can bore them to death when he reads them their Miranda rights."

As the van pulled in front of the suspects' house, with his vest on and his gun drawn, Adam suddenly got nervous. He'd been in on too many arrests to count and if he had been frightened, he didn't realize it until after the excitement was over. This time he kept remembering all the near disasters that had happened to him in the last two weeks.

Was he uptight because he kept screwing up, or did he keep screwing up because he was uptight? Either way, it wasn't a good time to get a case of the nerves. He refused to accept any other reason.

Everything that happened to him, every near disaster, could be explained by the fact that he was distracted. He needed to concentrate on the job at hand. It wasn't only his life he was endangering, but those around him as well. By the time they parked, he was in full cop mode.

The street was almost deserted. School kids were in class, and drug dealers were resting. It was too late for the morning rush and too early for the afternoon one. The police van with a cable company logo didn't arouse any suspicions. As the van turned the corner, a sudden afternoon thunderstorm blew in and anyone left on the street hurried inside. A perfectly timed clap of thunder covered the sound of the van door opening. The unit was able to deploy to their assigned positions without anyone noticing.

Nelson waited until everyone was in place and completely out of sight. Music from a video game spilled from the front room, confirming the brothers were home. He nodded at Steinberg and Adam, hidden on either side of the door. A stray leak sent ice cold drops of rain down the back of Adam's neck as he pressed himself against the old frame house.

Nelson rang the bell. As someone approached the other side of the door, he held up a brown paper bag and looked at the peephole, a king-sized smile on his baby face. "I wanted to return your belongings, Mr. Avalon."

A voice called toward the back of the house. "You hear that, Antwoin? I told you those motherfuckers wouldn't find a thing."

DeJean opened the door and reached for the bag. Nelson took a step back. DeJean leaned forward, stretching his arm out. "'Bout time," he said, just as he spotted Adam reaching for him. DeJean twisted, and threw the bag in Adam's face.

Adam swatted the bag aside. He pushed off on his sore foot, ignoring a sharp pain that told him he shouldn't have done that. DeJean swung a meaty fist at his face. The fist connected, but Adam grabbed his wrist and threw him to the floor.

DeJean was face down on the rotting porch with Adam's knee on his back and his hands cuffed behind him when Adam leaned close to his ear. "Just lay here quietly like a good fellow and that little love tap you gave me can be forgotten. Try to warn your brother, and your ass will never see daylight again." Adam increased the pressure on his knee, and DeJean couldn't have made a sound if his life depended on it, which it did. Before DeJean finished nodding, Steinberg had pulled Antwoin off the sofa and Nelson was cuffing him.

The raid with Nelson and Steinberg went perfectly. It was proof the only thing wrong with him was lack of concentration. Adam's jaw was sore, but that was a small price to pay for taking two dangerous criminals into custody.

The streets of Houston were safer because of the work he'd done, not just on the raid, but on the computer as well. The evidence he found was strong and would hold up in court.

The feeling of pride lasted on the ride home. It helped him face the chore that was coming. He changed quickly into casual clothes, but left the vest on, concealed by a light rain jacket. He put his weapon at the small of his back, covered by his shirt. His backup stayed on his ankle.

When he picked up Ruben at 7:30, he could feel the nerves start again. It was becoming more difficult to put Jillian's claims out of his mind.

Sure the shed was wobbly and he'd been distracted crossing the street, but that mirror should never have fallen. And having the large set of clippers stick in the ground two inches from his nose was beyond bizarre. Poor old Rover. He was sick, true, but he'd been responding to the insulin and seemed to be doing well. Adam refused to think about what had led him to face Hector alone.

"Are you ready, *compadre*? Let's get this thing in gear." Ruben was so big that with the addition of his vest, he looked like a mountain. Adam was sure he heard the springs protest when he eased himself onto the seat. He could picture the car, tilting to one side.

"I'm ready." Even he knew he didn't sound that way.

Ruben gave him a sidelong glance. "If you don't think this is a good idea, speak up now."

"It may not be a good idea, but it's the only one we've come up with, so let's get it over with. I don't like to think of that crooked sleaze-bag being in the department with honest officers any longer than necessary."

"We could always go for the direct approach—a Louisville Slugger to the kneecaps. That way he'd have to take disability and our problem would be solved."

Adam contemplated it for a minute. "I'm tempted, I have to admit. Angry as I am, I'm afraid once I started swinging I wouldn't be able to stop, and then where would we be? Down in the gutter with Marshall."

"Okay, but we'll keep it in the back of our minds. Sort of a Plan B if he doesn't take the hint."

"Deal."

The ride to Marshall's was spent in silence. Adam grew more nervous with every passing mile. He'd heard his father complain of getting the yips in golf and knew that was exactly what was wrong with him. Once you started worrying about it, you made it happen. The only thing to do, his father claimed, was make some type of change. It didn't matter what, just change something.

Three blocks from Marshall's house, he stopped the car and reached for his phone. He glanced over at Ruben, embarrassed, but kept dialing. When Jillian answered, he started talking immediately, not allowing time for him to change his mind or her to hang up.

"I need you to do me a favor. We're about to approach Marshall, and I have a problem."

"What is it?"

He tried to place her voice. It wasn't welcoming, but it wasn't angry. Cautious, he decided. "I can't concentrate. I keep looking for something to break and fall on me. I'm not saying I believe any of this, but I need to know Heather is busy somewhere else. Can you keep her occupied for an hour?"

"That would mean I had to talk to her, something I've been avoiding the last few days." She sighed. "Fine, I'll do it. Give me fifteen minutes."

He hung up, put his phone away, and glanced at his watch, but avoided looking at Ruben. Neither one said a word for the fifteen minutes. Finally, Adam squared his shoulders and started the engine.

Jillian slammed the palm of her hand against the steering wheel. Adam didn't understand how draining it was for her to talk with Heather. She covered herself with bug spray and headed for the park. On the way, she stopped at Dairy Queen and bought a banana split.

"All right, Heather, I'm here. Shall we get this over with?" The cicadas stopped singing when she spoke, but started again immediately.

"Is that a banana split? God, that looks good. I haven't seen one of those in years. I used to love them. Mama always bought me one on the way home from pageants as a treat if I did a good job. I don't suppose you'd let me have a bite?"

"You really think I'm a fool, don't you? Get this straight. I'm not letting you in. I'll never let you in. You can't have my body for an hour or an instant." She took a big bite of the banana split, licking hot fudge from her lips.

"You're such a bitch, Jillie. And you used to be a sweet little girl."

"If I am a bitch, I learned it from you. Now, can we get down to business?" The ice cream was starting to soften and a string of chocolate hung off the spoon.

Heather crossed her arms impatiently. "I don't know what business we have. You're mean and selfish and won't do anything to help me."

"Your story's so sad I could just cry, except for the part where you lied to me for all those years. Give it up. Admit it won't work and move on. Go join Mom and Dad. They're probably waiting for you."

Heather sat on the table next to Jillian, smoothing out her skirt. She was wearing a low-cut, bejeweled sundress and ankle-strap heels. Jillian didn't know what the outfit would have cost if it had actually been purchase in a store, but she was willing to bet it was more than she cleared in a month. Heather was almost-living proof that expensive and cheap weren't contradictory.

"Well then, you are a fool if that's what you think. I'll never give up. You robbed me of a life. I never got to have anything—no prom, no sweetheart, no adventures. I never even learned to drive, or had a grown-up kiss. I want to experience those things. If you won't give them to me, then I'll have to share yours."

"No, you won't. My life is mine. I'm not sharing. I didn't rob you of anything. You did it to yourself."

"Of course you did." Heather got up and started shaking her finger at Jillian. "You were told not to get out of bed. If you had stayed where you belonged, it wouldn't have happened."

"You were told never to touch the gun. If you had behaved, it wouldn't have happened." Jillian sat the half-eaten banana split on the table beside her.

"I'm sorry your life got cut short, Heather, really I am, but the part you did have was good. Mother took you all over the state to those pageants and spent time teaching you to sing and dance. She hardly looked at me once she realized I couldn't carry a tune and was chubby."

"You could have done it if you wanted to. I would have helped you. It would have been fun. But you were too stubborn to do something you knew meant so much to me and to Mama."

Heather sat again, but left more space between them. "You'll have to get used to it, Jillie. You're the one who can see me. You're the one who can hear me. You're the one who's going to have to live with me. I'm not going anywhere. I'm staying right here to live your life with you, and there's nothing you can do about it. If you want to try not speaking to me, go ahead. You know how well that's worked for your friends in the past. No, I'll be here forever. When you die, my face will be the last thing you see. Then I'll start keeping your kids company."

Jillian was so angry she didn't trust herself to speak.

"In fact, we should spend even more time together. I think you should move out of that apartment and come home. We could be roommates. We could watch TV and do things together. As a matter of fact, I think you should sell that business. Then we could be together all the time. You could buy a little dress shop, and I would help you run it. I'd be great at picking out inventory."

Jillian could imagine the trashy clothes Heather would pick out. They'd be bankrupt in six months.

"While we're talking about the changes you need to make, I don't like that boyfriend of yours. He's a smart-ass. Get rid of him. I like it better when you go for the big stupid kind that don't ask questions. Your other choice is to give up and let me in. I'll take good care of your body, I promise. I've already started checking on doctors who remove tattoos."

That was the final straw. Jillian didn't know if she would have called Adam a boyfriend, and she wasn't sure he was even a friend now. She was certain that whatever happened, it wasn't going to be Heather's decision. She picked up the remains of the banana split and threw it at Heather. It sailed through her face and landed on the grass behind her. "You want it so much, here, take it." She took her purse and swung it through Heather, first one direction and then the other. She kept swinging until her arm was tired.

Heather looked shocked and tried to move out of the way. She clearly didn't like the sensation. Jillian knew Heather went to The Galleria at night after it closed to look in the windows and study the fashions. Heather claimed she didn't like to go in the daytime because people passed right through her. Jillian always assumed she didn't like to be ignored, but maybe she could actually feel it, and the sensation was unpleasant.

This was something new. But was it anything she could use? She had to find a way to get rid of Heather. It was her only hope.

Chapter 30

Ruben stood to the side while Adam knocked on Marshall's door. He held the folder with the records and photos, but wasn't visible through the peephole. Marshall would feel less threatened if he thought only one person was at his door.

The porch light came on and Marshall opened the door to the width of the chain. "Well, if it isn't the famous Toe Jamb Campbell. Are you lost?"

"I've got a problem. I need some help with Calvin." He used Marshall's first name so it would seem more like a personal visit and put Marshall at ease. If Marshall refused to let them in, it would make everything more difficult.

"Could I come in and talk with you about it? I hate to disturb you. I hope it won't get you in trouble with the wife."

"It's only me," he said, closing the door slightly as he took the chain off. "Been that way for almost two years now."

From the looks of things, Marshall hadn't vacuumed or washed a dish in all that time.

"Sorry to hear that. I didn't know." Adam stepped in and Ruben followed close on his heels.

Marshall was suddenly more guarded. "What is this? Why is *Poncho Grande* here? He's supposed to be on sick leave." The alcohol on Marshall's breath was strong enough to strip varnish. Marshall must have been drunk to use that nickname in front of Ruben or Adam. Most men wouldn't use it if either of the detectives were in the building, maybe the city. Adam decided to ignore the insult in the interest of the case. Ruben must have felt the same way because he didn't say anything, although Adam could feel waves of anger radiating off his body.

"I told you, Ruben and I have a problem we need to talk to you about. Let's go sit down where I can show you something." He didn't wait for Marshall, but pushed through to the kitchen table. Without stopping to look around, Adam knew the place was a dump. The dirty dishes only told half the story. The empty bottles told the other half.

"Our problem has to do with a Luger P 08 that was turned in for demolition eighteen months ago, but was used in two homicides over the past few months."

Marshall was no amateur, and he was prepared for just such a question. "Hey, I only take them in. What happens down the road is out of my hands."

Adam nodded as if he understood and was after the next person on the list. "I know that, Marshall. You have no control over someone in property who might develop sticky fingers."

Ruben hadn't said a word, but he hadn't let go of the folder either.

"But here's my problem. You switched from pink forms to yellow ones two years ago, but you're still using the pink ones for special items. And none of those special items that got a pink form have showed up in property."

With that, Ruben laid the folder on the table and began to take out pages, one at a time. "This is the number of guns turned in for destruction the first six months you worked the front desk." Ruben reached for another piece of paper. "This is the number of guns turned in over the last six months. Here we have other types of weapons the first six months and the last. The same with drugs." He flipped over two more pages.

"Here we have purses, wallets, cash, anything of value. Do I need to show you how few of those have made their way to property lately?" Adam waited. He kept his face natural, but he couldn't control his heart rate. This was it. There was no turning back now.

"I told you—I pass them on. I can't be responsible for what happens to them after that." Marshall's forehead broke out in sweat and he kept glancing toward a bottle of bourbon.

Ruben took out several pictures and spread them in front of Marshall. "Can you explain why the items you use the pink forms on are the only ones that disappear?"

Suddenly Marshall pushed back from the table. "What's going on? You aren't on duty. And you. . ." He pointed at Adam. "You work homicide. If you're trying for some kind of shakedown, you're shit out of luck."

Adam leaned in and spoke softly. "This isn't a shakedown. It's your one chance at salvation."

Marshall froze. "What do you have in mind?"

"You're going to retire immediately. You've developed health problems. You get to keep your pension, your dignity, your reputation. And best of all, your freedom. All you have to do is tell us exactly what happened and then hand in your resignation."

They had reached the tricky part. Marshall could decide to fight the charges and it would get ugly, or he could decide to fight them and it would get dangerous.

Instead, he started to cry. "I don't know what happened. It was that dammed Luger. I saw it and I couldn't bear to have it destroyed. I kept thinking 'This is a piece of history. It belongs in a museum.' So I saved it."

"Then why didn't you give it to a museum?"

"Well, it wasn't really that old or unique, so I kept it. It was so easy I kept a few others. Then my wife left me and I was short of cash, so I sold them. It was only a few at first, so no one noticed. Then that same voice said, 'Go ahead. You deserve it. You've spent your life helping other people. Now it's time to help yourself.'"

Adam sat back. "What voice? You didn't say anything about a voice."

"That's what's so strange. It was a woman's voice. Why would I think in a woman's voice? Almost a little girl."

Adam would have sworn someone hit him in the gut. He couldn't breathe or move for several beats, but dealing with the problem at hand was all that mattered for now.

"Here's the deal we're offering you. We're taking everything with us tonight. Let's load it all in the trunk of my car—every gun, every ounce of drugs, everything of value. Tomorrow morning you retire. No two-weeks notice. You clean out your locker and go home. You aren't well. If you do that, and don't make a fuss, we never say a word."

Marshall looked almost relieved to have it over with. He nodded and rose from the table. "It's all in the garage," he said.

Adam backed his car into the driveway, close to the garage door. It took several trips to load everything into the trunk. Adam was hot, but Ruben was sweating and had turned white. "Sit for a few minutes, partner, I'll finish here. If anything happens to you, Mamacita will have my nuts in a grinder."

Finally, Marshall crammed the last box into the back seat. "That's everything," he said.

"Maybe," Adam said. "Let's check, just to be sure."

He and Ruben searched the entire house, looking in closets and under beds. Hidden beneath Marshall's pillow was a Smith and Wesson revolver, which they took. In Marshall's bathroom, they found several containers of pills and white powder, even a few baggies of crystal meth.

Adam shook his head. Now, there's a lethal combination—excessive firepower and a drug that makes you paranoid. They could have just waited. At the rate he was going, Marshall was due to have a complete meltdown at any time.

"Don't take those," Marshall begged. "I need them."

"I guess you won't have any trouble looking sick tomorrow." Ruben pulled the door closed behind him.

"That went better than we had any right to expect." Ruben's color was returning.

"It could have gotten ugly." Adam slumped in the car as the tension left his body.

"It still could. He's in there right now, trying to come up with a plan to make it all go away. If he shows up tomorrow morning and blames it on you, we're in deep shit. We need to find a place with no ties to either of us to stash this stuff until we can get rid of it permanently."

"Jillian has a storage shed behind the shooting range. I could put it in there temporarily."

"So y'all are speaking again?" Ruben tried to turn to face Adam, but there wasn't room in the car.

"I don't know about that, but she has a vested interest in seeing Marshall go down."

"Are we going to talk about the phone call, or pretend it didn't happen?"

Adam gripped the wheel and stared straight ahead. "We're going to pretend it didn't happen."

"Okay, but we'll need to pretend Marshall didn't hear a little girl's voice, too."

"I can do that."

"Have you made plans for disposing of this stuff permanently?"

"Not yet. I've had a few other things on my mind. Anyway, we can't do that until we're sure he's gone away for good. We still need the proof if he decides to fight it. The pictures of him taking the gun from Jillian are enough for me, but they won't convince IA."

Adam dropped Ruben at Mamacita's. As soon as the door closed, Adam pulled out his cell phone. He'd waited to call until Ruben was out of car. Again, he started talking as soon as she answered, not giving her time to hang up.

"It's over. We didn't have any trouble. He sold a lot, but he still had plenty. Guns, ammo, drugs, you name it, he had it. What about you? Did you have any trouble? I should never have asked you to do that for me."

Her voice was cool and clipped. "It's not something I can talk about over the phone. Where are you?"

"Turning onto I-45, headed north. Any chance I could store this stuff in your shed for a few days until we decide what to do with it? I don't trust Marshall not to come to my house looking for it. You gave a fake name and address on the form, so he doesn't know who you are."

"Yeah, for a few days, but only temporarily. Most of that stuff's illegal, and I don't want it on my property. I gave my real name the first time, although I can't imagine he'd keep an incriminating piece of paper like that. But who knows what Heather might do if she's angry enough."

By the time Adam reached the store, Jillian had the door to the shed open and a space cleared in the back, behind some boxes. He'd removed his vest before he got to Jillian's, but the night was humid and the shed was an oven, holding all the heat of the day. His shirt was sticking to him by the time he moved everything for the second time. A spot between his shoulders protested. Dust filled his nose and he fought back a sneeze.

He slammed the trunk and leaned against the car, wiping his face on his sleeve. "Tell me what happened after I called." Half his brain insisted he didn't want to know. The other half was determined to make sure Jillian was okay.

She looked around quickly but didn't answer. She motioned upstairs with her head and led the way. Once inside, she opened two beers and offered him one.

"I thought you wanted me to slow down on the drinking," he said.

"This might not be the time to quit drinking entirely." She gave a slight smile.

"Heather was in rare form tonight. She laid down several ultimatums. Get rid of you. Sell the store. Move home with her and open a dress shop that we both could run." Jillian laughed, but it wasn't the usual pleasant sound.

"Can you imagine me running a dress shop? And with Heather. That would be a laugh. You should see her taste in clothes. It runs from high school prom to Hollywood tacky. Otherwise, she threatened harm to you, Cara, and any future children I might have. If I don't like it, I can always give up and let her have my body. She promises to take good care of it as soon as she has the tattoos removed."

He loved those tattoos. No one was removing them. "What do you mean, move home with her. Where does she live?"

"In our old house. It's still there. I haven't sold it or anything, although I did turn off the utilities. It's just sitting there, unoccupied except for Heather and an occasional drug dealer that stops by."

"I guess I never thought of . . ."—he struggled for the word—"spirits needing a place to live."

Jillian shrugged her shoulders. "Everybody's got to be someplace, I suppose. That's how she knew the young girl that got shot. She and her friends used the house to do drugs until I called the police and had them run off."

"So she did know her. You said she was protecting Manny."

"I was feeling charitable that day. After all, she saved your life and Cara's when she sent Snake-Eye to check on things."

"I had things under control." He ducked his head and took a long, slow swallow of beer, savoring the cool liquid on the back of his throat.

"Sure you did. Snake-Eye told me all about it when

he explained how the little voice urged him to see if I was okay."

Adam thought Snake-Eye showed up for just the reason he gave. Because he'd been shorted on ammo.

"Maybe I can come over on Sunday and we'll move the stuff to your old house. Then you can blame it on drug dealers if someone finds it."

"We'll have to make sure Heather is occupied someplace else. It could get dangerous for you if she found out."

He kissed Jillian gently and started for home, still amazed that he was able to discuss Heather as if he believed in her.

Chapter 31

Marshall did exactly as he was told. He came in on Friday morning and put in for immediate retirement due to health issues. Looking at him, it was easy to believe he was sick, but Adam knew, as did anyone familiar with narcotics, that he was suffering from a bitching case of withdrawal.

It was late afternoon when Adam got a call from the security company that his alarm had gone off. He tried to hurry home, but rush hour traffic was in full swing and rain had slowed things to a crawl. His heart stopped when he saw the trunk of his car pried open in his driveway.

Two uniforms were waiting for him. The senior officer, a balding man with a paunch that reminded Adam what happened when you drank too many beers for too many years, stepped forward.

"No one was here when we arrived. We can stay and help you nail up the door if you need us to. Make a list of anything missing, and we'll stay on top of the pawn shops."

"I can take care of the door, thanks. I know you have other calls. I'll make that list and drop it by the station." Adam needed them to leave, fast. He didn't want his fellow officers to see him as a victim, and he certainly didn't want them to find any trace of Calvin Marshall.

His first stop was the garage. It looked like an angry whirlwind had vented its anger on the contents. Tools were everywhere. Anything breakable was destroyed. The old Chevy he'd been working on was dented and scratched, but relief flooded him when he realized the motor hadn't been touched. Only a car buff would realize the motor was the part he cared about.

He held his breath as he trudged to the backyard. The tool shed was upended and the contents scattered. Rover's grave had been partially dug up, but the rancid odor must have warned the intruder that it wasn't hidden treasure. For one moment he was glad Rover was already gone and hadn't been put in danger.

The back door had been kicked in, and it surprised him how violated he felt. Inside, everything was in shambles. He could find nothing missing, but everything he owned had been swept onto the floor.

The open trunk on his car left no doubt it was Marshall, and the old crook would have known exactly how much time he had before the police arrived.

Bile rose in Adam's throat and he took several deep breaths before changing into old clothes and tackling the mess that was his home. It seemed like déjà vu. Only this time the culprit was someone he could actually get his hands on. Thank God Ruben had the foresight to insist he not leave the weapons in his trunk last night.

After fifteen minutes of cleaning, Adam threw the broom across the floor and it crashed into a table leg. *To hell with this.* He latched the broken trunk of his car with Bungee cord and headed for Marshall's. Full dark was still an hour away and he couldn't afford to be seen, so he parked two houses down. He reached the back door and was about to kick it in when he decided to try the knob. Unlocked.

He opened it quietly and stepped inside. He didn't hear anything, but he slipped softly through the house. When he reached the back, he found Marshall lying on the bathroom floor.

Adam watched with disgust to see if he was breathing. It turned his stomach to think the pathetic specimen lying in his own vomit had been a police officer only a few hours before. Marshall's feet were facing the door, so Adam prodded them with his shoe. Nothing happened the first time, but when he tried again, Marshall lifted his head and opened one eye.

"Fuck," he said when he saw Adam. "Go ahead. Do your worst. I don't even care."

"If you don't care, where's the fun in that?"

Adam reached in Marshall's pocket and took out his billfold. It must have contained close to a thousand dollars. Adam took out $200 and put the rest back. "I'm going to need a new back door," he said.

Marshall rolled over and groaned.

After watching for another minute, Adam marched back to the kitchen. Even the thought of helping Marshall repelled him. The drug-addicted thief deserved whatever happened to him.

He pulled out the same chair he had used the night before, and sat. He gazed around the kitchen and sighed. It looked worse than his, and no one had vandalized it.

Finally he stood and searched the kitchen for an address book. He found one in the cabinet over the telephone and thumbed through it until he found an entry that simply said *Maggie*.

A female voice answered.

"This is a friend of Calvin Marshall's. I'm looking for his daughter." He couldn't believe he was helping the man who had trashed his home and spit on the badge that meant so much to him.

"We're not exactly on speaking terms at the moment. I can't help you," she eventually said.

"I don't care if you speak to him or not, but he's lying on his bathroom floor in big trouble and he needs someone to make decisions for him. If you don't want to do it, I can call 911 and let them handle it, although that's going to put him in a bigger mess than he's already in."

There was silence on the other end of the line, but Adam didn't break it. Twelve years on the force had taught him to wait out the most hardened criminal. Marshall's daughter didn't have a chance.

"If you're his friend, can't you take care of it?"

"I misspoke. We were never friends, even less so now. Last night I took all his drugs and destroyed them. He obviously spent the day looking for new ones. He needs to go to rehab, and he needs to do it tonight. If you'll come get him, I'll find a place that will take him."

"I'll be there in twenty minutes," she said and hung up before Adam could answer.

As he dialed the phone again, he realized how often he'd asked Jillian for help in such a short time. He couldn't remember anyone beside Ruben that he'd ever felt comfortable depending on. Jillian gave him the name of the rehab center she had used, and even called it for him. When she called back, Marshall had a slot and was expected anytime.

Maggie was about Jillian's age, but looked a hundred years older. Her face was drawn and pinched and her shoulders slumped. She was about seven months pregnant. The glow he had always heard about was definitely missing.

"I'll get him settled," she said. "But I'm not up to dealing with this long term. I've already told him I don't want him around the baby, and that was when I thought it was just alcohol."

Adam helped her get Marshall to his feet and out to her car. He then ran back in to grab a barf bowl and a towel. He locked the door behind him.

"This is the name of the place, and the address. They're expecting him. Someone will help get him out of the car for you. Whatever you decide to do, it's between the two of you. I'm not involved."

"I don't even know your name."

"Good, then you can't ask me for help."

Adam slept in the guest room again. Saturday morning, he started cleaning. Staying busy kept his mind from dwelling on Jillian and the empty place he felt inside. At noon, he borrowed his neighbor's pick-up and went to Home Depot for a new back door. It took most of the afternoon to install, even with Chester holding it in place. For some reason, he took the cat door out of the old one and saved it before putting the broken door in the trash.

When he finished, he looked up at the motion detector security light. He had angled it high so Rover wouldn't set it off. He flipped the breaker switch and pulled a chair under the light. As soon as he touched it with the screwdriver, a jolt of electricity threw him back, out of the chair and onto the deck.

"What the fuck?" His arm was tingling and his vision was blurry. He got up slowly, leaning on a chair, but the legs of the chair buckled and he fell again.

"This is the type of thing that happens to people who don't do as they're told."

Shit, no. He couldn't have heard that. He shook his head. His ears were ringing, sure, but why would he think it in a young, almost breathlessly girlish voice?

His eyes were starting to clear, except in one spot directly beside the table he was reaching for. He moved his hand quickly and reached toward another chair. The spot moved next to that chair. He stayed where he was and blinked several times. His heart raced like a junkie on meth, but his mind cleared as he studied the blurry area.

"Have you learned your lesson yet? Next time might not be a warning. I'm sure Jillie isn't worth all this."

He looked again. Standing in front of him was a young woman wearing a ruffled, flowery dress and reeking of some cloying perfume. She had long blond hair, a stunning figure, and would have been beautiful except for the hard, cold look that distorted her face.

He lowered his hand to the ground as if to steady himself, but picked up the screwdriver instead. He hurled it like a spear through her chest. A howl that put Rover's dying call to shame filled the air. The figure clasped her hands to her chest and looked at the spot where the screwdriver passed through. Her face contorted in rage.

"That was a big mistake." Her eyes were now icy daggers and her voice was deep and ominous. "Now it's personal. You'll be hearing from me, even after Jillie kicks your ass to the curb."

"I don't take orders from sniveling cowards who hide behind lies and threats," he said as the table next to him flew up in the air and crashed to the ground.

He shook his head and looked again. The apparition was gone, but the aroma of perfume remained.

He reached carefully for the second chair, stood, and threw up over the deck railing.

He hadn't returned his neighbor's pick-up, so he drove it. Although he had no idea if that would fool whatever he'd just seen. He got to Jillian's an hour before the store closed. Cara was working in the front when he went in. Her arm was out of the sling, and the bruises had faded to a sickly yellow. The swelling had gone down, but her face was still misshapen.

"Adam," she said, giving him a kiss. "I'm so glad to see you."

That made one person.

"You look like you're improving. How about Megan? I hope she wasn't too frightened."

"Not at all. She never knew anything happened."

"I really need to see Jillian. Is she around?"

"She's in the storeroom. Go on back."

When he saw Jillian, working on the computer, he

wrapped his arms around her and breathed in her fresh, clean scent.

"Any chance we could go upstairs to talk and let Cara close the store? I don't want to take any chances."

"You're worried Cara will think I'm crazy, too?"

He stepped back and looked her in the eyes. "I'm worried, all right, but not about Cara."

A curious light in her eyes, Jillian nodded and pushed back from her desk.

As soon as they reached her apartment, he turned to face her. "You told me you could see Heather plainly. What does she look like?"

She stared at him quizzically. "About my height, long blond hair, movie star figure."

"She's not a young girl?"

"No, she didn't like me growing when she didn't, so she kept up with me. She stopped growing at about twenty-one. The 'perfect age' she claimed. Her voice matured a little. She sounds like a young Marilyn Monroe."

Adam shook his head. "Maybe, when she started, but by the time she left she sounded more like Marilyn Manson."

"Wow. You must have really made her mad."

Jillian began digging in a drawer and pulled out a small photo. "Here she is in one of her pageants."

The picture showed a young girl in a flowered, ruffled dress holding a trophy. He didn't want to believe it, but there stood the girl he had seen, only ten years older.

Adam pulled Jillian over to the sofa and sat her down.

"I need you to tell me everything you can about Heather."

"I take it you two have finally met," she said. "Now what do you plan to do?"

Chapter 32

"Where do I start?" Jillian said. "What type of things do you want to know?"

"Everything." Adam leaned forward and ticked each item off on his fingers. "What can she do, what can't she do, what she likes or dislikes. Where does she hang out when she's not with you? What things do you do together? Why is she the way she is? I don't know what will help, so I need to know everything."

Jillian leaned back on the sofa. "During our last big hurricane, I went down to the storeroom for safety. I had a sleeping bag, candles, and a small TV. When the electricity went out and the TV went off, I lit the candles. I was just sitting there, listening to the wind howl and debris hit the roof. The entire building was shaking and groaning. I wasn't afraid, but it was eerie. Suddenly the candle blew out and it was pitch black. Then I was afraid. Heather's voice whispered in my ear. It was the only time I've even known her to come into the store. 'Now you know how I feel all the time,' she said and poof, she was gone."

Jillian hung her head as if ashamed to admit how frightened she'd been. "It was terrifying—the dark, the building groaning. I got flustered and couldn't find the matches or flashlight. I called out to Heather, begging her to light the candle. The candle came back on, but Heather never said a word, just left me there alone. That's why, no matter what she does, or how much evil she causes, I have to feel some sympathy for her."

"It must be frightening for her, especially when it first

happened." Adam took Jillian's hand and squeezed it. "Why doesn't she go. . . wherever those like her go?"

"She doesn't know how, and she's angry. She feels she was cheated out of a life, and she's determined to hang on somehow. If she can't talk me into letting her have my body, then she'll just follow me around and live my life with me, constantly asking me, 'What does it feel like? What does it taste like? What does it smell like?'"

"So she doesn't have use of any of her senses?" He took off his glasses and pinched the bridge of his nose, willing his mind into action.

"Well, she can hear, obviously. She can't hear anything we say if we're inside, but if I go out and call to her, she hears me and comes anywhere but here immediately."

"Can she hear what you're thinking?"

"No, she doesn't have ESP."

"Are you sure she can't smell anything?"

"Positive. She always asks what something smells like. She drenches herself in perfume, but I don't think she has any idea how much she puts on."

Adam began to pace. He always thought better when moving. "And she comes immediately, just poof?"

"It takes a couple of minutes. I think she likes to get dressed up and fix her hair, but it's almost immediately. She can see, also. Not through walls, from outside, but once inside, she sees things without digging around. At your house, she knew what was in cabinets or drawers without opening them or going through the trash. But she has to specifically look. It doesn't happen if she just passes through a room."

A plan was beginning to take shape, but it remained out of reach. "So you can hide things from her if she's not expecting them."

"That's right. I'm not sure about touch. I know she doesn't feel heat or cold, but she prefers tactile fabrics, like silk or cashmere. Yesterday, when I tried to hit her, she didn't like it at all. And she hates it when somebody walks through her. So she must be able to feel something."

"You hit her? Wish I could have seen that." Knowing how frightening Heather could be when she was angry, his heart swelled with pride to think of Jillian standing up to her.

"She wasn't too happy when I threw a screwdriver at her this morning, either. Do you think there's something solid about her? After all, she may have whispered hints to your mother and Billy, even to Eddie and Marshall, but she didn't convince Rover to break his own neck because she told him he was fat and lazy."

Jillian's eyes lit up. "There has to be. She didn't have any trouble pulling down your mirror, and that took a lot of strength."

"Now we know she's not all smoke and air. Maybe that remaining bit of flesh is what keeps her from moving on. What does she do when she's at home?"

Jillian took a sip of the coffee she'd brought upstairs. "I don't think she does much of anything. She spends most of the time in her room, looking at her trophies and scrapbooks. I know she tries on her old costumes. She goes into the living room and dreams of when we were a family and sat around watching TV. Mother had the garage converted into a studio so she probably goes in there and does her old routines. But some of the time, maybe a lot of the time, she just lays on her bed and sort of checks out. Not exactly sleeping, more like waiting."

Adam was beginning to get excited. "Does she ever go into the kitchen?"

"Heavens no, she didn't go into the kitchen when she was alive."

"What about the other rooms?"

"Not usually. She wouldn't have any reason to, would she? The only thing she'd want would be a mirror, and those in her room or the studio are better."

"So the house is still furnished?"

"When Daddy died, I locked the door and left. The last time I saw it was just before the hurricane hit. I went into the storage room to get a camp stove and a lantern."

"You haven't upped the insurance lately, have you?"

"I don't have any insurance on it. It ran out three months after Daddy died, and I never renewed it. I couldn't afford the premiums at the time."

Adam could tell she didn't like talking about this, but he pushed her anyway. Knowledge was power, or in this case protection. "You said curiosity was Heather's main motivation."

"She was only thirteen when she died. She looks grown-up because she chooses to. She's seen and learned a lot of things, but mentally she's a child trying to pretend to be an adult. Basically she's no different than a kid playing dress-up. Her big hang-up is adult relationships. She never got to have one and she wants to know what it's like. So she wants to watch, or at least have me tell her about it, but she has no idea of the emotional part."

Jillian got up and went to the window. "When I was younger, we did things together—watched TV, went to the movies, drove around—and I didn't mind telling her about my day at school and who said what to whom or who got into trouble. She knew most of the kids at school and liked hearing about them. As I got older, my tastes changed, and I wasn't interested in the same things she was. Maybe she was trying to understand, I don't know, but she started following me around, spying on me. She wanted more and more personal details that I wasn't willing to give."

Adam went to her and put his hands on her shoulders. He couldn't afford for her to break down now. He needed every bit of information he could get. He felt exposed, standing in front of the window, so he pulled the curtains closed. "Tell me about your house. Are there others close by?"

"We're the last house on a cul-de-sac. It's a two-story frame house with blue trim. Although I think it needs painting by now. There's nothing but woods behind us. The lots are huge, over an acre each. It's not a subdivision. That's how Mother got by with running a business from home. Our nearest neighbors are about a football field away."

She turned to Adam. "Do you remember in the eighties there was this TV show about some little girls, *Full House*?"

"I remember it. I didn't watch it."

"Neither did I. I was into sports and trying to please my dad. Heather wanted to watch it, but I knew Daddy wanted to watch a ball game, so I refused to put it on. The nearest family was the McElroy's, and they had two little girls about the age Heather was when she died. I would smile at Daddy and say, 'This is so nice. I'll bet the McElroy's are watching something silly like *Full House*.' That was my signal to Heather that she should go to the neighbor's to watch her show."

Jillian actually laughed. "That poor family, I know she creeped them out. Their dog would start to whimper and pee on the rug every time that show came on. They finally moved away, even though they loved having so much room. A family without kids lives there now, and they both work. They keep an eye on things for me and let me know if vagrants try to break in. They're not home now. They've gone to Mexico for two weeks."

"You don't always do what she wants. What about other people? If I'd been sitting at the desk instead of Marshall, could she have talked me into keeping the gun?" He gritted his teeth. No way a voice in his ear could make him turn his back on everything he believed in.

"I think you have to be leaning that way. It's more like a nudge to do something you wanted to do anyway but knew you shouldn't."

Decision made, Adam turned and stretched. Time to put his plan in action. "Do you have any decongestant?"

"Sure, it's in the bathroom. I didn't know you weren't feeling well."

Jillian ducked into the bathroom, and Adam retrieved the two beer bottles and carried them to the kitchen. As he put them in the trash, he checked under the sink and grabbed a bottle of drain cleaner.

"Where's that camp stove you said you had?"

"It's in that storage shed where we put the stuff from Marshall's house, which, by the way, I'd still like to get off my property."

"Don't worry. I have a plan. Unfortunately, it involves you having to talk to Heather again. But, with any luck, it's the last time you'll ever have to speak to her."

"Whatever you have in mind, be careful. She's dangerous when angry. She doesn't have any impulse control. I don't think you can scare her off."

"I agree. Frightening her won't do the job."

Adam waited until he was well away from Jillian's before he stopped at a CVS and bought a large box of Sudafed. Half a block farther was a Walgreen's. Why did they build them so close together? He went inside and bought another box. He didn't like the fact the decongestants were locked up and he had to ask someone to get them out, but Wal-Mart was even worse. There he had to take a card to the cashier and she sent someone for the box, meaning more than one person saw him.

On the seat of his neighbor's pick-up were two ball caps, one with an Astros logo, and the other a John Deere. He stopped at every drug store until he was several blocks from his house, switching caps, and brands of decongestants at each store.

A criminal's favorite trick, putting on a ball cap and calling it a disguise. Was that what he was about to become, a criminal?

Down the road, he found a Pep Boys, and bought two containers of anti-freeze. At Home Depot, he bought two jugs of drain cleaner, but was afraid to buy more at one place, so he drove on to an Ace Hardware and bought two more. He paid cash at each place, and had gone through Marshall's $200 and everything he had in his pocket by the time he got home.

The car was near empty by this time so he filled up at his usual station. He didn't mind using his credit card there, since it was a normal occurrence. He was hesitant to go to an ATM, so he fished out his emergency $500 from the back of his gun safe.

In his garage, he went first to the shelves on the side where he stored old, unused items. Next to an ancient, hand-cranked ice cream freezer, he found a petrified bag of rock salt. Its condition didn't matter, just the name on the bag. He also picked up a can of paint thinner and some old Mason jars. In the workshop section, he had two gallon containers of anti-freeze. He took the full one and left the one that had been opened. Brake cleaner, engine starting fluid, gun scrubber, and gasoline additive also went into the box he was filling.

He remembered the bottle of drain cleaner in the guest bath, and took that, some alcohol, and coffee filters also, along with a box of wooden matches and a couple of empty two-liter pop bottles. The box of coffee filters was new, so he pulled out three and set them by the coffee pot. Then he called Ruben. Bad enough that he'd chosen this path. Now he was pulling his friend into it also.

"Hey, old buddy, any chance I could come by early in the morning and borrow the key to your cabin?"

"You're welcome to it, but unless you're planning to take the boat out, I can't imagine what you'd want it for. It's not the nicest place to take a lady friend."

Ruben paused. "You're not seeing a married woman, are you?"

"Are you kidding? I can't handle single ones, what would I do with the complications of a married one? No, I just want to borrow the two-burner propane cooker we made." If only it was as simple as woman trouble.

"Are you planning a party and didn't invite me?"

"No."

"Is the stove in your kitchen broken?"

"Um, yeah. It's on the fritz." Crap. Ruben was a human lie detector.

"You're fucking with me, *compadre*, and I don't like it. Whatever you're up to, I'm coming with you. I hope you're not planning to dump those guns in the lake near my cabin. Someone would sure as shit see you do it, even if you waited till after dark. Sooner or later a storm would move things around or a drought would uncover something. If only one of those guns turns up in that lake, it'll send someone knocking on my door. They need to be destroyed completely."

Maybe, but how exactly was he going to manage that?

Chapter 33

Sunday morning, Adam picked Ruben up at nine o'clock. Friday's rain had washed the air clean and the sun was shining. They pulled off without saying a word, but Adam waved to Mamacita, standing in the doorway. One block later, Adam stopped in front of a drug store. "Would you mind getting me a box of Sudafed?" he asked. "The big box," he yelled as Ruben started into the store.

They stopped at several stores along the way. Sometimes Adam went in, sometimes he sent Ruben. At two hardware stores, he bought drain cleaner. At a camping store, he bought propane. By the time they reached the lake, Ruben was shifting uncomfortably in his seat.

"This is beginning to get expensive. Any chance I'm going to get my money back?"

"Not likely, but you'll have the satisfaction of knowing you've done your good deed for the day. For the year."

"Yeah, speaking of that, I don't know exactly what that good deed is, but I'm getting a bad feeling about what you have in mind. I think it's time you let me in on your plan."

Adam opened the car door and started up an overgrown path to the cabin. "No way. The less you know for sure, the better. It's for your own protection. Let's get that cooker. How much propane do you have?"

"Enough. I'm not ever getting my cooker back, am I?"

"I'll help you build a new one. What about those iodine water purification pills you bought over the Internet when you had that brilliant plan to camp out in the woods? Do you still have them?"

"You might as well take them, too."

When they returned to town, Ruben protested about being sent home. "I've been in on everything up till now. You might need my help to finish it. If this doesn't work, you're going to have one pissed-off ghost on your tail."

Damn. He'd never been able to put anything over on Ruben, but how he'd figured this one out was a mystery. "That's why you have to stay here. You're not even on her radar screen, and I'd like to keep it that way."

Adam filled the car again before he got home. This time he paid in cash. When he reached his house, he called his parents, mostly to indicate he'd been home. Now he'd involved them in his mess. If the shit ever hit the fan, his mother would forgive him, but his father would never look at him the same way.

He turned on the TV and ordered a pay-per-view boxing match. It wasn't much of an alibi, and wouldn't stand up if everything went south, but it was the best he could think of.

In the garage, he grabbed a box of rubber gloves, then changed clothes and left again. He'd done all he could to cover his tracks. He hadn't done anything illegal yet, and he already felt like a crook. How was he going to feel when he'd finished?

On the way to Jillian's, he stopped at a drive-through to buy a hamburger and milkshake. He hated to take the time, but he hadn't eaten all day and couldn't afford to run out of energy.

At four, he pulled up behind Jillian's. When he got out of the car, she was waiting, looking as determined as he felt.

"Here, put these on," he said, tossing her a pair of rubber gloves. "We have to wipe down every item with Windex before we load it in my trunk. Just using a cloth isn't good enough. We don't want any fingerprints to show up."

It took an hour, but they wiped down everything, even the items Adam had bought or found. They took off any labels that might indicate which store had sold the product. When they finished, it all went into the trunk of Adam's car.

"Okay, give me five minutes to get clear, then call Heather and tell her you want to meet. I'll need at least an hour, maybe more. Do you think you can keep her occupied that long?" Putting himself at risk was one thing, but endangering Jillian was a knife through his heart.

Jillian nodded. "How will I know when you're finished?"

"Keep your phone on vibrate. I'll let it ring three times to make sure you feel it, then hang up."

He squeezed her hand before he shut the car door, unsure if he'd live to see her again.

Jillian could feel her nerves acting up, but decided that was natural. Heather would expect her to be upset. She didn't try to fix her hair or make-up. It would give Heather something to complain about, and the more time she wasted, the better.

When she got to her car, she stood with the door open and called out, "I'm headed to the park, Heather. Let's see if we can talk about this."

On the way, she stopped at a 7-Eleven and bought a big Diet Coke and some Hostess Twinkies.

Heather was waiting when she arrived. "You look like a slob. Couldn't you have put on some make-up or changed your clothes? That hair-do is absurd, but if you're going to wear it that way, at least fix it."

"I haven't been in the mood to get dressed up lately." Jillian flopped on the table.

Heather was wearing skin-tight jeans with a logo on the pocket Jillian suspected most other women would have recognized. The fabric of her blouse screamed money. Her high heels had red soles. Jillian didn't know what they were, but she knew stars often wore them to red carpet events. Heather obviously thought she had the upper hand.

"Boo-hoo-hoo. Don't give me that sad story. I take it you've considered my offer."

"That wasn't an offer. That was a list of demands."

"Whatever it was, do we have an agreement?"

"I can't do it, Heather. Not all those things. Maybe we could compromise on some of them."

Heather ignored her and looked at the cup in her hand. "Is that a Coke?"

"Yes, can you see the bubbles?" Jillian swirled the cup until it foamed. "Look at this Twinkie." She broke it in half slowly, letting the cream layer string out. "Do you remember how much you liked these? Mother didn't want you to have them because you might gain weight, but I was already fat, so what difference did it make? Sometimes I'd hide one for you and you'd come to my room late at night to eat it."

"I remember eating your Twinkie, but it wasn't because you saved it for me. You hid it for yourself. You were selfish even then."

"I guess we have different memories."

Jillian glanced at her watch. It had been less than fifteen minutes. How was she going to keep this up for an hour?

"What's the matter, Jillie? Got a hot date?"

"As a matter of fact, I do. Adam said he wanted to come over later this evening to talk." Jillian made quotation marks with her fingers. "I imagine he wants to break up with me. You were right. Telling him was a big mistake."

"Well, that's one problem we won't have to argue about. I say good riddance. You can do better."

"Maybe, but I kind of liked him. I want your promise that if we break up, you'll quit bothering him. Forget about him entirely."

Heather ignored her. "Let's talk about the other things.

Are you ready to cooperate, or do I need to show you what can happen?"

Adam was right to take drastic steps. Even if she never spoke to him again, Heather would torment him for years to come.

"I said I would compromise, and that's what I'm willing to do." Her voice was rising, and she struggled to bring it under control. "I'll give up Adam. I know I can't have him, not after telling him about you. He's not the type to let it go and pretend he didn't hear me."

She threw the Twinkie in the trash, uneaten. "I'm not selling the business. I have no interest in running a dress shop and wouldn't be very good at it. The store belonged to Daddy and we're keeping it in the family. I'm not moving out of my apartment either. I like it there, and it suits me just fine. I will spend more time with you, though."

She waited to see what Heather would do, and she wasn't disappointed. Heather swung her arm at the table, and the cup of soda went flying.

"That's not what I said. I want you to live with me in our old house, like we used to."

Jillian spoke quietly, afraid the lies would catch in her throat. "It can't be like it used to be, Heather. Mother and Daddy are dead. It'll never be the same. What we can do is find a new way to be together. I'll turn the electricity back on and buy a TV, then I can come over in the evening and we can watch it together. There're lots of shows on now you'd like—reality shows, talent shows. Maybe we can go to the movies, or shopping. I'll take you for a ride in the country when the wildflowers are blooming."

"I'm willing to let you keep the store. It belongs to our family. But I want you to move home." Heather sounded determined, but not angry. At least not yet.

Jillian switched to another subject. If she agreed too easily, Heather wouldn't believe her. "There's something else I can't do. I can't go on a date and have you watching over my shoulder and making comments. It drives me crazy, and I'm not going to do it. I'll come home afterwards and tell you about it. At least about the date part—where we went, what we talked about, that type of thing. I'm not going to talk about the personal stuff. That has to be my business."

"I don't know why you think you have any say in this. I told you what would happen if you didn't do what I said."

"Come on, Heather. We have to work together on this. I think I've met you more than half way." She was exhausted. Dealing with Heather was harder than running ten miles.

"I gave in on the store, and that's all. If it bothers you that much, I won't talk to you while you're on a date, but I'm still coming along. And you are moving home."

"I tell you what, let's try it my way for a while and see how it works. I'll come by the house after Adam leaves. It probably won't take long for him to tell me he thinks I'm crazy and doesn't want to see me anymore. Then I'll tell you all about it—what he said, what I said, everything. There's just one thing. It's sort of spooky driving up to the house at night. I know there are all those candles on the coffee table. Could you light them for me before I get there? That way it won't seem so scary."

"I can't light candles, you know that."

If she couldn't convince Heather to try, all her efforts would be wasted, and Adam didn't have a chance. "Of course you can. If you can knock a cup off the table or cause a mirror to fall, you can light a candle. You lit one for me when I was hiding in the storeroom. Just wave your arms and say abracadabra, or whatever it is you do. Light them all. I can't see in the dark like you can."

"I'm sure I don't know what you're talking about. I've never been anywhere near the storeroom, but I suppose I could do it if I wanted to."

"Okay, now, I need to go to the drug store before Adam

comes over. Do you want to come with me? We could wander up and down the aisles and look at the make-up and stuff."

Heather followed Jillian to the car and sat in the front seat beside her. Jillian couldn't risk looking at her watch again, but she was able to glance at the dashboard clock. Twenty more minutes. She could do it. She'd drive slowly. Sweat began to trickle under her arms.

Chapter 34

Adam didn't have any trouble finding the house. Jillian's directions were clear. It was an interesting area, with an almost rural feel due to the distance between houses and the overgrown woods to the back. The house was sprawling and old, with off-white wood that was dingy with mildew around the base. The trim and front door had been painted blue, but the color had faded over time.

It may have been Heather's influence, but the house didn't have a welcoming feel. Pictures of children laughing and playing didn't spring to mind. He was certain it hadn't been a happy place for Jillian to grow up, but it was the perfect place for what he was about to do. It was a place where evil would feel right at home.

Driving up to the front of the house, he gripped the steering wheel and looked around cautiously. Was Heather gone, or just sleeping? He sat in the car for several minutes, hoping she'd make herself known if she saw him. Although what he'd do then, he had no idea. The air was laden with moisture, but the rain held off for a while.

Finally, he went to the back of the house and kicked in the door. He paused to see if there was any reaction, then hurried through to unlock the front. The stench of vomit and urine filled the air. Jillian was right. Heather had no sense of smell.

It took multiple trips to unload the car. Wearing the rubber gloves caused his hands to sweat and made every move more difficult. Leaving his car in the driveway worried him, but he'd put mud splatters on the license plates, and that was all he could manage.

He forced himself to go upstairs to Heather's bedroom, just in case, but there was no sign of her. The closet was open and contained several pageant ensembles, nothing else. The walls were lined with her trophies and ribbons. Pictures of her in various costumes sat on the dresser along with a single bottle of Opium perfume, complete with tassel. As he leaned forward to sniff the bottle, a chill ran down his spine. How many times had he noticed that scent over the last weeks without realizing what it was?

He finished unloading the weapons from the car. Some went under the bed in the master bedroom and others he put under the sofa. The rest he placed in the kitchen, spread out for easy reach. He placed any drug in a plastic pill bottle on the kitchen counter. The rest, especially the baggies of crystal meth, went into the master bathroom. He put them in a corner, next to a wall. They were out of sight from the main room and protected by the bend in the counter. The bathroom, like the rest of the house, hadn't been touched in twenty years. Probably not since Jillian's mother died. Signs vandals had used the home for drug parties were everywhere.

In the kitchen, he sat Jillian's camp stove and Ruben's two-burner cooker on the counter. He paused, looking at the cooker, already missing the carefree days he and Ruben had spent at the lake. It was unlikely that life would ever be the same for him. Tomorrow he could easily be dead or maimed or in jail. What would he do if he couldn't be a cop? Repairing cars no longer seemed a viable option. At least Jillian would be free, no matter what happened to him.

The kitchen was still fully stocked. He looked under the counter and pulled out the three largest pans he could find. There was a soup pot, a roasting pan, and a large saucepan. He dug through the drawers until he found a metal spoon with an extra long handle. It clattered as he dropped it onto the counter and he froze, listening for any sign of Heather.

Several of the gallon containers of antifreeze and drain cleaner went on the kitchen counter and others on the floor. He opened one of the bottles of drain cleaner and poured some in each pot, making certain to coat the sides and leave an inch in the bottom. If only he had time to let it corrode the inside of the pot, but he had no idea how long that took. It could be an hour or a week. At any rate, once started, he couldn't wait. Heather might notice his handiwork at any time.

Fumes were beginning to build, so he moved quickly. If he passed out before he finished and Heather found him, what would she do to Jillian? Some of the containers went into the bathroom, but he worried Heather would see them, so he hid them in the tub and drew the curtain. The other items he spread around the kitchen. He carried the empty bottles he'd found in his workshop trashcan outside the kitchen door and placed them in a large plastic bag.

The kitchen table and chairs were still there, although three of the chairs were broken. Of course, nothing about this was going to be easy. He found one chair that looked sturdy and made himself comfortable as he began opening the packages of decongestant. When he had a large pile, he found a mixing bowl and started crushing them. He left two boxes intact and hid them in the master bathroom.

He opened the lid to all the containers, along with a bottle of bleach he took from his laundry room, then held one of the drain cleaners above the counter and released his grip. The side split and the pungent liquid ran over the counter near the cookers and into the sink where he placed a bowl full of Clorox. He had to jump back to keep from getting splashed.

The arrangement of candles was still on the coffee table as Jillian had promised, but they were burned down to stubs, another sign of use by drug addicts. Two large, decorative candles on the mantel had also been used. Thank goodness he had planned ahead and included several candles in the box of items he brought from home. He had planned to drip wax on some plastic lids and stand the candles in it, but the burning in his eyes warned him lighting anything would be a dangerous mistake. Instead, he smashed the bottom of the candles onto the lids and stood them upright as best he could.

One candle he laid on its side, as if it had been knocked over.

Adam checked the house to be sure he had everything in order and nothing could be seen without going into the other rooms. Finally, hands trembling, he began to open the valves on the propane tanks. He carried two small tanks into the living room and put them under the sofa with the tip of the nozzle sticking out. He was afraid they would make a hissing sound that would give them away, but he didn't hear anything.

The odor was already becoming overpowering. If Heather had any sense of smell, she would immediately know something was wrong. Even without it, the fumes might burn her eyes. It couldn't be helped; there was no going back now. He hurried out of the house, closing the back door tightly and locking the front door behind him. The deep breaths he took as he ran for the car did as much to clear his mind as to clear his lungs.

Several miles down the road, he pulled behind a filling station and put the rubber gloves, the paper towels used to clean off fingerprints, and the blanket used to cover the bottom of his trunk into the dumpster. No one was watching, so he slipped into the restroom and washed his hands several times. He even splashed water on his face and the back of his neck.

He turned the car around and waited until he had driven well past the house in the opposite direction before fishing out the disposable phone that had been among the items taken from Marshall's stash.

"911 Operator. How may I assist you?"

Adam slurred his words. "I need to report a lab."

"A lab, sir? Like a dog?"

"No, like a meth lab. Where they mix up drugs."

"May I have your name, sir?"

"You have to find this lab. Before it blows up and kills people. The guy cooking the drugs is an idiot, a crack-head that's used too much of his own product. He got one year of chemistry at community college and he flunked that. Everything's open at once, and he's too dumb to even use Pyrex. He's using regular metal pots and pans. He thinks 'cause the first batch turned out okay that he knows what he's doing."

"Where is this lab, sir?"

"On Forest Bend. North side of the city, off the I-45 feeder. It's the last house on a dead-end street, and it's kind of blue-looking. Nobody lives there, and my bro...some people moved in and started cooking meth." He let his voice raise to near hysteria.

"Please stay on the line, sir, while I contact the police and fire department."

"If you send them SWAT guys, tell 'em to stay way back. I don't want nobody getting hurt. And that thing could blow any minute. You can already smell it from the street. Don't you hurt nobody in that house. They'll come out if they know they're surrounded and don't have no choice. Better the slammer than the cemetery." He didn't need to fake the concern in his voice at sending anyone into that house.

Adam turned off the phone and took out the battery, but drove until he was out of the area before breaking it into small pieces and dropping them out the window one at a time. He wanted the call to register as coming from a cell tower near the house, but he didn't want the pieces found anywhere close.

He took out his personal cell phone to signal Jillian, but cut it off before he finished dialing. He should have planned better. If the 911 call could be traced to a specific cell tower, so could his warning call to Jillian. Why hadn't he thought about that? Several miles passed while he contemplated the problem. It had been a couple of years at least since he'd seen a pay phone outside, or inside for that matter. Finally he called Ruben.

"I hate to ask, but I need one last favor. Would you call Jillian on her cell, let the phone ring two or three times, then hang up?"

"What the hell are you up to? Don't tell me you've involved her in whatever mess you have going. Have you got any idea what a dangerous game you're playing?"

"I can't talk about it now. When this is over, I'll tell you all about it, but for the moment I need you to trust me and make the fucking call. Can I count on you for that? It shouldn't get you in any trouble. She's had dinner at your house for Christsake. You could call her to see how she's doing." His voice rose with each word.

"I'm not worried about me, you fuck-head. I'm worried about you. I know you're up to something bad, and I don't want to see you go down. You're my partner, and I'm the one that should be watching your back. I know you like her, but she's a civilian, and she's not trained for this type of thing. She might not be able to hold up when they start questioning her."

"Of course, you're my partner, that's why you couldn't do it. Anyway, it had to be her. I'll explain it later, but if you'll do this for me, you will be watching my back. But it has to be done now. Can I count on you?"

"*Mierda*. Hang up the damn phone so I can make the call. Next time, include me from the beginning. It takes more than one mind to think of every possible disaster, and you aren't devious enough. At least, I never thought you were."

Jillian let Heather pick the radio station and they sang together until she reached the store.

They were standing at the back of the store reading humorous birthday cards and laughing when she felt her phone vibrate. She had a six-pack of beer in her cart, along with a package of glittery hair clips she was never going to use and a rose-colored blusher Heather had picked out for her. She had to admit it was a more flattering shade than the one sitting discarded in her dresser.

Except for the hair clips, she hadn't actually minded the time with Heather. Now that she wasn't carrying around so much guilt over Heather's death, she saw what it could have been like to have a sister. The first time had been an accident and not her fault. She knew that now. How was she going to handle the remorse when it was her responsibility? What right did she have to take Heather's life, such as it was? But could she ever trust Heather to stop hurting other people?

"Once we get rid of that pathetic loser boyfriend of yours, we can start to have some real fun." A female shopper passed through Heather without noticing, and Heather swatted at the gallon of milk she was carrying. The carton split open when it hit the floor, soaking the woman's pants and filling one shoe with cold milk. Heather's laugh sent chills down Jillian's spine.

Heather was still chuckling as she marched toward the front counter. "Come on, let's check out. I'll mess with the clerk's head so much he'll bag your things with a smile and never charge you for them."

"No, Heather, they have a camera. When the register doesn't add up, he might lose his job."

"So? I didn't like the way he looked at you anyhow, and he never even noticed me. It'll teach him a lesson."

Her heart sank. What had she been thinking? Heather wasn't ever going to change. This was the only way. "I better go now. I'll see you in a little while. Don't forget to light up the house for me."

Jillian started for her car, but turned back. "Goodbye, Heather, I'll see you soon."

Jillian was pacing by the back door when Adam pulled up. Her relief at seeing him unharmed was like a breath of fresh air.

"Come on in," she said. "We'll wait together." The thought of waiting in her apartment alone made her stomach cramp.

"No, I can't be here when the shit hits the fan. I won't involve you any further. How did things go on your end?"

"Fine, I guess." Jillian leaned in the open window. "She promised to light the candles for me."

"Good. Go upstairs immediately and call Cara. Talk about the schedule for next week or anything, but make some phone call to prove you were home."

"I did that the minute I hit the door. Then I logged on to the computer and paid some bills."

"You can call me if you hear anything. That won't seem strange because we already have a pattern of talking to each other. But you might not hear anything until tomorrow. Who knows how long it'll take them to find the owner? Or how aggressive they'll be once they locate you."

Great, another thing to worry about. Up till now, she'd only been concerned about Heather.

Jillian leaned in to kiss him and wrinkled her nose. "You better take a bath as soon as you get home."

"Don't worry. I'll be bathed and these clothes washed five minutes after I walk in."

In the shower, he soaped and shampooed twice. He even used the fingernail brush. He gathered his clothes for the washer, but stopped abruptly. Tomorrow was garbage day. He could see his neighbor's can sitting at the curb. He gathered everything, even his belt and shoes, and bagged it. Stepping silently out the back door, he slipped the bag in his neighbor's can.

Damn, he hated to lose that belt. It was expensive, but he'd seen too many crooks convicted because they hung onto something with their vic's blood on it.

So was he now in the same category as the low-life's he took off the street? Had he lost his moral compass? Was letting Snake-Eye leave the scene of a crime and dealing with Marshall on his own the first steps down a road he'd sworn never to travel?

It was something he'd have to think about. And for some reason, his thoughts seemed to be clearer than they'd been since the day he found Manny's body and first smelled that sickening perfume.

Chapter 35

On Monday afternoon, three plainclothes officers came into Jillian's store. Their cheap suits and city issue cars gave them away immediately. She steeled herself, unsure what would happen next.

The tall one with a receding hairline and old acne scars spoke first. "I'm Detective Hightower, and this is my partner, Detective Beavens." He pointed toward a slightly younger man with a severe overbite. Jillian immediately named him Bucky Beavens. "We're with the Narcotics Division."

He pointed to the third man who stood back somewhat and seemed more interested in looking around the store. "This is Agent Collinsworth. He's with the ATF. We're looking for J. R. Whitmeyer."

"That's me." She forced herself to smile. "What can I do for you gentlemen? Are you thinking about upgrading your department-issued weapons? If so, you've come to the right place. We carry a full line and give a substantial discount to peace officers."

Cara was standing in the door of the storage room, holding Megan and listening.

"No, ma'am. We're here about some property you own on Forest Bend."

"That old house? Don't tell me those hop-heads broke in again. Listen, I nailed the door shut, and I have a service cut the grass once a month in the summer. Some neighbors promised to watch the place and if they see activity, they contact me, and I call you to run them out. I don't know what else I can do. It's not a nuisance or an eyesore."

Hightower shook his head. "There was a problem last night. Someone tried to set up a meth lab and it caught fire."

The blood drained from her face. She didn't have to pretend she wasn't worried any longer. "Oh no, please tell me no one was hurt. I couldn't stand it if anyone got hurt."

"That's probably the only thing they did right. It looks like they all ran out the back door seconds before the place blew up. We've been checking the hospitals, but so far we haven't found any burn victims."

"Blew up? You said caught fire. What do you mean blew up? Did it catch the neighbor's houses on fire?" She held her breath, and fear clutched at her heart.

Beavens spoke for the first time. "Someone called it in moments before it blew, so the fire truck was already on its way. There wasn't any damage to other property. You wouldn't have any idea who called it in, would you?"

"Probably the Del La Garza's. They're the closest house and would have seen cars going in and out."

"They've been on vacation for a week." Hightower stared at Jillian, but she didn't blink. He shrugged and flipped his pocket spiral closed.

"Then I don't have a clue, unless it was a rival drug gang."

"We suspect it was a relative of the chemist, worried about his brother's safety," Collingsworth said. "There is another matter we're concerned about. The house was full of weapons." Collingsworth stepped closer to the counter.

"Aren't drug dealers known for keeping a cache of weapons nearby?"

"This looked more like a business."

"Hey," Jillian put her hands out. "I run a legitimate business here. You're welcome to look at my records. I can account for every piece. The storeroom has plenty of space to hold anything I can afford to buy. There's no reason for me to store things off premises."

"These seemed to be older weapons. Used pieces." Collingsworth had definitely taken over the questioning.

She straightened her back and tightened her lips. "I never deal in used equipment. New stuff only. I have no idea why there were weapons in that house. I haven't been there in over a year. It's the house I grew up in as a kid. I inherited it when my father died. I suppose I'm sentimental enough that I don't want to sell it, but practical enough that I don't want to live there."

Trying to project anger, not fear, she looked each officer in the eyes. "Mostly, I try not to think about it and hope one morning I'll wake up knowing what to do. I couldn't afford insurance premiums at the time, but now it'll probably cost me more to clean up than the premiums would have cost. What do they call that, risking a dime to save a penny?"

Cara stepped forward, holding Megan. "I've only been here a few weeks, but I've never seen any used merchandise come through the store. We don't take trade-ins, and J. R. doesn't deal out the back door. Everything's on the up-and-up, or I wouldn't be working here. Not with my baby on the premises."

The officers obviously didn't know what to make of a new mother and a baby vouching for Jillian's honesty.

"We were able to recover one weapon with a readable serial number. We traced it back to a man who says he turned it in for destruction several months ago."

Her stomach clenched. Exactly what Adam was trying to avoid.

Hightower pulled out a small notebook and began reading from it. "He claimed to have given it to a tall, skinny, bald-headed guy. Of course, he didn't keep any records of the transaction. We called both Headquarters and Central Division, and neither had anyone by that description working there."

That was true, technically. Marshall had retired. If they

kept prodding, they would figure it out, but if they accepted that answer, they would move in another direction. Adam worked out of Headquarters and they were connected so she didn't want them continuing that line of questioning.

"Who knows what he might have done with it? It's probably changed hands ten times since then."

"True. He's an upstanding citizen, but pretty old and a bit confused. He claims he took it someplace downtown, but he can't remember exactly where. Then he got lost driving home so his kids decided to put him in a retirement home. He's a dead end." Bucky Beavens obviously didn't have much faith in the mental abilities of older citizens.

Jillian tried not to show her relief. She thought they would never leave. Finally, they promised to keep her up on the investigation and let her know when she could begin cleaning the lot.

They left, but Jillian didn't think it would be a good idea to call Adam right away.

"If you want to drive out and look at it, I'll keep an eye on the store," Cara said.

Seeing the house in that state was the last thing Jillian wanted. If Heather was hanging around, it would be bad news. Still, it would look suspicious if she didn't go. She grabbed her purse and started for the door.

When she reached the lot, a fire truck blocked the road and investigators were sifting through the rubble. The fireplace was still standing along with one wall, but the rest was a smoldering mess. Debris was scattered in all directions.

A heavy weight settled on her shoulders. Why hadn't she come to see it one more time before it was gone?

Not all her memories of that house were unhappy. She'd known some good times, too. She approached one of the firemen.

"If you find any pictures intact, would you save them for me?"

"It's not very likely, Ma'am. What the fire didn't get, the water did. But if there's anything left, it'll be put to the side."

Jillian stood and watched for a few more minutes, but Heather didn't approach her. Of course, that didn't mean anything. With the police and firemen around, she would have gone someplace else.

It took all Jillian's courage to drive to the park. She sat on the table and waited, but didn't call Heather's name. After half an hour, she went home.

After work, Adam called Jillian from his home phone. He tried to sound casual. "Hi, Jillian. Are you okay?"

"Mostly. It looks like my old house was being used for a meth lab and it blew up last night. Three guys came to tell me about it this morning. I'm pretty upset."

They were careful not to say much over the phone.

"That's terrible. Why don't I come over? I'll bring something to eat, and you can tell me about it."

Adam picked up a double meat pizza and went straight to Jillian's.

"Don't worry about talking here," he said, squeezing both her hands. "They couldn't have bugged this place. Now, tell me about it. Did they act suspicious?"

"Maybe a little, but I think it was more for show than anything. You should have heard Cara stick up for me. One gun still had a serial number, and they traced it to a guy who claimed to have turned it in. I think they asked questions at Central Division and at Headquarters but didn't get anywhere. The guy had dementia, and there wasn't any receipt, so I don't think they'll follow up on that."

A chill shot down his spine. "Shit. The main thing we didn't want to happen. Is the house completely gone?"

"To the ground. You have a future as a demolition

expert if you want to change careers."

He held his breath as he asked the next question, but he had to know. "What about Heather? Have you heard from her?"

"I didn't see her at the house or in the park, but she could be waiting. Only time will tell for sure, but I didn't feel her."

"I don't feel her, either."

Jillian started crying. "She was my sister, and I killed her—twice."

He tried to put his arms around her, but she pulled away. "It wasn't your fault, honey. Not either time. It was a direct result of her own actions."

"I know that, but somehow it doesn't make me feel any better. I was too young to understand what happened when we were kids, so I didn't grieve. Now I've got to grieve for both times."

"We'll grieve together. I'll be right with you."

"I don't think so. There's no way you can grieve for somebody you never loved in the first place and who tried to kill you. Anyway, the police are looking for a connection to Headquarters and I don't think we should be seen together for a while. I never called you at your office, only on your cell phone or at home. Did you call me from your office phone?"

"No, always from my cell, or at home. Larry and Mike know about us, but this is one time I'm thankful the county and the city don't like to talk to each other. But if they do ask, you can't lie." The chill he felt earlier now encircled his heart. She was pulling away from him, and there was nothing he could do to stop her.

"Okay then, we should be safe. I don't think they'll check that hard."

"I'll step back and let you have the time you need, if that's what you really want." His voice caught, but he kept going. "I won't like it, but I'll do it for you. Don't wait too long. It would be a shame to let this slip through our fingers when the way is finally clear for us. I care about you. Don't forget that."

He left the pizza. He'd lost his appetite.

Adam waited anxiously beside the elevator when Ruben stopped by the station two weeks later to check in. He'd talked to his partner a couple of times, but hadn't gone to his apartment. He'd avoided Ruben just as he'd avoided Jillian. No point in putting them at risk, but it had been lonely, and the evenings crept past.

They walked together to Hard Luck's office and their boss waved them inside.

Ruben had lost weight, but he still filled the doorframe. "Wanted to let you know, the doc gave me the all-clear to start back to work next week. Full duty, he said. It's hard to believe, but I think I missed this place. Nothing like living with your mother to make the days crawl by."

"It's about time. What were you off, three months?"

"Five weeks. It just seemed longer. Anything happen while I was gone?" Ruben sank into the chair across from Hard Luck's desk and Adam took the one closer to the door.

Hard Luck faced Ruben, never glancing Adam's direction. "Your partner did a lot of slacking off. Said he was working on the Manny Dewitt case, but he had something else going on he didn't want to tell me about. You wouldn't happen to know what it was, would you?"

Adam sat up and blinked in surprise. Had Hard Luck known the whole time?

"All I know is if he said he was working on something important, he was. I got a nice surprise when I arrived this morning. A new guy was on the desk. He said Calvin Marshall retired. I was sure they'd carry him out of here feet first, or in handcuffs."

At least Ruben was standing up for him. He hadn't been sure he would.

"That old crook. I had my fingers crossed we'd get rid of him before he brought shame down on all of us. He left here in a hurry, looking like a cat that lost a fight. Surprise, surprise, someone called a few days later looking for a tall, skinny, bald guy who worked downtown. Nobody here could remember anyone who fit that description. I told them to try 61 Reasner Street and ask Central Division, and they went away. I think we dodged a bullet on that one."

Hard Luck pushed back from his desk and looked Ruben in the eyes, ignoring Adam. "That's another thing I don't suppose you know anything about?"

"Like I said, Adam would never let a hint of dirt blow back on this squad, not while you're in charge. He knows how you value your clean record. And he doesn't goof off on company time."

Adam's jaw dropped as the two men continued to talk about him is if he wasn't there.

"I know that. It's why I didn't dog him about what he was doing. I knew he was up to something when he asked for a picture of Marshall, but I thought he was only doing preliminary background investigation. When he had it figured out, I expected him to come to me with it. I would have helped him. I don't give a flying crap about my clean record, that's just my hard luck. When you get back to work, I want you to watch out for him. I don't want him going all Lone Ranger on me again. We're a team in this office, and we watch each other's back. He should have remembered that about me."

Adam stood and walked out of the room, but not before he heard Ruben's answer.

"He did, and if he'd needed you, he would have called. Relax, and know you can depend on him to take care of things without any mud splashing back on his fellow officers."

Adam returned to his desk and didn't acknowledge Ruben as he left the building. His eyes started to burn and he began vigorously cleaning his glasses. He deserved everything that had just happened and more. It may have felt like someone stabbed him in the back, but they hadn't. It was just two old friends reminding him that he should have trusted them.

Chapter 36

August was in full swing and the heat was almost visible, radiating off the pavement. Jillian watched Adam mowing the grass as she pulled her car into his driveway. Almost four months since she'd spoken to him, and she didn't have any idea if he'd be happy to see her.

His shirt was off and he was covered with a fine sheen of perspiration. He must have given up on his hair because it was buzzed short. Maybe she could convince him to let it grow back out. After all, that was what had attracted her to him in the first place.

He was wearing shorts with old tennis shoes and looked so good she wanted to just sit and watch, but he'd seen her car. When he tried to turn the mower off, she waved her arms and shook her head.

"You only have one strip left," she shouted, pointing to a single line of tall grass. "Finish up and put the mower away. I'll wait."

"Okay." He nodded, turning to cut the final swath.

He disappeared around the corner, and Jillian heard the gate open and close before the mower was turned off. When he reappeared, he had put on a T-shirt. It was damp and grass-stained.

She leaned against the side of the car as he came up and gave her an awkward kiss on the cheek. "I'm all sweaty," he said. "I hate to touch you."

"I have something that might help." She held up a six-pack of cold beer.

"Good plan. Let's go inside and see if we can figure out

what to do with that."

She handed him the beer and reached into the back seat. "I've got something I want to show you."

When she stood, she was holding a pet carrier with a small, yellow kitten. "This little fella showed up at my door a couple of weeks ago. I decided you might like him. He's already been fixed, so he won't blame you for it. Don't take him if you don't want to. I can always keep him, but I don't have a yard so he might be happier over here."

Adam went completely still. "That's very thoughtful of you. I appreciate it. Do you know I saved the pet entry off my old back door? I must have known I'd get another one someday."

At least he hadn't thrown her out yet. That was a good start.

He stuck his finger between the bars and the kitten immediately began to investigate it. He tilted his head to one side, studying her. "You're looking good, but something's different. Are you letting your hair grow?"

"I'm experimenting. I've spent so much of my life reacting to others, now I'm trying to see what I like."

"It looks pretty, but so did the spikes."

"Covering all your bases, are you?" The relaxed banter felt good after so much time alone. Maybe they could start fresh after all.

He placed a hand over his heart. "I'm a police officer. I'm trained to tell it like it is, not embellish."

The air-conditioning was a slice of heaven after only a few minutes standing outside. The living room was clean, but lived in, with newspapers on one end of the sofa and a bag of chips on the coffee table.

"Make yourself comfortable," Adam said. "I'll only be a sec. I want to get out of this shirt. It's sticking to me."

He went into the back room, and Jillian heard the shower, then the buzz of his electric razor. When he returned, he was wearing clean clothes and his hair was wet.

She'd taken the kitten out of the carrier and was playing with it on her lap when Adam sat beside her. He hadn't asked her about Heather and she appreciated it. It might take her a few minutes to work up to that.

He grabbed a beer and rolled the cold bottle against his neck. "Okay. Shall we drink to. . . Does he have a name?"

"I've been calling him Buddy, however, since he doesn't come when called anyway, I don't think it'll make any difference if you want to change it."

"To Buddy," Adam said. They clinked the bottles together.

He took the kitten on his lap. "What do you think, Buddy? Do you want to live here? I work strange hours, I'm grumpy in the morning, and I might be late feeding you, but other than that, I think you'll like it. The backyard is full of birds and squirrels to chase. An obnoxious dog lives across the street, but I think you can take him, even at your size."

Buddy climbed up his arm and began to purr.

"I think we have a deal. He wants to stay." He held Jillian's gaze. "What about you? Will you stay for a while?" She started to speak, but he hurried on before she could refuse. "You could bring me up-to-date on how you're doing and the happenings at the store. Is Cara getting along okay? I'll bet Megan has grown. What about Snake-Eye? I haven't heard a good Snake-Eye story in months."

Jillian held up her hands. "Whoa, that's a lot of questions. Snake-Eye is in rare form. He's decided to branch out into knife throwing. We had a gully-washer of a rain storm about a week ago, and he was outside looking for the knife he had just thrown so he got a bath of sorts."

Adam laughed. "Any bath would be an improvement, but I'm not sure a tropical storm would be enough to do the job completely."

"Megan." Jillian smiled at the thought of the baby she'd

grown so fond of. "I think she grows overnight because I swear she's bigger each morning. She's the one I'm going to miss."

"Is she going somewhere?"

"Cara's divorce and name change will be final soon and she's planning to move to another state. Trevor should be in prison for a long time, but she wants to make sure he can never find her. She doesn't want to be looking over her shoulder."

Buddy had fallen asleep on Adam's lap. "The gun and the threats mean he's going down for attempted murder, not just assault. That should keep him behind bars for quite a while."

"I know. I heard your testimony at the trial. I was sitting in the back of the room." Hiding. She hadn't been ready to speak to him yet. "The D.A. explained to Cara that the fact you're a police officer and the way you phrased your testimony, recalling exactly the threats he made and the things he did, carried a lot of weight with the jury."

"Tell Cara not to worry. She won't have to come back for parole hearings. I'll keep track of him and show up anytime they even think about letting him out."

Adam placed a sleeping Buddy on the sofa and reached for his beer. "You realize Trevor never did understand the guy behind the counter that day was a cop. When I testified, he kept elbowing his attorney, asking him why this police officer was testifying about what happened. 'How does he know what went down? He didn't see me smack her around. It was just some dopey pot head.' It didn't help him any with the jury."

"I'm going to miss Cara terribly, and she'll be hard to replace. In fact, I've already started looking so I'll have time to train someone before she goes. But still, you have to question her good sense for hooking up with Trevor at all."

He grinned. "Snake-Eye told me there's no mathematics

for attraction, and I suppose he has a point."

Jillian shifted on the sofa, tucking one leg under her and facing Adam. "I've realized how tied down I've been the last few years. Working six days a week and teaching classes a couple of nights means that I don't have any life outside the store. At the very least, I need to hire more help, people I can depend on. Not someone like Billy that, sweet as he was, couldn't be left alone for any length of time."

She took a deep breath and let it out. "So, I haven't decided yet, but I'm considering selling the store and becoming a nurse. I'll take some classes first, to see how I like it. The store's been in our family a long time, and it's my home, but it has so many memories, both good and bad, all jumbled up together. It's a big step, so I want to take it slowly."

"I can certainly see you as a nurse. You'd be a good one. But you're right. Selling the store would be a big change and you need to take it slowly." His eyes were soft behind his glasses. "You'll know what's right when the time comes."

She hadn't realized how much she needed someone she could talk to about what had happened. "I've already made so many little changes in the way I do things. I get out of the house more, go shopping, go to a movie. Did you notice I don't carry a gun anymore? In fact, I don't even carry a purse. Just put my driver's license and some money or a credit card in my back pocket. It's very liberating."

He leaned his head back and laughed. "You're the only person I know that would think not carrying a gun was rebellious."

"What about you? What have you been doing?"

"Well, my brother and his wife had their baby, a little boy." He took a picture off the bookcase and handed it to her. His mother was grinning and holding a baby with red cheeks and black hair that stood straight up. Jillian ran her thumb over the picture and smiled. No question the baby was a Campbell.

"My father came for a few days and helped me do some work around the house. We poured a cement platform for my tool shed and refinished the back deck. That weekend we went to Ruben's place on the lake and made him a new two-burner cooker, a much better one than he originally had, and Ruben took us fishing on his boat."

He took a long pull on his beer and looked at Jillian. "I took him to the restaurant you and I went to. I told him my friend liked the spinach ravioli. Later he asked me if he was going to get a chance to meet my friend. He looked disappointed when I said that didn't seem likely. I was pretty disappointed myself."

Jillian squeezed his hand. She hated causing him pain, but she'd needed the time to heal. The last months had been a roller coaster of emotions. "Tell me about Ruben. Is he back at work?"

"Ruben moved back to his apartment and is working full time. It's made me appreciate the importance of a partner I can depend on. The Toe Jamb nickname seems to have been forgotten, thank goodness. For a while, I was afraid I was going to have to transfer to another department, maybe another city."

Jillian held her breath, afraid to ask the next question. "I hope you didn't get into any trouble because of that sergeant."

He studied the beer bottle in his hand. "No one's ever figured out what happened with Calvin Marshall. The stories get wilder with each telling, everything from he inherited a fortune to he killed a man in a fight over drugs. The truth never even made a blip on the radar screen. He went to rehab, but he's still a prick, just a clean and sober prick."

Buddy yawned and stretched, then fell back asleep. Adam shifted. "I've kept my ears open, and there doesn't seem to be any questions about your house. The meth lab story's been accepted."

"They asked a lot of questions, but no one acted concerned. It felt routine. I sold the lot, but it took everything I made to clear it off, so there was no profit to arouse suspicion."

He stood and grabbed her hand, pulling her off the sofa. "Come on. Let's sit on the deck and enjoy the refinishing job that almost killed my back and knees."

As he opened the back door, the warm wood of the deck gleamed and welcomed her. An ancient oak put most of the surface in shade and a breeze cooled the air. She immediately noticed that he'd added a second Adirondack chair.

They sat, side by side, holding hands and watching a blue jay eye them suspiciously.

Jillian gave him a small smile. "You're avoiding my question. How are you dealing with everything that's happened?"

"Like you, one day at a time. I saw Heather with my own eyes, and she's still hard for me to accept. The things I did—letting Snake-Eye leave, going after Marshall on my own, and my God, blowing up a damn house—I wouldn't have considered before she entered my life. Yet, I don't regret any of them. In fact, I feel freer now. I don't look at everything as black and white. I'm still my father's son and believe in rules, but I can see shades of gray."

Adam looked into her eyes, and her heart lodged in her throat. "You still haven't told me about yourself. How do you feel about things? I'm assuming you haven't heard anything from Heather."

"Not a peep. I'm adjusting. I spent half my life trying to piss her off and the other half trying to appease her. Now I have to make decisions based on what *I* want to do, and that's harder than it sounds."

"You'll get it right, I have faith in you." He rubbed his

thumb across her knuckles.

"I went to the cemetery last week and took flowers to Heather's grave. I sat on the ground and talked to her. It was strange, but I got the most comfortable feeling. I have to believe there's special forgiveness for someone who dies so young. The air had been very still, and suddenly there was a warm breeze, and I felt everything was all right—she'd found a good place, probably with Mom and Dad. I think she's happy for the first time in a long while. So now I don't need to feel guilty about trying to find some happiness for myself."

Adam wiggled his eyebrows at her. "In that case, why don't we go back to my room and see if we can find some happiness right now?"

Jillian slapped his hand. "Not so fast there, Romeo. My plan was that we take it slow this time. Actually get to know each other first."

"I can live with that, as long as I'm in there somewhere. You know I love you, Jillian. I never realized how much until I thought I'd lost you. Waiting for you has been the hardest thing I've ever done. But it was worth it, if it brought you back to my door. And I'll wait longer, if I need to, but my plan is that we work on building a life together."

The protective wall she'd build around her heart crumbled and tears came to her eyes. "Keep up that kind of talk and you might get lucky."

He grinned. "I kept your toothbrush, just in case."

CPSIA information can be obtained at www.ICGtesting.com
Printed in the USA
LVOW011612191212

312426LV00001B/12/P

[5]